Cat Chase the Moon

ALSO BY SHIRLEY ROUSSEAU MURPHY

Cat in the Dark

Cat Raise the Dead

Cat Under Fire

Cat on the Edge

The Catsworld Portal

**BY SHIRLEY ROUSSEAU MURPHY AND
PAT J. J. MURPHY**

The Cat, the Devil, the Last Escape

The Cat, the Devil, and Lee Fontana

Cat Chase the Moon

A Joe Grey Mystery

Shirley Rousseau Murphy

An Imprint of HarperCollinsPublishers

CAT CHASE THE MOON. Copyright © 2019 by Shirley Rousseau Murphy. All rights reserved. Printed in the United States of America. No part of this book may be used or reproduced in any manner whatsoever without written permission except in the case of brief quotations embodied in critical articles and reviews. For information, address HarperCollins Publishers, 195 Broadway, New York, NY 10007.

HarperCollins books may be purchased for educational, business, or sales promotional use. For information, please email the Special Markets Department at SPsales@harpercollins.com.

FIRST HARPERLUXE EDITION

ISBN: 978-0-06-284574-0

HarperLuxe™ is a trademark of HarperCollins Publishers.

Library of Congress Cataloging-in-Publication Data is available upon request.

19 20 21 22 23   RS/LSC   10 9 8 7 6 5 4 3 2 1

To the memory of Bobby Long

Cat Chase the Moon

Prologue

The old man didn't want to wake up, he didn't want to get out of bed, he felt so heavy he longed only to drop back into sleep. Through the curtain of the east window the first smear of fog-dimmed sun sulked lifeless and depressing. Even the hens outside sounded dreary, as if they had no desire at all to lay an egg or peck at the scattered grain. The world was without joy, no smallest pleasure awaited him, no sound of Mindy running and laughing and talking to her pony, or galloping across the field.

It was two weeks since her parents had left, taking the child with them, taking his little granddaughter away to live in town, Mindy shouting, "I don't want to go! You can't make me go," crying so hard she nearly threw up. But of course they had taken her. Mindy was a brat when she was around her parents. She was nice as pie when she was just with him, or with her pony; she was full of life and fun. Why couldn't Nevin and Thelma have left her here? Now, every day, every hour that she was gone the emptiness grew worse. He'd thought it would get better, but it hadn't. No more than two weeks earlier he had begun to come to terms with Nell's death. Then the last of their three grown sons left so soon after his mother's funeral, taking Zeb's only grandchild away and not giving a damn if he was alone, never caring if he was still filled with pain over Nell's passing, never caring if Mindy might have been a solace to him. Never even wondering if he could manage the farm without a little help from Mindy.

Well, at least Nevin, his youngest, and his wife, Thelma, *had* waited until Nell was gone, they hadn't hurt Grandma like Varney had, his middle son leaving six months ago, walking out on Nell while she was so sick. (Ever since Mindy was born, all three grown boys called their mother Grandma.) Varney said he'd gotten a job in town, one too good to refuse. He didn't say what kind of job and Zeb didn't ask. Varney hadn't cared that he was breaking his dying mother's heart. Maybe her hurt over Varney's abandonment had made the cancer worse, Zeb would never know. Well, Varney's leaving hadn't been so bad in the end. Without his temper the house had been quieter for Nell.

But then his Nell died, of the pain and cancer or maybe of the medicine itself, how could anyone know? As soon as she was buried, Nevin and Thelma packed right up and moved into the village and never asked if Mindy could stay here with him. Mindy, with her curly brown hair, brown eyes, and turned-up nose, was twelve, bright and loving, and she was all he'd had left. Thelma might have let Mindy stay but she was too scared of Nevin to disobey him. Zeb and Nell had been married fifty years and just the one grandchild, and now suddenly everyone was gone. Zebulon Luther was alone.

Fifty years of marriage, a happy marriage. But as soon as his Nell passed, after all the illness, the last boy hauled out. Left Zeb when he wasn't so well, either, with the arthritis and the kidneys. Left him to do for himself, cook, keep up the garden and farm work, though there wasn't much of that anymore. He'd stopped haying some years back, when he was in his sixties. The two younger boys wouldn't hay, they had let the land go to weeds not even fit for pasture. And DeWayne, his oldest, had never taken to farming. He liked the city life, he liked to travel. Zeb didn't know how he made his living, he wondered a lot about that, but Zebulon seldom saw him.

Well, at least he had the two horses for company. But what good was the pony when the child missed him, and the pony missed her. *"You can't keep a horse in town!"* Thelma had mocked when Mindy begged. And the pony without Mindy was growing as lifeless and sad as Zeb himself.

Earlier this morning, before dawn, something had waked him; or maybe he was dreaming that cold eeriness, the moon drowning in thick fog above a battered body that lay struggling in an open grave; and above it stood the shadow of a big tomcat. He lay half awake and puzzled; but the dream faded and was gone. Shivering, he pulled the quilts up and crawled back into sleep.

1

The sea crashed behind Joe Grey, the tomcat standing tall on a heap of broken branches; the night's heavy fog admitted only a smear of light from the low moon, just enough to brighten the hushing waves. The sound of digging had drawn the gray tomcat up the beach to the little sandy park, to the oak tree that had long ago fallen, a dry and twisted relic from last spring's storms. The shoveling noise stopped abruptly when Joe Grey inadvertently stepped on a twig: a sudden silence cut the night, then the sound of running through the sand and dry grass among the scattered trees.

He couldn't see much of the runner in the heavy mist and tangled branches but he could tell it was a man, heavy footfalls among the dead branches. He could see dark clothes, a dark floppy hat, brim pulled down. Joe heard him hit the sidewalk, hard rubber-soled shoes, heard a car door open. Heard an engine start and the car pull away, a dark, long shadow in the mist. Joe leaped to the highest branch of the fallen tree, looked down where the man had been digging.

A body lay beside the dead tree where dirt had been scooped out. A half-dug grave in which a woman lay nearly buried, bruised and bloodied, fresh earth thrown over her lower body and legs—but she couldn't be dead, blood still flowed, her heart would still be beating.

At the edge of the grave, in the damp, heavy sand, he could see the shovel marks, small, sharp curves in the shape of those spades people carried in their cars for an emergency.

She was slim and tall, her long black hair was tangled but, except for the blood, clean and shining. She would be beautiful under the purple bruises across her face and what looked like purple finger marks circling her throat. Her right earring was missing, the lobe torn sharply in two: the two ragged flaps bleeding down her white shirt. Her left ear was red and bloody, swollen around a lump of smashed gold, as if the side of her head had been pounded against a log. Flecks of bark clung to her face.

Dropping down from one fallen branch to the next,

Joe Grey stepped into the half-dug grave and put his nose to her mouth. Yes, the faintest breath.

He pushed his mouth to hers, feeling weird at the contact; he breathed in and out, forcing air into her lungs until her gasping came stronger. Her right hand moved faintly. The tomcat, even after the dead bodies he had confronted at so many crime scenes, felt sick that the grave digger had meant, apparently, to bury her alive.

A patrol car passed slowly, making its rounds. The fog was so thick the officer didn't see a thing among the tangled tree branches nor would he have heard any strangled cry, over the static of his radio. As the unit passed, Joe considered yelling out for help.

Right, and have the guy's strobe light catch him, a tomcat, yelling *Help!* and then running. Worse, Joe knew most of the officers and they knew him, dark gray tomcat, white paws and thin white strip down his gray face. He was in and out of the station all the time, was practically the station cat. For a cop to see him here on what would turn out to be a crime scene wasn't smart. One more puzzle for the department, Joe Grey nosing around a crime scene at just about the time the "phantom snitch" called in the report—if he could find a phone. His presence here would be one more coincidence he didn't need. He prayed that Haley would pull over, get out of the car, find the half-buried victim himself and call the dispatcher—while Joe fled among the rubble of the wild little park and vanished.

When the officer had noticed nothing suspicious among the fallen and tangled trees, when the car had passed and turned back toward the village, when Joe was convinced the woman would keep breathing on her own, he raced for a ramshackle cottage at the edge of the shore. Leaping to a sill, he clawed his way through the rusty screen and slid open the rickety window. This house was the only relic in the long line of seafront homes, the rest all restored to elegance or replaced by new dwellings. This old place smelled of cats but he didn't see any.

Slipping through the dim kitchen he found a phone in the hall. He called 911 and relayed his message, then beat it out of there, the torn screen clawing at his fur. Racing back across the dead-end street, crossing the narrow lane where it ended at the sea, he kicked away pawprints in the drifted sand—but there were cats in the village. Why would he be suspected of being the phantom caller? He had been faced with this dilemma before and never been caught. Slipping out of sight among the fallen branches just as the first siren screamed, he searched hastily for the woman's purse, for a billfold or ID, but found nothing. She was still breathing but the oozing blood had slowed, not a good sign. He was looking for the shovel her attacker might have buried when the medics screeched to a halt, cop cars behind them; Joe Grey dove into the tall grass and bushes and was gone.

He watched from across the street as the medics worked on her: oxygen, all kinds of tubes, then loaded her into the ambulance. He would know little more until the information was on Captain Harper's desk, until he could saunter into the chief's office and have a look at the report.

Ordinarily Joe would stay after the medics left, would watch from the bushes to see if the cops found any clues he'd missed. But this was Saturday morning and he was already late. His tabby lady would be waiting with her striped ears back, her striped tail switching, sitting rigid among the small children on the library window seat, her green eyes flashing at his tardiness.

How many tough tomcats spent their Saturday mornings in the library among a bunch of snively little kids listening to story hour? How many patrons smiled with amusement at Joe and the other four cats snuggled among the children: Joe's lady, Dulcie. Their grown kitten, Courtney. (Courtney's two brothers were otherwise occupied.) Tortoiseshell Kit and her mate, red tabby Pan, as macho a tomcat as Joe Grey himself, all curled up among warm and cuddling children listening to a tale of magic.

But the cats were there for more than the story. Intently they watched for the mysterious man who had appeared these last few Saturdays prowling among the books, striking their curiosity and sometimes their concern.

Ever since Dulcie, who was Molena Point's official library cat, first saw the shadowy figure slip behind the book stacks and stand watching the children, the cats' curiosity had drawn them. Browsing among the books, he kept his eyes on one lone child, then another.

Public libraries were not the welcome retreats they had once been, peaceful and safe. These days, even small libraries had guards on the premises. Plainclothes officers walked through the paneled, silent rooms, sometimes arresting a stoned man, taking him away to sleep it off in jail. All across the country, addicts were frequenting the book rooms, hiding their stashes among the shelved volumes or concluding their sales in the towns' most innocent refuges. It was not uncommon, at closing hour, for a librarian to find a drugged man asleep in a soft chair, a newspaper spread over his face.

Molena Point Library was a handsome building with pale stone walls, mullioned windows, and carpeted floors, a peaceful retreat set back from the sidewalk by a deep garden graced with flowers, small ornamental trees, and stone benches. This morning when Joe Grey had entered, trotting among the blooms and up four stone steps, crossing the stone porch to the carved oak door and pushing inside, he knew he was laughed at, but in a friendly way. Most of the patrons knew him. Padding down six steps to the big reading room, sauntering across in plain sight of half a dozen elderly men sitting in comfortable chairs reading, he had leaped onto the wide, cushioned window seat and settled down beside his tabby lady in the lap of a blond little girl who smelled of peppermint. Two women at a reading table watched the five cats among the children and laughed and whispered to each other. Three old men smiled, and one laughed softly. *Smile if you want,* Joe thought, half amused himself. *Better than a couple of drug dealers settling in, waiting for their contacts.*

He heard from across the village the short blast of a police siren that made him want to leap away and follow, racing across the rooftops as he usually did. But Dulcie gave him a look that settled him down. Every siren wasn't a major crime; this one could be anything: traffic violation, fender bender. Or a domestic argument. They'd had plenty of those since Zeb Luther's family all moved out, leaving the old man alone.

Moved in across the street from Joe, shouting altercations in the middle of the night that woke Joe and his housemates and left them all cranky, to say nothing of enraging the neighbors.

He was wondering if the adults in the library were listening to the story, too, only pretending to read the papers. And, speak of the devil, here came his quarrelsome new neighbor Thelma in the front door dragging her little girl. At once Mindy broke away and ran to the window seat, crowding in at the end. But when she spotted Joe and started to scramble to him, the librarian Wilma Getz, Dulcie's silver-haired housemate, told her kindly to sit down where she was. The tale Wilma was reading was one of the Narnia books; the boys and girls were already entranced, as were the cats, drawn to the war-refugee children and the secret world they found at the back of a closet—but soon again the cats' attention was drawn away to the open balcony, to the second-floor bookshelves that looked down on the reading room. Even as the world of Narnia unfolded in snow and ice, a figure appeared on the balcony among the deepest row of bookshelves. In the shadows he was hardly visible. As on every other Saturday morning, he was watching the children. The same man, the shadow of his close-clipped, pointed beard, dark cap pulled down over shaggy, dark hair. *Why* was he watching the children? Or was he watching the cats, was he some kind of mentally obsessed cat fancier?

Not liking to be stared at, and quick-tempered, Joe wanted to race across the room, leap up through the rail, knock the man down and question him until he knew what the guy wanted.

Oh, right! And tell the whole world I can talk.

The man stood still for a while, looking, watching brown-haired Mindy, Joe's new neighbor. But then he turned away, faded into the shadows of the back row of bookshelves, and glided toward the stairs that led down to the main floor. Joe knew that Wilma Getz watched him, too, as she read aloud the tale of Narnia.

The next the cats saw of the man he was at the non-fiction shelves just across the room, flipping through bright, oversized books. He was wearing thin pigskin gloves, expensive ones, new and pale. He carried half a dozen books to a table, spread them out, and began to make long, careful notes from the front and back pages of each. While he recorded his references he would glance up now and then around the room or at their little group. Joe wanted to wander over, hop casually on the table and see what subjects he was recording from the title pages and index, what pictures he was lingering over. The tomcat was about to slide down and pad across to take an innocent look when a nailed paw stopped him and Dulcie's green eyes pulled him back. She could see he was warming up for trouble, she could sense his rising challenge.

It was at that moment that Officer McFarland came in the front door, brown hair uncombed, dressed in badly worn jeans, wrinkled cotton shirt, a stubble of beard, looking more like a vagrant than the neatly groomed young cop he usually was.

He spotted the stranger, picked up a newspaper off the hanging rack and sat down across the room, half out of sight behind its pages. At the other end of the window seat, tortoiseshell Kit and red tabby Pan watched McFarland. And they keenly watched the intruder, who remained for some time working away at his notes, calm and preoccupied. His little beard was perfectly trimmed and neat compared to his shaggy hair and wrinkled cap. At last, apparently finished, he returned the books to the shelves and left the library.

The cats watched him through the big, curved window. He crossed the garden, moved around the corner, and disappeared up the side street. In a moment McFarland put down his paper and slipped away following him. Joe wanted to scramble up to the roof and track them, but Dulcie gave him another look, a look that said, *He knows you're watching him.* He scowled back at her. After all, the man had really done nothing wrong.

Except that everything he did was off-key.

Was he planning to kidnap one of the children? It happened often enough, all over the country. Or had he been watching the cats? Maybe watching Courtney? But that was silly, there were calico cats all over the village, what would he want with this one? Joe looked at his beautiful daughter, the delicate black bracelets around her right front leg. He would kill anyone who touched her. So would Dulcie—and Courtney could land a few bloody strikes herself, the kitten having learned to fight early on, from her two teasing brothers.

When story hour was finished, when the children broke away talking and laughing, running, checking out books, meeting their mothers, Kit and Pan streaked out the front door belatedly following Officer McFarland. Dulcie and Courtney, thinking of a late breakfast, followed Wilma into her office; but Joe Grey never hesitated, he charged on past them through her office, through the cat door into the alley, up the bougainvillea vine onto the roof, and raced toward the side street, where Kit and Pan followed McFarland below. All three saw McFarland turn the corner then pull back as the shadowy man entered the Swiss Café.

McFarland moved on up the street among a crowd of tourists and stepped into an old car parked at the curb. Slumping down, he used the newspaper guise. Jimmie had been in the library last Saturday, but had left before the snooping stranger did. Maybe he'd followed the man several times, maybe knew his habits. This wasn't a case yet, it was a question, a quiet surveillance.

Joe Grey watched four little girls and two women crowd into the café—well, the snooper couldn't snatch a child from that crowd. Growing restless, knowing McFarland would stay with the guy, knowing that if something ugly happened he'd hear sirens, Joe took off fast, hitting the roofs with determined paws, heading back to Dulcie and Courtney, who would be waiting in Wilma's office.

Though he did wonder if by now the chief had returned from the hospital, should have gotten what information he could on the battered woman—if she could talk at all, with that black-and-blue throat. If her windpipe wasn't torn or collapsed, the tomcat thought sickly; and his mind was on both cases, the nearly dead woman, a beautiful woman and not a sign of ID that he had found; and then the shadowy prowler. If the man was watching one of the children, if he meant to kidnap a child, this was the worst crime of all.

Or, at that moment, Joe Grey thought it was.

One Saturday, Joe had seen Jimmie McFarland photograph the guy's footprints after he'd crossed the polished floor of the front entrance; and both Dulcie and Kit had seen Jimmie taking fingerprints one evening after the library had closed—and Joe couldn't shake his unease, couldn't forget the chill gleam in the man's pale eyes.

What Joe Grey didn't see, nor did Jimmie McFarland, was the prowler slip into a men's shop, casually lift two shirts and several jackets off a rack, smile and nod at a salesman, and take them into a dressing room. No one saw him facing the mirror removing the mustache and his cap with the tangled hair attached to it. They didn't see him take out a handkerchief and wipe his handsome bald head until it shone, didn't see him fold the objects of disguise, wrap the handkerchief smoothly around them, and slip the package in his own jacket pocket. Departing the store, he left the new clothes neatly on their hangers in the dressing room. He thanked the nearest salesman, the first one was with a customer. He stopped at the front counter to buy two pairs of socks which he paid for with cash, and he was gone.

That was why, when Jimmie and his fellow officers kept a watch for the library prowler as they went about their routes, no one ever did see him—or didn't know that they saw him.

But now, Joe slipped into Wilma's office to snuggle down with his family—though he didn't stay long.

2

et him go, you can't change him," Wilma said as Joe Grey soon raced out the cat door. Dulcie started after him, but then she sighed and turned back. Half of her wanted to follow Joe, to see what he'd find; the other half told her to stay out of it. The guy was interested in children, not cats. Anyway, Officer Mc-Farland was on his tail. And *they* could shadow him all over the village, from the rooftops, until they picked up a clue or two, until they had enough to call in valuable information that Jimmie McFarland might miss.

But neither the cats nor Jimmie picked up much more information. Except for what, later, Courtney herself found out, to her dismay.

Now, Wilma sat down in her desk chair, took the

clip from her long gray hair where the children had tangled it, brushed it smooth and reclipped it. Dulcie's housemate was a tall, strong woman, a retired federal parole officer and now a part-time reference librarian. She loved best reading to the children, just as she read to Dulcie and Courtney at home, just as she had read to all three of Dulcie's kittens until Courtney's brothers moved away, starting their own lives.

Dulcie had lived with Wilma since she was a kitten; she was less than a year old when she discovered that she could speak. Her first words, blurted out without thought, had shocked them both. They had stared at each other in frightened silence. That moment had changed their lives forever.

They were alarmed and frightened, but then all at once they found themselves talking up a storm, both woman and cat wild with delight at being able to communicate.

Soon their household was a different place. They shared every thought, every memory. They were like long-lost roommates newly reunited, trading every secret. Or *nearly* every secret. Dulcie might leave out some of her and Joe's most frightening adventures, though Wilma eventually learned about most of them and either scolded or laughed at them. Dulcie had learned to read, as Wilma read to her, the pretty tabby picking out the sound of each word, then of each letter. She learned the written word fast, took great delight in that new joy as she learned to pick out words on the computer. Soon Dulcie, listening to her own muse, found her head full of poems that she had to write down, and they were both amazed. The word pictures were simply there, something in her cat nature heard the cadences and had to save them, had to read them back to herself.

Even now, trying to ease her fear of the prowler, she padded across the desk to the computer, clenched her paws tight, and gently touching the keys, she opened her own personal document and started a new page— seeking to drown her fear of the prowling man, to calm that fluttering feeling that made her paws tremble. Whatever he wanted, she hoped Jimmie McFarland nailed him, and soon.

Now, longing to bring back the fairy-tale joy of Narnia, wanting to return to that magical world and drive back the ugly parts of life, she began a poem,

White witch before the moon,
Cold witch, cold as moon . . .
Little animals turned to stone,
Moonlight on them
Cold, alone . . .

But these were frightening words, and no others would come. Despite the fun of the book, the evil in it mixed too well with the man on the balcony, driving the goodness away. She looked at Courtney, expecting to see a shiver of fear in her young daughter's amber eyes—but Courtney was not upset. Courtney the dreamer was still deep in the wonders of Narnia, still in the ice and snow, still with the magical beavers, hardly thinking of the stranger in the shadows. "Anyway," Courtney said, reading her mother's look, "anyway, he's gone now. And what harm did he do?"

Wilma, with a glance at Dulcie, took calico Courtney in her arms and they headed out the back door for her car. *For home and safety,* Dulcie thought. While at the same moment, up on the roofs Joe Grey was streaking for the police department, for his own brand of safety among MPPD's family of cops.

The old man, having left his truck parked against the heavy bushes beside the grocery, was coming out of his lawyer's office feeling better. Maybe he wasn't as old and half dead as he'd thought. Finally getting his will and trust in order, signing the last papers. Wiping out everyone but little Mindy and the two trustees he had chosen, leaving her the house and land, the two horses, the tractor and haying machines, and what money he had—which was more than his three sons knew—he felt more like the old Zebulon Luther once more. He figured no one would take better care of Mindy than Police Chief Harper and Charlie, his redheaded wife. He lived close enough to the Harper ranch to ride over there sometimes, or to see Charlie riding by on her sorrel mare, to stop and talk with her for a while or ask her in for coffee. Sometimes Charlie would bake a carrot cake or bring him a bag of oatmeal cookies. He and Mindy kept that secret, the two hiding them and sharing them alone. Yes, Charlie and Max would make fine guardians, if it came to that. Zeb knew a lot about Max Harper, and all of it good except for what Thelma and Nevin said, and that translated easily into the real truth.

His attorney, Eric Lock, was an easygoing guy raised in Montana, and about Zebulon's own age. It was mighty nice of him coming into the office on a Saturday. He insisted on getting the Harpers' written permission before finalizing the trust. It didn't give Zeb custody but it gave him a leg up, to take better care of his granddaughter. Lock took care of it all, and Zeb, leaving his office, felt pretty good.

He pulled back as Thelma and Mindy passed by, headed on down the block. He was so excited to see his granddaughter he started to run over and grab her up and hug her. Instead, he pulled deeper into the shadows of a camera shop, stood watching her sadly as she disappeared.

He could see a black stretch limo parked down the street and he got a glimpse of the driver, crew-cut white hair as his third and oldest son straightened his cap. What was DeWayne doing here in the village? He'd thought he was on the East Coast. Zebulon hadn't seen his oldest son in more than three years and he never heard from him, never a call or a letter, nor did he expect any. DeWayne dressed the best of the three boys, was the slickest. Had a fancy girlfriend, everything he did was to act big-time—but Zeb never saw the boy. DeWayne had e-mailed the girlfriend's picture to Varney, not to his own father.

DeWayne was in South America for a while, then returned to drive limos for a small company in San Francisco. Even when he came down here, he never called or stopped by.

Well, he was here now. Zeb guessed with the car show, with all the tourists in town, more limos had been hired.

Or did DeWayne's presence mean something more? In this crowd, he could sure figure a way to pick up some loose cash. DeWayne had sticky fingers even worse than his brothers.

Zeb had tried for years to change them but they wouldn't listen so what was the use? He and Nell had done everything they knew to keep them straight; their crimes were never anything too bad, as far as he knew: misdemeanors like minor stealing, shoplifting. He and Nell had ended up not prying into their business, life was easier that way. To talk about it only made Nell sicker.

He turned away when Charlie Harper and that young female building contractor, Ryan Flannery, came out of the PD and, some distance behind them, the chief. Max Harper was in uniform today, not in his usual jeans and boots.

He waited until Max had pulled out, and Mindy and Thelma had gone on. He didn't want Mindy to see him here in town and shout "Grandpa!" and run up to him making a fuss, no matter how much he missed her. Heading back down the street for his truck, he felt in his pocket for his grocery list. Lonely old man shopping to cook for himself like so many single "seniors" in the village, left to waste alone; and his cooking never tasted as good as Nell's had, or even Thelma's, after she took over. Glancing back once at the courthouse, he saw a cat on the roof behind him but paid little attention; except he wondered if he should get a cat. For the mice. And, to be honest, for the company, a warm, friendly animal to cuddle down with at night.

From the roof of Molena Point PD, Joe Grey hardly noticed the old man; he seemed vaguely familiar, some local Joe had seen around. The tomcat had backed halfway down the oak trunk by the department's glass door when Charlie Harper and Joe's own housemate, dark-haired Ryan Flannery, came out, her tousled bob lightly flecked with sawdust, her carpenter's tools still hanging at her belt. Charlie Harper's red hair was tied back with a pink scarf, she was wearing a pink T-shirt, new jeans, and sandals. Looked like she'd meant to go out to lunch with Max and had been stood up by some emergency or official appointment. Too bad. Some distance behind them, the chief appeared, dressed in uniform as was Detective Dallas Garza, the two heading for the chief's squad car. Max turned to wave to Charlie, and she blew him a kiss. He glanced at Joe, frowned, and the two cops were gone, turning out into village traffic—and Joe would have to wait until they returned to get any information about the woman he had found, or about the library snooper. Maybe they'd have something soon, with McFarland tailing the guy.

He could slip in the station and prowl Max's desk.

But eavesdropping when the detectives were present was better than snooping alone through the chief's notes and reports. Listening to Max and his staff toss a problem around while Joe himself sat reading Max's handwritten notes and scanning the computer screen usually added up to a bundle of facts worth waiting for.

Now, he dropped on down the oak tree and followed Ryan and Charlie who looked like they were headed for lunch. Ryan had just come from work, khaki shirt and work pants, and heavy boots. When she saw Joe, she grinned and beckoned to him. He followed them down the sidewalk and into the flowery little tearoom that Ryan had said no cop would ever be caught entering. As the door swung closed Ryan caught the heavy glass, Joe slid through, and they made for an isolated corner table, passing the elderly tearoom cat asleep on the window seat. The old fellow hardly stirred, hardly opened his eyes when he caught a whiff of Joe Grey. There were no other cats in the room at the moment, though most of the tables were taken.

Joe leaped into the corner chair between Ryan and Charlie, and Ryan ordered for him, Joe's ear twitch of agreement at a smoked-salmon sandwich, hold the bread, and a crab salad, hold the mayo. When the waitress had left, Charlie launched softly into a discussion of facts that Ryan must already know, thus telling Joe what he hadn't had a chance to hear in the chief's office where he'd been headed.

Charlie said, "Max meant to get to the hospital early, see that battered woman again that the medics picked up, then have a quick lunch. But he's running late for some meeting, he stayed at the hospital quite a while. She's in bad shape, the guy almost broke her neck. She was lucky someone found her." She didn't glance down at Joe but she stroked him lovingly—and Joe could feel her shudder, as he did himself, thinking of the woman nearly buried alive. He looked up at Charlie and rubbed his head back and forth against her caressing hand.

"She's still on life support," Charlie said. "She can hardly speak, her throat is so injured. Looks like she speaks Spanish more easily, maybe one of the Latin American countries. Dallas will sort out what the other guys miss."

"What made her attacker leave so suddenly?" Ryan said softly, looking down at Joe Grey. "Lucky for her someone came along. I've seen enough grisly murders, but to be buried alive . . ." She leaned down to hug Joe Grey and kiss the top of his head. It embarrassed him for her to kiss him, even when they were home alone. She said, "I wish I'd learned Spanish when Dallas was living with us." Ryan's two uncles had moved in with her dad and the three little girls after their mother died.

Dallas was her mother's brother, the Latino half of the family, with his dark hair and nearly black eyes. Ryan had the dark hair, but her green eyes were like her dad's, Mike Flannery, and his brother Scotty's. The Scots-Irish part of the family. *And tempers to match,* Joe thought, smiling.

"And then later this morning," Charlie said, talking to Ryan as she filled Joe in, "another street robbery. Victim was carrying a canvas bag with cash, another bank deposit."

That brought the tomcat to attention. He'd heard nothing about this. He must have been lolling with the kiddies at story hour when that went down. Maybe that was where the siren they'd heard was heading.

"It was out in the valley," Charlie said. "That victim's in emergency, too."

"I think . . ." Ryan paused, looked startled as the front door opened and their new neighbors, the brown-haired little girl and her plain, unhappy mother, came in. Mindy spotted Charlie and took off running. She threw her arms around her redheaded neighbor, who often rode the trails with her—but Thelma grabbed the child, pulled her across the room, and sat down with their backs to them but where they could see out the window. Mindy looked around at Joe as if she would grab him, too, but at her mother's look she sat still.

Joe just looked at her. He had had enough of the Luther family since Thelma and Nevin and Mindy moved in with Varney. Nevin was the youngest, Varney the middle brother. He'd moved into the rental across from Joe Grey's house about six months ago. Neither Joe, Ryan, nor Clyde had had a full night's sleep since the other three joined him. The two brothers were always at it, shouting and arguing over nothing. Joe, when he was in at night—which wasn't often—had slept in the kitchen with Snowball and the big silver Weimaraner where they couldn't hear so clearly; the aging, loving, nonspeaking little white cat considered the Weimaraner her protector. She slept nearly buried between the big dog's chest and paws. Joe Grey would lie draped over Rock's flank, their gray coloring so similar it was hard to tell cat from dog.

"I keep wondering," Ryan said softly, "if there's a connection between the battered woman and the street robberies. I don't know why there would be, except that during the car festival there's big money around. And these last three robberies, two of them just before the bank closed, were all large cash deposits from restaurants that are crowded to the hilt. Bar owners getting rid of their surplus cash."

Restaurant bars usually got rid of what cash they could before the crowds gathered. Dinner customers most often paid by credit card, while those at the bar shelled out greenbacks. Joe knew that from slipping into any number of village restaurants, watching the crowd from some dark corner as he spied on a suspect, collecting information that he could pass anonymously to Max Harper—if he wasn't tossed out by the maître d', thrown unceremoniously out in the parking lot, angry and clawing. Ryan glanced at him, a teasing look in her eyes. "This latest robbery just after the bank closed, no sign of a witness, even the phantom snitch missed the action. But then, that was clear up the valley."

"But there *was* a witness," Charlie said, looking at Ryan. "That robbery, *after* the Mid-Valley Bank closed. Though the witness didn't see much, she couldn't run after him. She was way pregnant and pushing two kids in a stroller—Max said so pregnant that if she'd chased the robber she might have delivered right there on the street. She whipped out her phone and called the dispatcher, but the small squad working that area was clear up the valley, and the guy got away.

"She called the medics, too," she said, laughing. "Baby boy, born on the medics' stretcher before they even got her in the ambulance.

"She said the man was dressed in dark gray and a tan jacket, old jogging shoes, cap pulled down over dark shaggy hair. She didn't see his face, he fled around a corner and she didn't see or hear a car." Charlie pushed back her red hair. "Max was mad as hell that they lost him." She lowered her voice when a black limo pulled up in front of the tea shop, the driver in black uniform, black cap; they could see someone tall slumped in the backseat, only a shadow behind the dark glass.

The driver got out and came in, crossing the room directly to Thelma Luther's table. Dark auburn hair, liver-colored freckles running into his sideburns and scalp. He sat down, they said nothing but looked at each other comfortably. The moment he appeared, the shop cat woke, hissed fiercely at him, and fled for the kitchen.

Mindy, having had little response from Joe Grey but a growl, raced at once for the older cat. She snatched him up near the back door; but she held him gently, petting him despite his angry snarls. Joe Grey, with the window seat empty, flew across the room and jumped up on the padded bench that stood against the window, sitting tall as he took silent possession, smugly defending the warm place the old cat had abandoned.

The driver was a middle-aged man, of middle height. Joe didn't like his eyes, they were small and mean. He ordered coffee and a sweet roll, a second one to go. When the waitress had left, he turned to Thelma.

"We've changed our plans, we're moving on for a few days."

Her look was puzzled, questioning.

"Too many tourists. I thought Car Show Week would be good cover, tourists thick as cockroaches. I'd *counted* on cops everywhere, but not *this* many and not at three in the morning. Early last night, Maurita began to get edgy, there was a big fight. She doesn't like the crowds, either, you know how temperamental she is."

Thelma looked at him nervously.

"The bars close at one," he said. "I thought the village would quiet down but it doesn't."

Of course it quiets down, Joe Grey thought. Last night—this morning—I was out at three, middle of town, all over town. Quiet as a tomb. The thought of a tomb made him claw nervously at the seat cushion.

"But you've . . ." Thelma began.

The man nodded. "We'd already done the casing. Maurita did the inventory, she knows her business. But then afterward when she was done . . ." He paused, looked uncertain. "Afterward, she just fell apart, lost her nerve. She was shaking and she started crying. They fought, and she began throwing things in her suitcase. He stomped out, called her some pretty raunchy names, and left the motel. She took off alone in one of the backup cars, headed for San Francisco, she said. He let her go. They'll both cool down by morning.

"We'll put it off until the crowd eases up. Hit San Francisco for the rest of the week, until these tourists thin out and the cops pull back, and pull back their part-time crew." He was speaking softly. He glanced several times at Ryan and Charlie but there was no way they could hear him; it would take a cat, a cat sitting alert and close to him, to hear the auburn-haired man's whisper.

Max *had* brought in extra forces, because of the trouble they'd had at last year's car show: robberies, three small riots that filled up the jail, and despite the tight surveillance at the show itself, two thefts of antique cars that had been parked on the village street, each worth over a million.

The driver rose. "Got to get to work. We'll be in touch. Our little company, getting this gig with ALS, we don't want to blow that." American Limo, which served Molena Point and up the coast, was a big corporation, but even they hired smaller companies to fill in during the busiest times. The man paid his check, picked up the wrapped sweet bun, and left.

Little Mindy was still in the kitchen, waitresses

stepping around her as she restrained and petted the old cat, some of the women frowning because she was in the way, some just smiling; the shaggy old cat looked somewhat happier now that he was being petted, until one of the waitresses reached to pick him up and toss him out and he started snarling again and striking at her. Joe abandoned the scene, turning back to the window as the limo pulled away. He got the license number and just caught the little sticker with the name of the company, Maitre D' Limo.

Whatever that's about, he thought, *it's sure as hell dicey. It can't hurt to give the chief a call. I wish Thelma had mentioned the guy's name. They seemed casual enough, almost like family. Or does Thelma have something going, on the side?*

3

As Joe leaped into Ryan's red king cab she pulled her notebook from the center console and wrote down the license number he gave her: the make of the limo, the logo that said ALS.

Driving home, they caught a glimpse of Charlie's red hair in her SUV, headed toward the gallery that handled her work, and Joe told Ryan about the man who'd been casing the library. Ryan and Charlie had already heard the rough details in Max's office before the chief left for lunch, and she knew that Jimmie McFarland was tailing the stalker or whatever he was. She looked over at Joe, frowning. "It could be nothing. Some guy doing research for a college class or a private project, that's the way Max seemed to take it—

except," she said, "he does have McFarland keeping an eye on him."

"And what has Jimmie found out?"

"Not much so far," Ryan said. "He's checked for prints—but in a library? Fingerprints all over the place. And when the guy took the books from the shelf he was wearing pigskin gloves. That's what set Max off. Do you know how clumsy it is to flip through books and try to write down notes while wearing gloves?"

Joe snorted. "Try that with cat paws, see what you get."

She couldn't help grinning. But then, looking over at him, she turned solemn. "What's happening to the village, Joe? We always have some crime, a murder or two, a few burglaries, just like every town—a few really bad ones, that *you've* helped solve, that might never have been sorted out without our phantom snitch, without the evidence you've tipped to Max and the department."

She turned a corner, stopping for a half dozen giggling young tourists, and turned to look at Joe. "That poor beaten woman, half buried alive, that gives me the sick shudders. It *was* you who tipped Max off?"

"Yes, and scared the killer off," he said, "when I stepped on a dry twig. I couldn't see much of him in the fog, just his shadow, heavyset or heavy coat; hard to tell much, except he was tall. Did anyone find the shovel? Did they find anything after I belted out of there?"

"Max didn't say. Except there was dirt on the curb where the snitch . . ."—she grinned—"where you said her attacker had parked."

"Did anyone report the torn screen across the street," Joe said, "where I made the call?"

She shook her head. "Max didn't mention it. With that old house, who would notice? In that house, all the screens could be rotted. Now, with the fog cleared, Kathleen and Davis are working the area." She glanced at him. "You don't think they'll find pawprints around the phone?"

"That house has cats, I could smell them."

As she pulled into their drive, across the street in front of Varney Luther's rental, he and Nevin were standing in the scruffy yard close together arguing in each other's faces—not loud, not mad, just arguing. Maybe that was natural behavior, Joe thought. Maybe they grew up that way. At least they weren't pounding each other in the middle of the street again, where someone would call the station. Neither one wanted to go to jail, Joe knew enough about them to know that. One more loud fistfight, Max had told them, and they'd be in the lockup.

When Thelma pulled up, parking her old green Volvo in front, the two brothers scowled at her and at Mindy and went in the house. Getting out hastily, Thelma followed them, dragging Mindy by the hand—and looking back at the squad car that had been easing along some distance behind her.

The patrol unit pulled on up, Chief Harper sat a few minutes, double-parked, looking at the Luthers' rental. The old, plastered building was set back from the street farther than the larger houses on either side. It had once been a cramped duplex. Now, with the removal of several interior walls, it afforded room for Varney, for Nevin and Thelma, and a tiny room for the child. Joe and Dulcie had prowled it months ago among timbers and Sheetrock during the reconstruction before Varney ever moved in. Ryan's firm hadn't done the work. The landlord had gotten someone cheap. Cheap and shoddy, Joe thought, not anywhere near Ryan's high professional standards.

Max's squad car sat a few more moments, the chief looking at the now-empty yard, then he moved ahead and turned into the Damens' drive, parking beside Ryan's king cab.

"I wish," Joe said, "those two had been pounding each other so bad that Max would *have* to lock them up."

As Max got out of the squad car, Clyde's Jaguar came up the street and slid into the remaining space. Stepping out he raised a hand to Max, leaned in through Ryan's window to kiss her, but looked suspiciously at Joe Grey. Why did Clyde always suspect he was up to some kind of trouble?

"Anything for lunch?" Clyde said as he and Max headed for the front door. "Max hasn't eaten."

"Those impromptu meetings take forever," Max said, "and accomplish nothing."

Ryan moved on inside to the big kitchen, where she started coffee and began to make sandwiches. "What happened at the hospital, Max? Oh, the woman isn't dead?"

"She's still with us, and doing better than anyone thought. Still in a lot of pain. A cracked jaw, they've wired that up. She can't talk much. Amazing that there's nothing worse broken. Two ribs, a number of small bones, a lot of deep bruises."

Ryan opened a fresh loaf of rye, spread on cream cheese, layered on salami, buttered the outsides and laid them on the grill, two for Max, two for Clyde, and despite the fact that Joe had just eaten, one for the tomcat.

Max sat down in his usual place, pushing aside the neatly opened morning paper which, Joe noticed, did not mention the open grave and attempted murder. It featured instead the winners of the state's high school spelling bee, a big spread above the fold. And, below the fold, a young black bear that had wandered into the village from a nearby canyon. The bear had escaped two foot-patrol officers by climbing a pine tree near the village church. Now, this morning, he was drawing quite a crowd.

Max said, "We managed to dodge the press on the open grave. The woman was already tucked away in the emergency room with guards. Reporters were up front asking questions. They got no answers. Still no match for her prints, and no ID. But I want her out of there, too many civilians nosing up and down the halls." He looked at Clyde. "I still can't believe what you said about the cat."

Joe nearly choked on his sandwich. He looked at Clyde, shocked, his yellow eyes narrowed. *What are you doing? What the hell did you tell Max?*

Clyde dealt out a handful of napkins and poured fresh coffee. "That sort of talent isn't as unusual as you think, cats and dogs scenting to find the start of cancer, find a whole list of diseases. *And,* some of those animals have already been proven to help heal their patients."

Joe relaxed, or nearly so. Except, they had to be talking about Joe's young son, Buffin, who had found his healing talents while nursing a little dog at Dr. Firetti's clinic. Max didn't need to know any more, he was already too often puzzled by Joe and his family. What had Clyde told him, what had he suggested?

"I've been looking at cats on the Internet," Clyde said. "A cat up in Oregon who knew when someone was going to die. He wouldn't leave their bed, cuddling against them trying to soothe them as long as they were alive. Maybe it's the same thing with the healing."

Max shrugged. "I suppose," he said doubtfully. "Like the scent detection of a good drug dog. Except drug dogs are trained to the skill. These sensing animals, if there is such a thing, would have to be *born* with the ability. And as to healing . . ."

Clyde picked up half his sandwich. "Same with healing. Ask John Firetti. He said the first time the kitten was in the clinic he hopped right up into that pup's cage, snuggled up to the sick dog, and at once the dog wagged his tail and rested against Buffin. In a little while the dog was smiling and wanting to get up, wanting to walk around, acting as if the pain was gone." Though Clyde himself was still puzzled over the event.

Ryan said, "John Firetti will tell you, he'll tell you what Buffin can do. Besides, what harm to try? You *said* if the woman doesn't get better in Recovery the hospital wants her in a nursing home, that she needs more quiet and rest." She looked at Max quietly. "She needs to get well enough to give you some information. And maybe Buffin can help heal her. She'll have good care, good nurses, she'll be just five minutes from Emergency. Why not try it?"

The chief said nothing.

"Having a pet," Ryan said, "a little cat to cuddle, could calm her, might cheer her where nothing else would." But Ryan knew that Joe's buff kitten could do more than just calm a patient.

Max said, "No nursing home would bother with an animal. And the cost . . . My budget won't handle guards twenty-four/seven."

"That new little nursing home over near the foreign car sales," Ryan said, "near Clyde's shop. They're small. Ten patients, and they're nice people, I know the manager and one of the nurses. I could talk with them. It isn't far from the vet clinic, John Firetti could check on Buffin, check on them both," she said, grinning. "It has no business sign, it looks like an ordinary house. Mirrored windows so when the lights are off you can't see in, alarms on all the windows. The owner and two of the nurses carry, and are well trained. Is she well enough to go there?"

"And," Max said, "if her attacker sees us move her? Sees the ambulance and follows it, knows she's there? Is waiting for another chance at her before she talks? We have guards on her room, but if he catches us moving her out . . ."

"You're a cop, you can figure that out. Dress her as a medic, switch with a woman medic bringing in a patient? Send her away in the supposedly empty ambulance . . . Is she well enough to walk? Drive the 'empty' ambulance into the fire station like they always do, and switch her into an old car?"

Max sighed. Arguing with Ryan was as bad as arguing with Charlie. Except that Ryan didn't give him the hug-and-kiss routine that his redheaded wife would, to soften him up. He got up, frowning. "No more arguments, we'll talk about it later."

"Wilma's coming to dinner," she said, waiting for the next round, letting him think about it. "And the Greenlaws. Potluck. Charlie said she'd drop by from the gallery if they finish early enough. What about you?"

"Not tonight. I think I'll head back to the hospital. At least she speaks English, Dallas found out that much—as garbled as it was with her wired jaw and her bruised throat."

This grisly attempted burial would hold Max and the detectives twenty-four/seven until they nailed the near-murderer; the chief had no notion that the case pulled at Joe Grey in the same intense manner. Max thanked

Ryan for the sandwich, gave her an unexpected kiss on the forehead, and left them, swinging out the front door and into his squad car. Joe watched him from the living room window as he cruised slowly by the Luther house, giving the place another look-over.

What so interested him about their bickering neighbors? Well, domestic cases *could* turn into big trouble, could explode in a flash. A good cop was always watchful; such conflict, even from a distance, always put an officer on alert.

Joe Grey dug his claws into the back of the couch, wondering if Max knew something that he didn't. Was there a connection between the Luthers and some other crime? The library prowler? The beaten woman?

Maybe he'd hit the station later, stretch out on Harper's bookcase, try to put the pieces together.

4

It was over three weeks after Nevin and Thelma
and Mindy moved out and left him that Zeb found
the letter. He found it on a Friday, the day Mindy had
always started begging about going to the library for
Saturday. He wondered if Thelma was taking her to
story hour since they'd moved away from the ranch
and into the village, with the library and shops right
there close. Thelma always grumbled about story
hour, she didn't like sitting around listening to what
she called "kiddies' books." The librarian, Ms. Getz,
said you had to grow up, grow truly mature in the way
you looked at life, before you began to enjoy reading
again the best children's stories.

Well, this Friday he'd gone out to the road to get
the mail and the paper, all junk mail usually that he'd

throw in the trash. Except his bank statement was in there and he tossed it on the table. Varney had had his mail forwarded to a post office box when he left six months ago. Nevin and Thelma did the same just a few days before they moved out.

Before they left, Zeb had hardly ever brought in the mail. Mindy did it, or Nevin. Zeb didn't get much mail himself, only an occasional postcard from a cousin or some old friend or one of Nell's friends; and their statement. Just to be sure he hadn't missed anything, he shuffled methodically through the junk ads, tossed them in the trash, and turned to pick up the bank statement.

But this wasn't his statement. It was Nevin's. And not Nevin and Thelma's regular account. Just Nevin Luther, alone. And it wasn't from their bank, either, the one in the village. This was from the Bank of Walnut Creek, way up the coast.

Nevin had never had an account in that bank. Why would he? Why drive way up there? Zeb had never seen a statement marked like this. He sat down at the kitchen table with the envelope before him, deciding if he should open it or direct it on, mark it "wrong address"? It wasn't his business.

He made himself a cup of coffee. Waiting while it brewed, he sat staring at the bank logo and at Nevin's neatly typed name, with this address. Maybe the bank had made a mistake when they were sorting out changes of address on the computer.

Pouring his coffee, sitting down again, he ripped open the envelope before he had time to think about it, wasn't even careful how he tore it. Pulled out the statement and stared at the front page where it gave the monthly total, which made him gag on his coffee.

Total assets: $1,271,899.10. *One million?* He read it again.

Total liabilities: $0.00.

Qualifying balance: $1,271,899.10. One million, two hundred and seventy-one thousand, eight hundred and ninety-nine dollars, and ten cents.

Zeb sat for a long time. He checked the amounts and dates of the individual deposits. None were too large, but many were just a few days apart. Took a lot of gas to drive up there that often. Would Nevin have done the banking by mail? That wasn't like him, he didn't trust the mail. He refilled his coffee cup and made a ham sandwich. Went out to the shed, picked up the two dozen newspapers stacked neatly on top of an empty crate, papers he kept for blocking the doors during a flooding rain and for sopping up water when he defrosted the freezer. The discarded papers were pretty much in order.

It took him the rest of the afternoon to find and tear out the pages with articles about the recent increase in bank-withdrawal thefts. And all the time thinking about where Nevin would have put the rest of the statements.

If Varney or Thelma knew nothing about this, Nevin might have figured it was safer to leave them here. He began to search the house, Nevin and Thelma's room first, closet, between the mattress and the springs, the dresser. He found them wrapped in a woolen sweater that Thelma had told Nevin to keep in a zippered plastic bag because of moths. A thin stack of statements with a rubber band around them, folded inside the gray sweater. The same bank, the top one dated the month before the current one, which he slipped in with the others.

Zeb woke real early Saturday morning. He fed and watered the horses, made one phone call, one of the few real friends he had left in the world. He and Robert Blake had ridden broncs together when they were young. Young and strong—and rode the bulls, too, crazy kids. He left the ranch in the old truck, the only transportation he had.

He swung through the village; he was there at eight when the UPS store opened. He made copies of all the statements, at a machine where he was somewhat shielded from the view of prying eyes. He didn't copy the clippings. He put the copies in a brown envelope and shoved that under the floor mat on the driver's side. He returned to the house, put the original statements back the way he'd found them, with the new one, folded into the sweater. He was in Santa Cruz by mid-morning, turning in at his friend's used-car lot.

Robert had pulled one of his cars up to the front of the lot, ones he hadn't done much cosmetics on yet though he'd maybe fixed up the engines, replaced a few tires. This one was just what he wanted, eighteen-year-old Ford coupe, blue paint so faded it was almost gray. It had nearly new tires, though, and Rob had washed it and polished it as best he could. They hitched the car behind the truck with a car dolly, so Zeb could haul it safely home. They had a beer, shot the bull for a few minutes. Zeb paid for the car with his credit card, which he had used for Nell's medical bills. He was home again around one, he had plenty of time. Passing the Harpers' ranch he noted Charlie's SUV parked by the house, the light in her studio reflecting against the hay barn.

At home he unhitched the car and backed it deep in the shed, tucked the envelope of copied statements in his pocket. Parked the truck just outside where he always did. He checked his watch again. This was Saturday, the best night to try, but he had plenty of time. He knew that little area, it was closer than the village, he knew most of the shopkeepers. The bank stayed open until six on Saturdays so people could deposit their pay, and the restaurant owners could make big deposits to nearly empty their safes before the busiest night of the week when robberies would be lucrative. Restaurant safes were weaker than a bank vault.

Throwing a saddle on his bay gelding he headed at a jog then an easy canter for the Harper place. It was Charlie who had taught Mindy to guide a horse with body movement, easy and nice, a little pressure, a little shift of weight.

He could see Charlie in the kitchen pouring a cup of coffee. She waved him in, and reached for another cup. She had cut her curly red hair short, a bright cap where it used to be a long flaming tangle tied back out of the wind.

Throwing his reins over the hitching rack near the pasture fence, he entered through the all-purpose front door into a big, tile-floored mud room, hooks for jackets, shelves for boots, long sink for scrubbing up hands and arms, pots of flowers on the windowsill. One door stood open to the kitchen, another to the big, high-raftered living room that looked out across the pastures to the sea. When he entered the kitchen, Charlie looked at his expression for a long minute, gave him a hello hug and led him to the table. He didn't visit often without phoning, didn't visit for no reason. She looked at the brown envelope he laid on the table, her bright, freckled face puzzled and then uneasy. She reached to the kitchen counter, fetched a plate of gingerbread; looked back at the envelope then at Zebulon, waiting.

"Would you hide it for me where no one else will find it? Well, if Max finds it, that's okay. At my house, nothing's very secure. Hide it from Max and not tell him unless he *does* find it. Or until the time is right. Is that putting too much on a cop's wife?"

Charlie laughed. "Can you tell me what it is, or is that a secret, too?"

"It's copies of Nevin's bank statements, a bank up the coast. I don't know if they mean anything. I think they do, and that Max will want them. The originals are in Nevin's dresser. Are you okay with them here, or do they put you in trouble?"

Charlie touched the shoulder holster under her light vest, and grinned at him. The statements would be safe here. She took the envelope, stepped into the living room and behind the fireplace. He heard a stone slide, then a lock click and turn several times. Heard a metal door open.

She returned without the envelope, her stardust of

freckles bright with interest, her green eyes wide with questions she wouldn't ask. Whatever this was about, she knew he had his reasons. That he was doing the right thing, or getting ready to do it. She knew Zeb wouldn't make trouble for Max.

As for Zeb, he trusted Charlie as he trusted the chief himself. He finished his coffee and gingerbread. He rose, gave her a hug, left quietly out the mud entry. He untied his gelding and headed home, the back way again, they were hardly seen as the bay moved quietly through the woods. At home Zeb unsaddled him, rubbed him down, and went inside to his room.

He had a little nap, drifting off wondering how all this would turn out, wondering if he was making too much of nothing.

He was up and left the house around five, drove in to the shopping center across Highway One from the village: newer grocery, drugstore, lots of casual restaurants and shops, fire station across the side road. He'd liked Molena Point when it was smaller, when this here land was all dairy barns and pastures, before the village started to outgrow itself.

He pulled into a small alley behind the drugstore where he could see the backs of a row of restaurants; and just across the blacktop, cars parked before the bank, its fluorescent lights reflected in their windows.

He killed the engine and sat in his car watching for a possible shopkeeper on his way to make a deposit.

Yes, he didn't wait long and here came Jon Jaarel driving into the lot in his new, white Lexus hatchback. Older, blond man, his once athletic trim still thin but going soft. Jon pulled in carefully between a bread delivery truck and a tall, rented camper, a narrow space where he wouldn't readily be seen by some pickpocket; the way Jaarel acted, Zeb knew he had money on him. As Jaarel opened the door and started to step out, his trench coat pooched in front as if he were pregnant. In the shadows of the tall vehicles, a car drew up nosing into the narrow space between Jaarel's door and the truck; the driver swung out, bundled up in the chill dusk, heavy jacket, hood pulled up. As Jaarel stepped out, the driver hauled back and slammed the door against Jaarel, knocking him hard into his own steering wheel and slamming the door against him. Jaarel struggled as the robber leaned in, ripped open Jaarel's trench coat, snatched out the money bag, and slammed the door in Jon Jaarel's face, a terrible blow. And the man was gone, barely a flash of his green car as he spun and sped away.

Jaarel lay still in his white hatchback, bleeding, as Thelma's car disappeared among the shops and small streets.

Nevin. The robber was Nevin.

Shamed and shocked, Zebulon wanted to run across and help Jaarel but he didn't have the nerve to be seen there. He was certain Jon was dead, the way the blood was gushing. And what if Nevin saw him? Grabbing his old phone, he hit the emergency button and alerted the local branch of the fire department, which was right across the highway. He backed out of the alley looking for Nevin but didn't see him. Didn't see any cops. He drove sedately up a side street as an ambulance screamed out of the station and across the main road.

Joe Grey waited, pacing with hunger, for their friends to arrive with their potluck supper offerings. At last here came Wilma, sliding out of her car carrying a wrapped casserole, Dulcie and Courtney leaping out behind her, noses to the air sniffing the good smell of her tamale pie. As Wilma headed for the kitchen, the Greenlaws double-parked in the drive. Kit and Pan jumped out of the black Lincoln Town Car and raced in the house, Pedric behind them carrying a tray covered with clear wrap that smelled like a field of ripe strawberries. Joe was rearing up sniffing the good scents of supper when they heard, from across the street, a car start. Curious, Joe raced to the front window to look, the other cats crowding behind him. Thelma's car, the green Volvo, was just turning the corner up toward Highway One, Nevin driving. Thelma stood in the yard looking sour, then turned back in the house scowling and dragging Mindy behind her. Maybe Nevin was going to the store, they always fought over that. Nevin said it was Thelma's place to do the shopping. She said she'd shop if he'd cook, but he never did. Maybe he'd said her car needed running so the battery wouldn't die.

Abandoning the sleazy couple, the cats returned to the kitchen; the big room was full of talk and laughter, the sounds of plates and silverware, and the aroma of supper and of the garlic bread that Charlie had just brought in. She didn't have to say, *Max is working.* He usually was. Clyde was saying, "It's Dulcie and Courtney and Kit that I worry about—it's the sweet cuddly ones that a cat dealer would steal and sell."

Joe gave Clyde a hard look. "You're saying I'm not sweet and cuddly?"

"Sweet as syrup," Clyde said, cuffing him on the shoulder. "Who wouldn't love to steal a mean-looking tomcat with teeth like rapiers?"

But the idea of a cat thief was too bizarre. "Why would anyone steal a cat?" Joe said. "If that guy knew we could speak, he'd have snatched us all up long ago. And why come to the library for an ordinary cat, there are cats all over the village, neighborhood cats wandering everywhere. As far as cuddly, little children are the cuddly ones. Little kids are kidnapped all the time."

But then he was sorry he'd said that, the thought of what happened to those kids made his paws go cold and his stomach queasy—and Clyde looked at Joe a long time. He said, "And there sure as hell aren't cats like Courtney all over the village, with her picture in half the history books. What about those books he was poring over, what was that about? All McFarland said when he looked later, after the guy had put the books back, was that they were from the shelves on ancient art."

Dulcie said, "The watcher looked a lot like the bank robber that pregnant woman described. Dark rumpled clothes, long black hair, wrinkled cap, old worn-out coat. It could be the same guy . . . And *he* stole a bundle of money."

Clyde shook his head. "How would a robbery fit in with his prowling the library, watching cats and children?" He glanced at the Greenlaws and at Wilma. "I think the cats would be smart to stay in tonight."

Before anyone could argue, Ryan said, "Dinner," loud enough to stop a barrage of hot feline arguments. She had set out the cats' plates in grand style on the kitchen counter, each with a blue place mat, each with a nice serving of Wilma's tamale pie, garlic bread,

Ryan's fresh green salad, and half a strawberry tart. No one paid much attention to the sirens from up the hill at the shopping center, such wails were common from the smaller fire station that served the valley— fire trucks and maybe an ambulance headed to one of the fancy older folks' communities: elderly people living together, many with no real family and too often needing medical help. Dulcie looked at Joe, feeling suddenly sad for those lonely folks—and feeling sad for herself and for Joe, now that their kittens were nearly full grown, the boys already off on their own and Courtney so wild with adventure that she would be leaving home soon. Dulcie looked at Joe. "I miss the boys."

Joe rubbed his head against hers. "So do I, but they're growing up, they're doing what they want to do. Buffin has settled in, like a miracle, to what he was meant to be."

He twitched a whisker. "And doesn't that make John Firetti happy. It's like having a new hospital assistant, only better. And for now, Striker's happy there, too. Now, our two kittens are all the doctor and Mary have to comfort them, since Misto died."

Dulcie smiled, her ears up again. "Maybe we haven't lost Striker, maybe he'll hang around the cop shop more than you guess."

Courtney exchanged a glance with Kit, a look of understanding. Courtney *did* miss her brothers—but perhaps only a little, now that she had her mama and Wilma all to herself, the three of them had the house to themselves, and *she,* the one remaining kitten, had things pretty much as she wanted.

But Striker and Buffin, the two stars in the Firetti household, had what they wanted, too. They got to wander the hospital, they got to go to the shore every morning and evening to watch John and Mary feed the wild ferals.

Courtney got to do that sometimes, running on the shore among the wild beach cats, leaving her own pawprints in the wet sand. *But,* she thought, *what will my grown-up life be like? Buffin has found his place, he healed that little dog and sent him home happy, and he's healed more. Dr. Firetti says he has a rare talent. And Striker, all claws and teeth, he wants to chase the bad guys like our daddy. But there's something more, too, for Striker. Some other talent, I can sense it; but no one knows yet what that is.*

But what will I do with my life? This right-now-today life? And she thought, *even this very village sometimes brings back such strange memories. Brings back long-past times, Medieval times that, when I wake, I can't stop wondering about.*

In the library she would look at her own pictures in ancient books, see herself in woven tapestries, yet when she tried to remember more about those long-ago ages, she knew that *right now* in this life, something maybe even more exciting waited for her, that a wonderful adventure waited, she could sense it like a bright glow all around her. She thought about that mystery all through dinner.

Afterward, when the cats and humans gathered in the living room by the fire, no one turned on the TV or a radio, no one knew there had been another robbery, another theft of money that had been headed for deposit in the bank. No one knew that the victim was dead.

Max Harper was still in the hospital with the woman from the grave when a second call came through from the dispatcher to his cell phone. Though the rescue units and his officers were careful not to pass information on to the news media, the local paper would have this one soon enough.

The caller wasn't his regular snitch, wasn't the familiar voice he was used to. Though the man's style was the same, passing on the information quickly, and immediately hanging up. And, like Max's usual snitch, his phone was untraceable. Likely an ancient cell phone with no GPS. The voice was that of an old man, shaky, frightened, and distraught. This disturbed him. He wasn't in the mood to deal with another mangled body, this one decidedly dead. For one of the few times in his life Max Harper called in one of the detectives to work the case with the attending coroner—Jane Cameron might be young and beautiful, but she was a tough investigator, she had just been promoted in rank, and she didn't get sick at the sight of a gory corpse.

The old man grew more and more upset as he drove the back way to Highway One and up past the turn-off to the Harpers' ranch. There was no one outside in the pastures to see him drive by and head up his own lane for home.

Having left the scene as the sirens came screaming, he had felt steady enough then, filled with a sense that he'd done the right thing. That he might have saved Jon Jaarel's life.

Could there have been any life left in the man after that brutal attack? What if it *was* murder, what if Nevin *had* killed him?

That was when his stomach really started to churn, when he began to feel pale and sick. Nevin, his own son . . . Over the years he'd known when Nevin was in trouble, and had tried to ignore it; and he had tried to keep the boy's earlier troublemaking from Nell.

As he approached his empty house, evening began to close down around him. He couldn't stop thinking about Jon Jaarel, injured and bloodied. The hardworking restaurant owner was a kind, steady man. Zeb prayed that he was alive yet was pretty sure he wasn't. The old man was filled with a hollow emptiness, with futility at the brutal ways of his own boys, his own family.

He should have made a second call to the dispatcher, should have told Harper who the attacker was. He hadn't seen Nevin full face in the dark but he saw enough to be sure; and he was sure that was Thelma's car. He was sick inside, he didn't know what to do, he felt so unsteady he could hardly drive.

How could he report his own son? All bundled up in old clothes like that, like a homeless man. He had moved so fast to get away that Zeb really hadn't seen his face. He never saw which way Nevin went, he'd been too busy calling the medics—but he knew. He knew, from the way the man moved. He knew the body language of his boys.

This wasn't the first bank-deposit robbery in the shopping area or in the village; and maybe Varney and Nevin were both responsible.

Pulling up before the house feeling even sicker, he saw his old truck sitting there and remembered to hide the car, get it out of sight. He wouldn't want one of the boys to see he had another car. In case he . . . What? Decided to follow them, to see what else they were up to?

After he backed into the shed in the far corner and got out, he felt so shaky that he had to brace himself against the swinging wooden shed door as he closed it. Going inside he gripped the porch rail then the back door, then hung on to a kitchen chair as he sat down at the table. He wished he had some whiskey; there was no liquor in the house. What do you do when you feel scared hollow right down to your very soul?

He couldn't even call the PD and ask if Jon Jaarel was alive; and ask if they'd caught the thief. Even if his phone was so old that it didn't have GPS he was afraid to make another call. How did he know what kind of equipment the cops used?

He sat still for a long time, his head bent on his clenched hands. At last he went in the living room and lay down on the couch. He covered himself with Nell's quilt and closed his eyes. His own boy. One of his boys. He guessed in the dark it could have been Varney but he was almost certain it was Nevin. He felt as weak as an old, old horse about to go under. Was there a place in the hereafter for worn-out horses and worn-out old men with nothing to look forward to? His life was gone. Nell gone, and the three boys turned out like this. Mindy was the only decent one, and the boys and Thelma had taken her away.

Max Harper was bound to find who did the killing—if Jaarel *was* dead. And then prison for the boy, or worse. And, he thought, if both boys were involved, if both were convicted even for short sentences, what would happen to Mindy?

Would Harper leave her in the care of her mother?

But Thelma would refuse to come back here. No telling where she'd take Mindy. Likely she'd head for the city. Turning over, not wanting to think any more, he felt himself drop into a hard, deep sleep. He wouldn't have thought he could sleep, in this state. He felt himself fall into a black emptiness that, he'd read once, came from depression or fear.

On the Damens' roof, late after supper, the cats sat watching the chill fog roll in, its promise making them smile. Soon the streets and rooftops would be all but hidden, they could slip away and go anywhere they wanted, totally unseen. Their human families couldn't object to that. Who could see a cat in this hazy over-cast? Already a long white tail of thick ocean mist crept low along the face of the hills, a dark dragon making its way up the valley, obliterating the lower fields. It would soon grow longer and wider to cover all the hills and valley and then sink down to hide the village.

Then it would be hunting time. No one to see and snatch up a prowling cat as they slipped down from the roofs and maybe to the little park to have another look for the earring—if the cops hadn't found it, or the guy hadn't taken it with him.

The earring was tiny. It might be crushed, but it could still be lying in the sand, lost or buried where the earth was soft and deep. It might never be discovered unless sensitive cat paws dug into every corner of the park and maybe beyond. Could you smell gold? Joe didn't think so, but he very much wanted that little piece of evidence.

The victim's testimony would be powerful, as would the cops' color photos of her lying bleeding and nearly dead, half buried in the rough grave—this, backed by minute bits of evidence the detectives had collected. But to have the torn-off earring with her blood on it and maybe bits of torn flesh and, hopefully, both sets of fingerprints—that should go even further toward convicting the guy, if they ever caught him.

5

The only sound the three lady cats could hear through the heavy fog was the hush of the sea from four blocks down where the injured woman had been found, where the two tomcats had already disappeared searching for the earring or maybe for other clues the cops might have missed, though that wasn't likely. Dulcie and Kit and Courtney had stopped *"for only a minute"* in the heavy haze to peer through a softly lit shop window. Standing on their hind paws, their front paws on the sill, their tails twitching, their noses pressed to the glass, they admired the lovely dresses, the tight pants and vests, and they imagined how it would feel to be real human ladies all dressed up.

The only glow to cut the mist was the faint light from the windows and, overhead, the diffused gleam of the fog-scarfed moon. In the thick haze, the three furry shoppers were only the faintest shadows, and at this hour, who was to see them? The streets were empty, the haze so thick you couldn't have seen a streetlight even if there had been any. Not a soul, no one here to laugh at the cute kitties looking in the shops, no one to be amused at them as the library patrons had been. The fog turned Dulcie's dark tabby stripes silver, and softened the orange of Courtney's bright patchwork; vapor so heavy it feathered Kit's tortoiseshell fur into curly tangles. They felt smug that they had slipped out of Clyde's house against orders only long after the Damens slept, when the fog was so thick that no one could see them anyway—and who would kidnap a cat!

Now, the girl cats didn't speak, even if the street was empty, but they could guess each other's thoughts. Dulcie's green eyes were bright with the dream of being a tall, beautiful woman, elegant in the red silk dress; Kit admired the lady wearing khaki hiking shorts and a leather vest—not that Dulcie or Kit would want to stay in human form, they just wanted to know how it would feel, how they would look. Courtney, unlike her striped mother and tortoiseshell Kit, did not often imagine herself as a lovely human. Truly, only a few of their special breed *could* change. Courtney dreamed of other kinds of magic, of centuries long gone, of ancient realms deep in her memory. As the other two lingered, she moved around the corner to peer in the end window at a soft-toned rain cape which, if she were human, would go well with her calico hair. *Would I still be calico?* Amused, she moved along toward the corner window looking at handsome luggage, at satin stoles, fancy hats and silk scarves, dreaming each into scenes from distant times.

When next Dulcie looked, Courtney had disappeared.

Galloping after her, skidding around the corner, Dulcie expected to see her daughter farther down the side street still peering in windows. She and Kit ran along the building mewing softly. Not seeing Courtney they stared across the street to the other stores, photography shop, art shop, small café—they found her scent, crossed to that side, and ran following her trail behind potted flowers and under porches. Courtney wasn't one to play tricks on her mother. Or, not usually. At the end of the next block her trail ran along beside a stucco wall, they could smell where she had rubbed against it—but suddenly her scent was joined by the smell of a man. Someone they didn't know. Then just as suddenly Courtney's scent vanished. As if he had picked her up?

They air-scented for her, but they smelled only blood. Human blood—and they smelled Courtney's anger, her rage. They hoped she'd clawed him good, hoped he'd dropped her, not liking her sharp rapiers. They could find no trail as if she had run from him. Was he still carrying her as she raked him? Had he hurt her? They followed his trail and the blood trail until the smells stopped at the curb.

Now they smelled canvas. A canvas bag? Then the hot stink of exhaust, and of tires taking off. Little pieces of bloody, torn canvas lay on the wet street. Why hadn't Courtney cried out, why hadn't she yowled for help? They followed his fresh tire tracks fast along the fog-wet street. At the next intersection, the marks of five cars coming out of driveways, turning as if headed for the freeway, maybe for a long drive to work; these crossed over the marks that the cats followed. But one car had turned around in the intersection smearing the other wet tracks, mixing them all up. Kit confusedly raced away down Ocean Avenue to find Joe and Pan, to find help. Dulcie was shaking with fear when the tomcats came running.

Joe licked Dulcie's face. "We'll find her, she can't have gone far."

"Joe, a man grabbed her. We didn't see him, we didn't recognize his smell. He *took* her, he caught her, took her away in a car. We smelled *his* blood, she must have fought hard, scratched him good. What will he do to her?" She was sick with terror. "Can we tell the cops? Will they listen? Will the department put out a BOL for a cat?"

"Harper might," Joe said, "if Clyde or Ryan ask him. If Charlie asks him." He was scared as hell, too. "We need help, now." Without another word he hit the roofs scrambling up a sagging vine and over the peaks for home, for his two housemates; Dulcie headed for her own home with Wilma, streaking along the sidewalk, Kit running beside her, stopping to scent at the bushes, to smell every shop door, peer under every porch, sniff at every car and into every dark corner praying that Courtney had gotten away from him. They searched behind every flower box, up every tree, through the fog-heavy night for the little cat's scent and bright colors, all the time praying, *He hasn't hurt her. Oh, he hasn't hurt Courtney.* Dulcie's heart was pounding. *What has he done to her, what does he want with my baby?* And in her mind she saw Courtney lying hurt and alone, trapped inside a bag, unable to free herself.

6

But Courtney wasn't hurt. She was quite safe, at least for the moment, though she was still mad as hell. What did he want with her? Having driven only a few blocks, with her in the bag on the floor of the front seat, he had turned into a drive and killed the engine. When he lifted the bag out of the car, that was when she nearly got away, pushing through the hole she'd torn, yowling and spitting. He'd clutched the bag closed, carried her through one door and then another; doors close together as if he'd crossed a small room, and closing each behind him. She tried to think which direction they had come, where she might be.

He opened another door and carried her up a hard stairway, his shoes scuffing on something that sounded like rubber matting. Up the flight of steps and through another door that he slammed behind him, too, and he dumped the bag on the floor. She lay shivering. She had gone through a whole range of emotions—terror, rage, and earlier when he had stuffed her in the bag holding her mouth shut, she had been so wild she'd ripped the bag nearly apart. Now, lying in the bag undisturbed, she listened. When he didn't move or speak, she clawed her way out through the bloody hole she'd made.

She was in an upstairs apartment.

She could have run but she didn't. She stood looking up at her captor. But this was not the prowler in the library. This man was quite different. His head and face were clean shaven, smooth and lightly tanned; his eyes were as blue as her kitten eyes had been, before they turned a deep amber. He was well groomed and clean, neatly dressed. He looked down at her with interest, and then with a smile of gentle caring—and did she see a touch of amusement? Maybe because she was scowling at him? He did not look cruel. Strange that even at first, capturing her on the street, he had carried her so gently that he hadn't hurt her, even though she'd fought and ripped at him. Most of the blood was his. Even gripping her by the back of her neck so tightly, he had been careful not to injure her, he had endured her slashing without striking back.

But did his gentle look hold something else, too? For

an instant she had the sense of a big, friendly-appearing dog peering down innocently at a smaller animal that he meant, the next moment, to tear apart.

But that was foolish. He stroked her back then patted the cushions of the brocade couch inviting her up. "Come, my dear. Make yourself comfortable. You'll enjoy living here. Don't be afraid. You can see that the apartment is lovely, and the antiques shop downstairs, which will be yours later, all the beautiful furniture and sculpture to rub against. Come up, my dear, and make yourself at home." And he fluffed up the folded throw at one end.

She leaped to the couch onto the cashmere throw, but she sat tall and still, full of defiance. All this elegance had begun to make her uneasy—yet the living room *was* lovely: ivory satin draperies closing out the night; lovely, carved antique chairs and chests. Wilma had taught her a little about antiques but she didn't know enough to sort these out. There were stained-glass lamps, too, and a rich Persian rug all in deep tones that had felt thick and soft under her paws.

"You'll so love living here—until we go on to New York, of course. Until you really become famous. Then, oh, you'll love living in such elegance." And he smiled and knelt and stroked her back in just the right way. How could he intend any harm?

He sat down at the other end of the couch, comfortable and easy. "You will be happy with me, my dear, and with our adventures. You will know luxuries you would find nowhere else, not in this day. And you will soon be famous. Oh, very famous when our project is complete. You will be on television, in the magazines, and then we will go for the movies. What can you learn, my dear? Can you learn tricks? That would be a nice touch. Oh, you will be idolized in the city."

His grand words began to excite her . . . but then they made her shiver. Were those words what her daddy called con talk, enticing promises that Joe Grey said meant trouble? *Big trouble*, the tomcat had said. *You might find that out soon enough if you're not a wary young cat.*

But the visions this man painted for her glowed too bright in her imagination, galleries richer even than this beautiful apartment, richer than his grand downstairs showroom where she and Dulcie and Kit had sometimes looked in the windows at his lovely wares. She had seen him then, waiting on customers when they had thought he was just another shopper.

And now, when she looked down at the coffee table, at the small silver tray of business cards, they said: *Ulrich Seaver, SEAVER'S ANTIQUES.* The cards were all in gold and silver as elegant as the shop. He was saying, "First we'll go to the San Francisco gallery, you will be the star, and that show is already scheduled. We'll get a nice start there, I'll have the brochures printed by then, I already have the copy ready."

How could he "have the show already scheduled"— whatever exactly that meant—before he was sure he could catch her or even find her? When he couldn't be sure at all that she would be his star?

She was certain, by now, that he didn't know she could speak. She could tell by his expression that he didn't imagine she understood him, his look didn't change as if he expected her response. He didn't wait to see her brighten with joy at what he told her. He was talking only so his voice would reassure her, hoping that his gentle tone would make her feel safe and loved.

Or maybe he was talking, too, to congratulate himself on the project that lay ahead. *That he thinks lies ahead,* she thought warily.

Maybe it was her color, her markings, that he thought would charm people, like the pictures in the library books.

Could he be connected to that shaggy library prowler? If they were both interested in the old tapestries . . . Maybe Seaver had pored over them just as the prowler had? Were they partners? But where was that man now? And how would those pictures make her famous anyway? For people to see her, then see the same cat in the old tapestries? Why would anyone care? And how strange that the two would be connected, this bald, sleek, well-dressed man, and the library prowler as shaggy as a street person?

He looked at her solemnly. "I wish you could understand me, my dear. I wish you could answer me, could tell me how excited you would be at our new adventure. What an amazement that will be, what fun we'll have."

Yes, Courtney thought with another shiver, *and what would you do if I did speak? What would you do with me then?* And the fear returned, the bright glamour fading to mist.

She stiffened as he rose, but he only turned away. "I will leave you to explore, my dear." He opened the pale cream draperies to the foggy dawn. "You will find breakfast in the kitchen. A sand box in the laundry room. You will see the gallery later, you will see the paintings and tapestries of you that I have so far collected, and photos of those I have ordered. Those pieces will remain at the New York gallery when they arrive." He held out his hand to see if she would be gentle or if she would try to scratch again. She swallowed her uncertainty, swallowed her resurging temper, and sniffed hesitantly at his fingers. He smiled with satisfaction, as if they had finally made friends, then he went downstairs to the shop, locking the door behind him.

Free to roam the apartment, she first checked every window but they were all locked tight. In the kitchen, on a tray on the floor, there was fresh salmon and clean water. She didn't want to eat, her stomach was already roiling. But her fear had made her thirsty, and she drank. She wished, for the first time in her short life, that she could take human form as some speaking cats could do. If she could become a human person she could get out of there in a second, could break a window with a chair, open it, turn back into a cat and be gone across the rooftops.

But she couldn't change. That was a rare skill indeed, belonging to only a few of her kind.

In less than a year of kittenhood, she had learned a lot, from her mama and Joe Grey, from Kit and Pan and from their human friends; had learned a lot when Wilma read to her. Her and Dulcie's tall, gray-haired housemate was an ex–federal parole officer, she knew about the human world and, somehow, she knew how to share it in easy terms with a little cat.

Well, and she had learned from her brothers, too. She could fight as hard as Striker and Buffin. She would fight Seaver again even harder if he tried to harm her. Though he hadn't so far. Even when she left him good and bloodied he hadn't hit her, and she didn't think he would.

She had learned to fight from her brothers and from her pa, and learned to swear from them, too. If he touched her with cruel intent just once, she would fight as hard as they, she would kill the bastard, she would shred Ulrich Seaver.

He said she would be happy and famous and that he had wonderful plans for her, but now those words, so softly spoken, made her feel sick again; her emotions swung back and forth until she didn't know what she believed. The sense of luxury, of being loved by this kind-appearing, elegant stranger, slowly vanished as she prowled the apartment searching for a way out. Searching, the fear returned; she was all at sixes and sevens, she didn't know what she believed.

She entered the bedroom last, after she'd prowled the living room and through the big open kitchen with an eating area that looked out on the street. The bedroom had a view of Ocean Avenue, and a connected small, bright bathroom. It was these rooms that held her, staring with surprise.

In the bathroom, a lady's powder box, bottles of lady's makeup, and a few lace-edged towels. And in the bedroom, in one of two closets, ladies' clothes, finely tailored suits and blouses, sleek dresses; lovely shoes with low heels. A woman's expensive purses on the top shelf, everything neat and dust-free.

A woman lived with him, but where was she? Seaver hadn't mentioned her, not once. When he referred to "we," she had thought he meant herself: Courtney and Seaver. But had he meant the woman? A wife? There was no picture of her on the dresser, no framed wedding pictures as there were in her own human friends' homes. Maybe his wife had just taken a trip, leaving him to tend the shop. Or maybe she had gone herself to try to capture the calico cat for whom they had such plans.

Thinking about this, she hopped to the bedroom window to look down on the main street. It was then that she saw the cats below and her human friends, saw almost everyone she knew down on the streets among the shoppers, saw them searching for her. Saw Pan stalking the rooftops, saw Kit across the street peering in among the shadowed peaks—saw her own parents prowling a little garden between buildings; they appeared to be calling her name but she knew they were softly mewling, that was all they dared to do.

She saw Charlie Harper enter a dress shop, maybe to put up a poster. She was carrying a thick roll of heavy paper, her red hair reflecting in the windows. Courtney watched Ryan and Clyde, Joe's housemates, tacking up posters, too, or taping them to windows. Both were wearing old jeans, faded T-shirts, and baseball caps, ordinary and unremarkable.

Each poster had a big calico drawing of her, her own face, her own right front leg with the three black bracelets, a picture as lifelike as if she were looking in a mirror. That was Charlie Harper's drawing, sharply reproduced above the words REWARD: ONE THOUSAND DOLLARS.

One thousand dollars! Oh my! She backed away, shocked that anyone would lay out money like that. She might be young but she read the paper and she listened to her human friends. She didn't know what the stock market was except it was all about trading and Clyde said even a thousand dollars was a "nice piece of money." Was *she* worth a thousand dollars? And she was more confused than ever.

Until now, she'd been thinking only about herself trapped in this apartment. One minute imagining her grand new future, people crowding to see the tapestries of her past lives and to learn their ancient stories *and to look at her*! The next minute she'd been filled with cold fear at what such a future might really mean, the two emotions racing back and forth, muddling her head until she didn't know what to think.

She thought about the woman nearly dead out there

in the sand, beaten and almost buried alive. Was that Seaver's wife? Was that where she was? Was there more to his plan, more to this seemingly kind man than she imagined? Why hadn't Seaver mentioned his wife's name as he talked about the gallery exhibits? Had she refused to help him in some ugly plot that involved more than stealing a cat, and he had beaten and tried to kill her? Maybe they had fought, maybe he thought he *had* killed her, he was trying to bury her when something frightened him, made him run, made him leave her there half alive? If that woman was his wife, maybe Courtney's own kidnapping was part of some far more grisly scheme? Letting her imagination run, she tried to think how to escape. *I could be alone with a killer and no one knows where I am. Everyone is out searching for me, they're all looking, my parents, my friends all hurrying out on this cold morning while I'm thinking only of myself, of what Seaver really means to do to me.*

She began to examine the windows again, trying to find one that was loose, one that she could claw open and at least cry out her meows. But this apartment, as Joe Grey might have said, was built like a steel jail cell.

7

J oe Grey was searching frantically for Courtney when he skidded to a halt before a newspaper stand, scanning the details of a bank-money theft and murder last evening that he'd known nothing about. It happened shortly after they sat down to supper. But there wasn't much story there, it looked like Max had held out a lot. Joe got more details when he saw Clyde on the next corner—by now everyone, cat and human friends alike, was out looking for Courtney. Even a few cops were watching as they went about their patrols. When Joe and Clyde stepped into an alley behind some trash cans where they could talk, Clyde gave him a few more specifics: how fast the rough-voiced snitch clicked off, and his words exactly as Joe would have said them . . .

"But *I* didn't make that call, I was . . ."

"Max knows it wasn't his regular snitch, he said the voice was totally different, but the message was just as brief, as businesslike and curt. He kept as much out of the paper as he could, until he gets it sorted out."

That was often Max's way, when a crime looked dicey. Joe could understand that. In fact, he realized, the half-buried woman had been kept out of the papers and off the TV completely. Even the crime tape had vanished as soon as the detectives finished investigating the site and filling in the grave.

Earlier that predawn, when Courtney first went missing in the small hours, Joe had raced home in the dark and fog to wake Clyde and Ryan to tell them she had vanished, that they needed help, that they couldn't find her anywhere; that she was there with Kit and Dulcie one minute, and gone the next. At his alarm his housemates had risen, scrambled into their clothes, and they were gone before daylight, the three of them looking for the little calico, as was Wilma, and soon the Greenlaws. All this, long before the morning paper came out.

Wilma had called Charlie on her cell, so not to wake Max. But Max was at the station. Charlie, in her pajamas, had gone to her studio, found a drawing she had done recently of Courtney. Putting heavy paper in the copier, she ran off two hundred posters with the words

REWARD: ONE THOUSAND DOLLARS at the bottom, and with several phone numbers that could be called. She was dressed and half out the door headed for her SUV when Max got home. He raised an eyebrow at the stack of signs. She said, "Something's happened to Courtney. Wilma called. The kitten's gone. The posters . . . Everyone's out looking."

"I know. Someone called the station. Hell, Charlie, those cats wander the village all the time—and Courtney's not a kitten, she's nearly grown. What does Wilma mean, gone?"

"She said it was pitch-dark when all the cats woke her barging in through the cat door and into her bedroom. They were meowing and crying, very upset. And Courtney, she wasn't with them. They kept crying and clawing at the skirt of her robe. 'Courtney?' she asked them, and they yowled louder."

She looked up at Max. "You think dogs are smarter than cats, but I don't think so. They were trying to tell her as best they could, that was the only way they *could* tell her. They were too shaken over Courtney's disappearance for her to have just wandered off." She could imagine what they were really crying out, a narrative no cop could believe.

"Wilma tried to calm them but they kept running back and forth between her and the door. She thought maybe Courtney had been hit by a car. She pulled on her clothes, grabbed her cell phone and followed them, they all piled in the car, heading for the village.

"It was then she got the call," Charlie said. "Someone in the village, in an upstairs apartment just off Ocean—a Robby Arlen. He had gotten out of bed to close the window, he saw a young calico cat wandering the street below, he described the stripes on her leg. He knew Wilma had a kitten like that, he had seen it in the library when he took his granddaughter to story hour. He said she went on up the street and disappeared in the shadows. It was still dark, just the moonlit fog. He said that in a minute the other cats she hangs out with, he thought some of them were Wilma's, they came up the street looking all around, meowing, excited, searching and nearly frantic. He was sure they were looking for the kitten, he said there was no other explanation, said it was the strangest thing he'd ever seen. He apologized for waking her, but he was worried—he's one of the CatFriends group. He's out helping look."

Charlie wondered if she was talking too much.

Max looked at her for a long time. He said nothing.

"I've got to go," she said. "Robby told Wilma some of them ran up the street as if maybe they'd caught her scent. Then in a while they came back, their tails and ears down, and started searching around the shops. He said he started back to bed, then grabbed up his phone and called her."

"Is Wilma all right? Has she been having bouts of . . . ?"

She stared at him. *"Dementia? My aunt Wilma?"* That made her furious. "Of course not. She's sound as a rock. Something happened to that kitten. Maybe someone stole her."

"Cats don't get stolen, Charlie. Why would someone . . . ?" But there *were* reasons to steal a cat, ones Max didn't like to mention.

As Charlie left, he started a pot of coffee, frowning. He had wanted to make breakfast for her but she wouldn't wait even for a sip of coffee; carrying the stack of posters, she was already headed for town.

It seemed like something weird happened with those cats every week or two. You could have dogs, and no problem, but cats . . . Though he knew that wasn't true, dogs could get into almost as much trouble; except these cats always seemed too closely involved with some village crime.

And still, as he puzzled over the cats and the calico kitten, most of his mind was on the snitch's call last evening, that gravelly old man's voice; and on the crushed body. Though that guy hadn't been his regular snitch, not with that rusty voice, he *had* had the same brief way of passing on information; he had given Max the same kind of short, curt facts as his own snitch would—describing the robbery, describing the murder that Kathleen and the coroner were now investigating.

It was amazing that someone as delicate and beautiful as Kathleen Ray could deal with the gory coroner's job with no trouble, no pallor and shakes, no throwing up on the job. That was why Dr. Bern liked working with her.

Charlie, on her way to hang posters, found Joe and Wilma on Ocean Avenue searching between the shops; she pulled over and parked. She could see others, cat and human, looking for the calico and softly calling her. Wilma, Charlie's tall, gray-haired aunt, picked Joe up and slipped into the passenger seat of Charlie's car. They sat for a few moments, Charlie combing out her short, tangled red hair, she and Wilma getting their stories straight on what they had told Max, or what they would tell him.

Charlie had wanted to leave out the part about a man stealing Courtney. She didn't know what kind of city council brouhaha that would cause, what kind of position that would put Max in if his officers went pounding on doors and searching the shops for a cat; though she didn't think Max would ever suggest that. All she wanted was a story that Max would believe, and that might encourage his men to keep an eye out for Courtney without puzzling questions. Courtney had been stolen, in Charlie's mind the pictures and tapestries of her had prompted the theft, there was no other way to look at the kidnapping.

As full daylight crept into the village, the cats' human friends were all out nailing or taping up Charlie's posters, and of course still searching for Courtney, walking the little courtyards between buildings, peering under porches, under and over fences, among huge pots of flowering trees and bushes, looking down occasional alleys that held only grubby garbage cans. Had the small calico escaped from her captor, or did she lie somewhere hurt, or worse?

And while everyone looked for her, Courtney was just as fiercely searching for a way out. In the chill morning, when Seaver went downstairs to ready the shop for opening, she prowled the apartment once again from window to window, seeking a loose latch, for a way to freedom. She had awakened on the couch edgy and frightened, and knowing she was done with dreaming of Seaver's bright and impossible future— she was cold and frightened one moment, excited the next; and she began again to wonder where his missing wife had gone. Perhaps she *wasn't* the woman in the grave? Maybe he hadn't tried to kill her? Whatever he'd done with her, and whatever plans he had for Courtney herself, she wanted only to be out of there.

Putting aside thoughts of grand gallery exhibits and the TV shows he'd promised featuring her, still she prowled the apartment pawing at the locks, her ears down, her calico tail lashing. Peering out the tall glass windows she could see her mama and daddy and the other cats down on the streets with her human friends, all looking for her. She wanted to wrap her paws around every one of them, she wanted to be held, wanted to be loved by those she trusted, she wanted to be safe.

The way the windows were set into deep stone sills, though she could see down, it would be hard for anyone below to get a glimpse of her up here. She watched Joe Grey scramble to the roofs searching the windows of other apartments, but even when she stood up tall, looking across, and scratching down the glass, there were too many reflections, slants of first sunlight bouncing off other buildings so he must not see her at all. His ears flat, he backed down the oak tree again, she watched him pause beside another newsstand and rear up to read the front page of the *Gazette* that had just been put in the rack. Could that be about *her*? But soon he went racing away once more, heading for the courthouse, for MPPD.

8

Joe Grey entered through the bulletproof glass doors of MPPD on the heels of two garbagemen marching a dirty-faced young boy between them. Their truck was parked in the red zone. The taller, better-groomed city servant held a young calico cat close against his shoulder, held her tight but gently. Joe, only glimpsing her, thought for a second it was Courtney but then saw that it was not. He felt further dismay when he realized that his office friend, blond, plump Mabel Farthy, was not at the dispatcher's desk with her welcoming smile. Instead, sour-faced EvaJean Simpson scowled at the calico, at the dirty, fighting boy being dragged through the door, and at the garbagemen. She gave Joe himself a poisonous stare.

The real surprise was that the waiting room was half

full of calico cats, each in a battered carrier, the cages lined up in the far corner between the long counter and the window. Joe pushed in behind the garbagemen and fighting kid and ducked under a folding chair, searching through the bars of each cage for Courtney.

She wasn't there, no one looked back at him with eager amber eyes, no one yowled out to her daddy.

Where had these cats come from? Had they been collected by sticky-fingered little thieves like that kid, after reading Charlie's posters? Clean, healthy neighborhood cats maybe snatched from their own front porches, each "rescuer" eager for his thousand dollars.

Money they'll never see, Joe thought, extending his claws.

He was only partly hidden in the chair's shadow. In a minute EvaJean would see him and make a royal fuss—once she was finished dressing down the garbagemen. "That cat does not belong here. Look at the poster, at the phone numbers. Call them, call the shelter, call those rescue people. All this fuss over a cat. This is a police department, not an animal pound."

The man with the cat fetched an empty cage from those stacked to one side. He put the cat gently in, gave her a last pet, and set the cage with the others.

EvaJean said, "I suppose you want to book that boy. People don't realize . . ."

"We don't need to book him. Just take his name and address and file a complaint. We already gave him a talking-to that ought to cool him for a while. If he pulls something like this again, you can take care of him."

"I don't take care of little boys, or cats. I want him and those cats out of here."

The glass door opened and Charlie Harper came in. She nodded curtly to EvaJean and began collecting the cats in their cages. The two men helped her carry the calicos out to her SUV where she had backed into the red zone and opened the rear door. She carried in some extra cages, for further contributions.

"Where will you take them?" said the shorter, unshaven man.

"To the vet, to be checked for an identification. You know, those implanted chips. If we can't find all the owners, we'll take those cats to our shelter." She glanced under the chair at Joe Grey, her green eyes laughing as he left the shadows and walked boldly past EvaJean's counter, following Charlie as she headed for the hall and Max's office.

"The cat can't go back there," the clerk said sourly. "Catch him, Mrs. Harper. Take him away. Your husband doesn't need a cat in there, he's in a meeting."

Charlie smiled. "Joe spends half his life in that office, he's been in meetings before. You're a temp, EvaJean.

You're signed up to work here all week, until Mabel gets back. You wouldn't want to be in the chief's bad graces all week, let alone the rest of the department?"

EvaJean's look was snake-cold. Ignoring Charlie, she turned away to the copy machine.

But Charlie didn't want to break into the meeting. She loaded the last of the caged cats in her SUV and took off for Dr. Firetti's. Joe Grey smiled as he sauntered on down the hall and pushed into the chief's office through the slightly open door. If Max was in a meeting, it would most likely be about yesterday evening's murder and robbery and their connection to the other bank thefts. Maybe he'd also hear some casual mention of missing Courtney, maybe some of the guys were keeping an eye out as they went about their patrols. To a cop, a vanished cat doesn't compete with theft and murder. But maybe Charlie *had* sweet-talked Max into seeing that his men keep a lookout. Courtney *was* Joe Grey's own kitten, and most of the officers considered Joe family, a part of the department, though they had no idea that Joe, so many times, had helped them wrap up a case.

Now, maybe it was their turn to help Joe.

Max and three detectives were crowded around the desk examining half a dozen pages of what looked like the coroner's preliminary report, with graphs, colored photographs, charts, and various printouts. Leaping to the desk, Joe pushed comfortably between Detective Juana Davis and the chief. Max looked down at him like, *What the hell do you want?* Maybe he was grumpy from being awakened at three in the morning.

Juana's dark eyes smiled down at Joe, and she scratched his ears. Her black hair had just been cut, straight black bangs, smooth black bob above her collar, a few streaks of gray that gave it a nice flair. Her black uniform smelled of her two young cats. Max Harper's western shirt and jeans smelled of horses. Across the desk, Dallas Garza looked at Joe with interest just as Max was looking, Dallas's dark Latin eyes half amused, half questioning. "Why do you always show up when new information has just hit the desk?"

"Leave the poor cat alone," Juana said. "Look how frazzled he is, he's probably been out half the night hunting for his kitten. Looks like the whole village is looking for her."

"Not the *whole* village," Dallas said, reaching to pet Joe. "Though there are a lot of people wandering around and looking in windows. I know Joe's bright, but to hunt for hours for his lost kitten?" He looked up at Detective Davis. "Hell, Juana, she'll show up."

Pretending ignorance, Joe stepped delicately around Max's assorted papers, onto the edges of camera views and X-rays of the robbery victim's injured head, of his bloody neck and shoulder. That whole upper part of his body had been hit when the thief slammed the door on him, grisly color shots of blood and crushed bone. The victim's foot and leg were twisted and looked broken. The coroner's written report lay right in front of him, facing Max. Joe would have to read it upside down, but he didn't think that would fly. A cat reading right side up, nose to the page, would be incriminating enough. He caught the name, Jon Jaarel. Jaarel's charming bar and grill had been a Molena Point landmark for years. Now Jaarel was gone, Joe thought sadly. And would the treasured restaurant soon vanish, too?

"The killer must have thrown all his weight against that door," Dallas said.

For some reason, Joe had the strange feeling that when the robber slammed the car door, he didn't mean to *kill* Jaarel. A man so eager for the money that he did in his victim with more speed than thought, striking fast but clumsily.

And who was the witness, the unknown snitch who had called Max?

Max's careful notes were there. The snitch had given him a more detailed description of the crime than Joe himself usually gave—yet this snitch had offered little to describe the killer, he said he hardly saw the man.

Well, Joe's own tips were often just as disjointed: details left out or confused in the fast action of the crime. A witness couldn't catch everything. And how could the killer vanish so quickly in that small, crowded shopping center?

But Max and Juana Davis were talking about what to do with Joe's own case, as he thought of it. Whether to transfer the woman from the hospital to a nursing home where she could rest and heal, under police guard, when Kit came bolting in through Max's door, wild-eyed. Joe crouched to leap down. Had she found Courtney? Had something terrible happened? She could say nothing until he'd raced out behind her, until they'd bolted to the roof and were alone, Joe nervous with worst-case scenarios.

In the office behind them Harper, Davis, and Garza stared after the cats, uncomfortably puzzled. "Cats," Dallas said. "Flighty as a drunk squirrel."

Juana smiled indulgently, thinking of her own cats. "Who knows what's in their minds?"

Max's expression didn't change, no one knew what he was thinking.

9

It was Kit who found Courtney, who came bolting down the sidewalk and in through the door of MPPD dodging two cops coming out. Ignoring Eva-Jean, she fled into Max's office following Joe's scent, so excited she could hardly help but shout out the whole story.

She had, searching for the calico, coming along the alley behind Seaver's Antiques, stopped suddenly and sniffed at the garbage truck that was idling there as two men dumped the week's collection. The back of the building had carved molding, and the front of the two-story structure facing the street was even more ornate: fancily decorated framing all along the windows and above the shop's wide glass door. Maybe the building was Victorian or maybe a mix of styles, but it seemed to fit the village. Kit stood inhaling the violent stink of garbage—but then sharply above that odor she caught the sweet scent of Courtney. Every cat has his own aroma, there was no doubt the calico was here, or had been. Staring into the truck's open tailgate, she was gripped by fear. Was Courtney in there among the trash, and hurt? Had she been picked up by accident, too injured to leap away or cry out?

Kit climbed up to look in, feeling sick at the thoughts that filled her. She turned to look for Dulcie who was down the alley behind her. She mewed, calling her, asking for help, she felt sicker as the men continued emptying trash cans and Courtney's scent came stronger.

Yes, it was from one of the cans. She dodged the empty bin as they tossed it down. It bounced twice and nearly hit her, rolled across the alley and hit the brick wall of the building on the other side. She approached the can warily, stuck her head in and sniffed again.

She could see kitty litter clinging to the can's sides where someone had emptied Courtney's cat box. She whirled around and meowed again. Dulcie had paused to scent at a garage door; she looked up at Kit, raced to the truck, and now *she* got a full whiff of Courtney. At the same moment they heard a noise from above, a sound like claws on glass.

The men were getting back in the truck.

Before they could drive away Dulcie shouldered Kit aside and leaped to the truck's hot hood, scorching her paws: the scratching from above came louder. Dulcie jumped from the hood to the top of the closed cab, Kit right behind her, as the truck began to move.

"Damn cats," said the driver, "cats all over this town."

Above, through the apartment window, the flash of white and orange was still wildly clawing.

Hearts pounding, they flew from the truck across space to the wide, decorative ledge that ran beneath the second-floor windows, its concrete curlicues embellished with pigeon droppings. Courtney peered out at them, her busy paws raking glass, her amber eyes flashing. The iron frames that bound the windows looked as solid as an iron safe.

"We need Joe," Kit said, "we need help."

Dulcie rubbed her face against the glass, loving her child, as Kit raced away across the rooftops for where she'd last seen Joe Grey. There she dropped down the twisted oak and in through the glass door behind a pair of cops, ignoring EvaJean, praying Joe was there. Yes, she followed Joe's fresh scent, ignoring EvaJean's tirade. When she burst into Max's office, the tomcat knew by her expression that she'd found Courtney. He leaped down from the desk and they fled the station—glass door, oak tree, courthouse roof—and raced six blocks of jagged peaks headed for the antiques shop, Joe Grey hissing, "Where is she? Where is Courtney, and where is Dulcie?"

"Dulcie's with her. I don't know where Pan is, hunting for her somewhere." That was all she had the breath to say.

By the time Kit and Joe reached Seaver's Antiques, Courtney had moved along the inside of the upstairs windows to the front of the building. On the outside, on the ledge, Dulcie followed, the two together trying every window. Maybe Courtney had already tried them, alone, while Seaver was downstairs in the shop; Joe could hear customers down there. Joe was so glad to see Courtney he almost yowled. But as he tried to help them loosen a slider, the attempt seemed useless, those windows looked like they didn't open at all, looked like they'd been installed to stay forever. They tried another and another, but nothing gave.

Pressing their ears to the glass, and whispering, the three cats could just hear each other. Courtney said, "This is not the same man as in the library. This one's bald, no beard or mustache—bald all over. I think this man is Ulrich Seaver."

"But why did he capture you?" Dulcie said. "He's . . ."

"Did he hurt you?" Joe said. "What does he want? Why . . . ?"

"So far, he's been kind to me, nice salmon, a soft blanket."

"But after that, what?" Joe said crossly.

"He wants to make a show cat of her," Dulcie said with fury. "He has some of the old tapestries, the real ones all in frames, and he has a gallery in San Francisco and has a museum show booked in New York just of her . . ."

"And I'll have my own Web site with colored pictures and maybe a movie and . . ."

Joe hissed and growled at his daughter. "What kind of damn foolishness has he been feeding you! You get your tail out of there, Courtney, and do it now! Before he skins and frames *you*!"

"I can't get out," she said demurely. "I've tried every window. But he told me, at night when he locks the big glass doors he'll let me downstairs. All by myself," she said, gloating.

She looked at Dulcie and Joe and Kit, her eyes sparkling. "He carried me all around the store when there were no customers, but he locked the glass doors first. Oh, it's beautiful, he turns the lights real soft and there are damask couches and marble statues and gold screens and all kinds of ancient, carved furniture and cloisonné vases, I read the little signs. And things I don't know what they are and can't name them. At night I'll have the whole store to myself, until he comes to get me in the morning and then I'll have the upstairs and a breakfast of salmon before he opens the downstairs doors to let customers in."

They all just looked at her.

"There is one thing," Courtney whispered. "A woman. A woman lives here—but she isn't here now. She must be elegant, she has tailored suits and expensive shoes, I looked in the closets. Is she his wife? They share a bedroom, lacy nightgowns and panties in the drawers, but no pictures of her and he didn't mention her. He doesn't seem to have any letters from her, I went through a stack of mail on the desk. How long has she been gone? There are two cars in the garage." Courtney looked at her daddy. "Has she disappeared? Could *she* be the woman in the grave?"

Joe was amazed at how much the young cat already knew about the ways of the human world. He said, "She's in the hospital. Max and the detectives were talking about it." As he sat thinking, a flock of pigeons dove down at the sill; when one pecked at him, he struck and hissed at it, and they flew on.

"There was no ID on that battered woman, they got no make on her fingerprints, nothing in AFIS, nothing anywhere that the department can find. If that woman is Seaver's wife she'd have some kind of identification, her prints would bring up a driver's license or maybe city records."

"But the woman is gone," Courtney said. "No purse, no billfold or driver's license, I looked all over the apartment. And she wears gold earrings, a whole drawer full of them, the kind with the little rings or buttons to hold them on."

"For pierced ears," Dulcie said. "When he lets you downstairs at night, can't you open any of those windows?"

"They're all like these. Except the powder room window. A tiny one, but even it has metal bars outside."

"Piece of cake," Joe said. "We can handle that small window and we can sure squeeze through the bars."

Courtney flicked her bright tail.

Joe said, "We wait until afternoon when he's busy with a customer, we slip in, hide under the couches, in dark places." He looked at Courtney. "Tonight after he locks up, goes upstairs and lets you down into the store, we get to work. The five of us ought to be able to . . ."

"The latch is a metal tab," Courtney said, "about four inches long. I think a person is supposed to squeeze it, then slide the glass open." She looked uncertain. "Can we do that? I tried, but paws aren't very good for squeezing. I guess the screen is on the outside but I can't see it, the glass is that . . ."

"Obscure glass?" Joe said. "With a bumpy surface? We can take care of the screen earlier, from outside." He went silent as footsteps came up from downstairs, then the turn of the doorknob.

When the apartment door opened Courtney was curled up on a blanket, on the big chair below the window. There was no other cat to be seen, the window ledge was blank, decorated only by pigeon droppings. A lone pigeon fluttered down to land on the carved rim: but it looked at the cats and it was gone again, in a flurry of wings. And as Courtney pretended to sleep on her blanket, she thought about Joe's plan.

But then she wondered. Did she really want to get away yet?

What she wanted, before she escaped, was to find Seaver's missing wife or find out who that woman was. Find out if it was she who had been beaten and nearly buried alive—find out if Seaver had done that. Sometimes he really *did* give her the shivers.

She wanted to stay until she found out if he was what he pretended to be.

Or did she? If he had beaten, nearly killed that woman, she wanted out of there *now*. Even as a little voice in the back of her head sang of glamour, of museums and bright magazine pictures, she saw too clearly the body that Joe had described and the bloody grave, and her own kitten blood filled with ice.

Shivering, she tucked deeper under the blanket thinking of ways she might force open that downstairs window.

10

Late that evening, with the store's lights dimmed and the big glass doors securely locked, Joe, Dulcie, Pan, and Kit waited, hidden under the antique furniture, for the upstairs door to open. When at last it did open and Courtney came out, she paused on the top step, looking up at Seaver. He smiled and leaned down and petted her and handed her a little treat. "Go on, my dear, the antiques store is yours now. Have a good time. It's a lovely place for you to roam, to get used to the finer furnishings among which you will be living. I'm sure you won't scratch anything, I know you'll be a good girl."

His words made Courtney want to throw up. She glanced up at him innocently, as sweetly as she could manage, and raced down the steps. Moving out of his sight, she leaped to the top of a small, hand-carved writing desk that stood against the inner wall. The subtly lit display windows formed a background to the rich brocades, golden pitchers, gilded chairs all artfully arranged. She sat looking out among the shadows. She listened to the upstairs door close. Slowly, in the whisper of light from the windows, the shadows began to take shape, to morph into vague forms that only a cat could see. She sat watching until at last a cat slipped out, then another, each watching the door above in case it might open again.

Dulcie appeared from under a settee, Kit and Pan from behind a china cabinet. Then Joe Grey from an elegantly arranged tangle of gold satin draped over a chair. As he reared up, the tomcat's silver-gray coat glowed against the gold like another piece of rare artwork.

Courtney sat tall on the desk before them, between a 1900 silver centaur priced at eight thousand dollars, and a seventeenth-century stone lion at twenty thousand, each price on a little card slipped beneath the object. Joe Grey, looking up at her, knew she was the most beautiful of the three. When finally she leaped down she led them winding through the store and into the little powder room with its gilt mirror, lace-edged curtains, and hand-painted tile.

The window had bars behind the ruffles. The spaces between the outside, decorative iron grill were too small for a human but plenty big for a cat. Joe Grey returned to the showroom and dragged an antique wicker stool into the powder room, pushing it beneath the closed window.

Earlier, before the store closed, before they had sneaked in, the four cats had inspected from outside the little window with its fancy barrier—and with a row of heavy wooden shipping crates, marked with Seaver's address, lined up against the outside wall. Crates set up on heavy timbers and covered with plastic to keep them dry, containers used presumably for antiques coming into the store, and for sending sold treasures out again.

Joe Grey had, standing on the tallest crate and using his claws, already loosened two of the flimsy turn-screws of the window screen. Now, with little effort, one could ease out one corner of the screen. With a good swipe of determined claws, one could bring down the whole thing if he chose.

Now, inside the powder room standing on the wicker stool, Joe and Pan tackled the wide metal window latch with their paws—white paw, red tabby, white paw, red overlapping, pressing as hard as they could while the three girl cats held the stool steady.

The latch barely moved. Straining, they pressed

harder. They changed positions so they could pull. Pulling and pressing, wiggling it back and forth, they began to loosen it.

The latch gave all at once. Whack. The window slid open right in their faces.

With that half of the window open, Joe Grey leaned out through the bars and pushed one corner of the screen loose. They slid through and were out of there in a tumble . . .

All but Courtney.

Balanced on the sill ready to leap out, she paused and looked back. She stepped back inside onto the decorative tile counter, stood looking out at the four cats below her, at three tails lashing, and one very angry tomcat, his short tail down, his ears flat, his yellow eyes blazing up at her. "Get the hell out of there!"

"I'm not going. I'm staying. Just for a little while. I'll slide the window almost shut so I can get out again later."

"*What the hell do you mean, staying? What do you mean, later?* You can't *stay.* Why do you think we went to all this trouble! Get the hell down from there, get out here NOW, Courtney. Out here with us NOW! Do it NOW."

She looked through the bars at her daddy, both cats' ears back, Joe's scowl so fierce he frightened her, and her own amber eyes flashed defiantly. "I will stay here for now. I want to know if that woman is his wife, that woman lying in the hospital all beaten up. I want to know if that's where his wife went, I want to know if it was Seaver who nearly buried her alive. I mean to stay until I find out."

"If she's Seaver's wife, the cops would have a make on her prints," Joe said. "They'd *know* who she is. The guys at the department would know her, would have seen her around. I don't even know if he *has* a wife."

"What if she's his girlfriend?" Courtney said. "A . . . what do you call it? A pickup. Maybe someone with false identities, the way criminals do, the way you told me about? So Seaver knew the cops wouldn't find anything."

Joe Grey sighed. Sometimes he wished he'd keep his big mouth shut. Besides her faulty logic, and an imagination Courtney must have picked up from Kit, what kind of child had he raised? "Come out from there, Courtney. Come out NOW . . ." But then they all heard it, the upstairs door open, footsteps coming down. Courtney slid the window nearly closed and beat it into the shadows under a couch just as Seaver's dark silhouette appeared.

He came down, sat down at his desk, switched on the light, and picked up a ledger. The cats had fled through the powder room window, making not the slightest sound. But Joe Grey turned and was slipping back to remain watching when the phone rang. Seaver picked up.

Joe eased up onto the crate, lying just beneath the window with his ear to the crack. "Yes?" Seaver said, then was silent for a long moment, then began tapping his pencil on the blotter. "That won't work, you ninny. She's not . . ." Another wait, then he laughed. "You *are* kidding? Everyone in town *knows* her. That red hair . . . What do you *think* would happen? She's the chief of police's wife, you dummy. You don't need a shill, a 'lady companion,' to make your rounds of the store. Do an appraisal as best you can without expert advice, just get on with it then drift away into the crowds."

Silence, then, "Well, of course she was better. That can't be helped now."

Another, longer pause, then . . . "Oh, right. Just an afternoon of shopping to help out a neighbor. So your father *is* her neighbor. Has she ever met *you*? She and Harper have only been married a few years, she was straight down from San Francisco, she didn't know anyone but her aunt. No. I don't want any part of that and neither do you. You try that, any of you try it, and we're done, I'm out of it. The cops've likely *seen* you going in or out my back door. If *you* get in trouble, we're all in the muck. Just go on the way you were."

There was a tiny click from the other end. Seaver stared at the phone, and banged down the receiver. He sat a minute, swearing softly, then put the ledger in a drawer as if bored with his bookwork, turned off the light, and went back upstairs. Courtney watched him, sleepy and innocent, from a brocade couch.

Outside, the minute Seaver was gone, Joe Grey was off the crates and catching up with the other three where they waited in the alley behind the store—but suddenly Dulcie wasn't with them. She flew past Joe, leaped to the crate, eased the window open and *she* was inside. Inside with Courtney, with her child. Joe Grey didn't stop her, she had that intent mothering look when it was best to leave her alone. What did she have in mind? Was she going to babysit all night? She was as stubborn as her kitten, as stubborn as Joe himself—but he did feel better with Dulcie on guard. He stood in the weeds looking up at the sky; the fog had cleared, the moon was bright. A perfect night to hunt. But they had better things to do. He and Kit and Pan, crouched in the alley, laid out their plan; then Kit slipped back to hiss through the window, to tell Courtney and Dulcie what they meant to do—and hoping Courtney wouldn't go all stubborn again.

When Kit returned to the alley, each cat headed home to tell their respective housemates that they'd found Courtney—though they were all three still angry at the young calico's hardheadedness. They would go to Wilma to tell her the news, and to Kit and Pan's old couple, and to Ryan and Clyde.

As they parted, Pan said, "Courtney will be all right. He's treated her well this far, he hasn't hurt her. If he thinks he can make money off her, why would he harm her? And, if he does get mean, she's safer with one of us here each night, to fight and to go for the phone."

Their plan seemed simple enough. Each cat's housemate would alert their few human friends who knew the cats could speak, would tell them they'd found Courtney, tell them the cats' routines and where she was, but they would tell no one else. They would leave the posters up, pretend to still be looking for her; they would not alert even the other members of CatFriends who did not know the cats could talk.

If they took down the posters, if everyone in the village knew she'd been found, Seaver would begin to watch for what kind of trick she was up to. And when she did escape, after the trouble he'd gone to to find and catch her the first time, during a second hunt she might not be safe anywhere.

Each evening before the store closed, one of the cats,

taking turns, would slip inside. Would watch the young clerk leave, watch Seaver lock the glass doors securing his valuable wares. They would watch Seaver go back upstairs, watch him let Courtney out of his apartment, watch her race down—and once the clerk left, the rest of the night would be theirs.

If the chosen cat couldn't slip in through the open front doors unseen, he or she would wait until pale, thin Bert had locked up, scuffling footsteps, heavy coat pulled tight around him as he headed home. When all was quiet, the chosen guard, eyes aglow and tail switching, would crawl in through the powder room window between the bars, under the loose screen and through the barely open glass, to spend the softly lit night with Courtney among gold-decorated and price-less antiques. With a phone on the desk and one in the back room, if something happened they could call the Damens or Wilma or the cops—why would he hurt her if he wanted to make a show cat of her?

But still, Joe was all atremble. The time would come, he knew, when the next step in Seaver's plan would take shape, a plan that might carry Seaver's calico prize miles away, first to the gallery in the city and then clear across the country, and how would they find her, then?

11

Joe Grey went on with the others, leaving Courtney and Dulcie in the antiques store but worrying about them both. On the rooftops he parted from Kit and Pan, their two tails, one golden, the other fluffy dark, flipping away under the risen moon as they headed home to their tree house—to Lucinda and Pedric, and to call Wilma.

And Joe raced home over the shingles, his claws scritching as he balanced across heavy oak branches. He heard music playing from the cottages below and smelled late suppers cooking. Then, close to home, the loud and familiar rancor of angry voices. Another Luther Domestic.

Did they have to be so loud? Couldn't they fight quietly? Did all that shouting help release their anger?

Thelma's and Nevin's voices came from the house, they were in their bedroom but they might as well have been outside in the yard putting on a two-person play for the neighbors who stood, now, staring in through the window. What were they fighting about this time? What had happened now?

Mindy crouched outside in the bushes beneath the kitchen window, wiping her nose on the arm of the sweater she'd pulled around her. Her silent shaking wasn't from the cold. From where she huddled, the way the windows were open, she could hear her parents' every word clearly, something about bank statements, and about "Too loose around the cops," at which Nevin gave a snorting laugh. Joe climbed into the cypress tree outside their window, its furry branches dense as a jungle—that was when he saw Zeb Luther parked around the corner in an old, faded car, not his own truck, his window down as he listened. Peering through the branches, Joe could just pick out the old man, his ragged gray hair, faded flannel shirt, and worn leather jacket. Mindy's grandfather. Ryan had said he hadn't come to visit since the family moved in, she had heard Mindy shouting at her mother and crying about that. What was he doing here this time of night? Spying, listening instead of coming right on in?

This was the man Joe had seen in the village peering

across the street into the tearoom at Thelma and Mindy and the freckled auburn-haired man. Joe had seen him standing outside the PD, too, looking uncertain, as if he was trying to decide whether to go in, his frown reflecting some painful decision that had interested Joe even then. The old man who had at last turned away shaking his head, looking so sad. If he hadn't been such an old man, Joe would have thought he was crying.

Now, the tomcat didn't think Nevin and Thelma could see Nevin's father from the bedroom, the way he was parked and with the tree in the way. They faced each other hissing and snarling like fighting cats themselves, they sure didn't care who heard them. Not a speck of dignity, Joe thought, nor did they have much feeling for their frightened little girl crouched under their window listening.

But then the subject grew more explicit, Thelma hissed something so quietly that Joe missed it and Nevin snarled angrily, "The hell I won't and what right do you have to tell me what to do?" Thelma stared down at the neighbors in the street and told him to lower his voice. Joe Grey, in his tree, drew closer.

"You'll go *now*!" Thelma snapped. "Right now! And you'll *stay* away, the farther the better. You think them cops won't have figured it out? You think they won't come . . . ?"

"I'm not leaving until I find that envelope. *You* think the old bastard won't go digging into it? What the hell do you . . ." His voice was like daggers. "It's over a week since I called the bank and they said they'd mailed it and I'm not leaving without it. And the rest of the statements, as well. Just like him to go prying around among my papers. I don't need him poking into my stuff and I don't need *you* poking into my business! And what were you doing with my checkbook? You had to dig deep to find it in my dresser. Give it to me now." There was a sound as if he'd slapped her. Joe saw her draw back looking shocked.

"Bastard!" she snarled and slapped him in return. "Why the hell did you leave it lying around if you didn't want me to see it! And that stack of statements. I told you, bring everything with you. Why didn't . . . ?"

When Joe looked up, Zebulon and his battered car were gone.

So, Joe thought, Nevin moves out of the family house, leaves some of his records and papers. Changes their mail from the rural address to a village PO box. There's a mix-up at the post office, his bank statement is delivered to the old address. Zebulon gets curious and opens it. And—what? What's so important? What's in the bank that Nevin doesn't want the old man to know about? Or maybe that Thelma doesn't know everything about? Who does the couple's banking? Does Nevin do it all? Maybe more money in that account than she thinks they have? Maybe lots more?

"And then you move that money up the coast," she said. "Why did you put it way up there in the first place, that was really stupid."

"I'm moving it farther than that, first thing in the morning. And to more than one bank, more places than you'll ever know. Hell, Thelma. You know where a good part of the money *you* stole is at, and some of mine and Varney's, too. The rest of it's none of your business, you needn't bother yourself about it."

"If the cops find last night's money, maybe with blood on it, you're in big trouble, Nevin. And where does that put me! You were using my car when that went down! If you go to jail on that kind of charge, they collar me as an accessory even when *I* didn't do anything. I land in jail, and where does that leave the kid? Your father can't take care of her."

"I'm out of here before they find me. If they put you in jail, if they ID your car—or maybe find evidence that you and Varney have been into the robbing, too— they'll lock you both up, put the kid in child care and you won't have to worry about her."

In the shadows of the yard Mindy left the bushes and slipped in the back door. In a minute Joe could see her in her own bedroom standing nearly out of sight within the thin curtains and he could hear a muffled sniffle. He wanted to leap up and snuggle her; as cranky as Mindy could be, or as sweet, she was, after all, only a confused and needful little girl, hurt and afraid. He was sickened by this family's lack of love for her, and for each other. He wondered what *would* happen to her. A child whose only real family, in her own mind, was her grandfather. Whose only other solace was the companionship of her pony.

Joe had heard her tell Thelma, in a lonely little voice, that she only wanted to be home with Grandpa and Tango, heard Thelma's cold laugh. "You're no better off with a helpless old man and a dumb horse. What good could either of *them* do you!" and that was the end of that.

A child with a father and two uncles who didn't give a damn for her, and a mother who, if she did care, didn't show it. Thelma didn't know how to love a child, maybe she had no love in her. There didn't seem much else in her, either. Though she might talk tough to Nevin and threaten him, she apparently didn't do anything to change his way of life. It looked to Joe like she just followed along in the same path.

If that murder and robbery last night *was* Nevin's

work, the thought gave the tomcat shivers: a body crushed to death in a car door.

Nevin and Thelma went silent when a police car came by outside. Nevin looked out the window, watched it cruise quietly away tailing the car it followed, maybe just tourists rubbernecking. But the cop car shook Nevin; he began hastily throwing clothes, a razor, and various toilet articles in a duffel bag and in a few minutes he was gone, out the bedroom, silent as he crossed the living room. Joe heard him quietly open and close the front door, watched him cross the drive and slide into his gray Suzuki, heard the engine as he backed out and took off.

Thelma, still in her robe, crawled into bed and turned out the light. You'd think she would come into Mindy's room, give her a little hug and some sympathy, spend some time with her to ease the pain of her daddy leaving. But no way.

Maybe better, though, if she left the child alone; Mindy was still crying and Thelma would only say something mean.

Joe watched Mindy's light go out but he didn't hear the rustle of covers as if she was getting into bed. He slipped to her sill where he could see in. She was still dressed in jeans and a shirt, and was pulling on a bulkier sweater. She put her ear to the wall of her parents' room. Joe heard only silence, and so must she. In a minute she softly opened her bedroom door, he could hear her slipping along the hall, headed for the kitchen.

Coming down from the tree, Joe went around the side to the kitchen window. Leaping up and hanging from the sill, he could hear her talking, could see her at the wall phone. His ear to the glass, he could hear her whisper—the gist of which was that her daddy had left, that maybe he wasn't coming back and good riddance.

"You're not home yet. Why didn't you take your cell phone? I saw you parked here, I wanted to sneak over but . . . He's coming *there,* Grandpa," she said, sniffling. "Coming to get some papers, he acted like you stole them. He's in a mean mood, real mean. Oh, when you get home please pick up the recording, please see the flashing light when you come in—then get out of there. Go back in the woods or to the Harpers'. Hurry, he's already left, maybe ten minutes. Don't stay there, Grandpa, I'm afraid of him." She was sobbing again. She choked, "I love you, I pray you get my message," and she hung up.

12

Joe watched Mindy make a peanut butter sandwich and pour a glass of milk. He watched her leave the kitchen taking her lone supper down the hall. He climbed the cypress again and looked in her bedroom window—not like a human voyeur, he thought, amused, but feeling only pity. Now the room was dimly lit, she had turned on two tiny night-lights plugged in just above the floor; she sat up in bed, in her clothes, wolfing the sandwich and gulping the milk between sobs. Did she turn on those lights every night to give herself comfort? He wondered if she'd done that at her grandfather's house or only here where she felt alone and unwanted. Her red sweater hung on the bedpost, her shoes and socks lay underneath, her school backpack beside them, he could see a white T-shirt stuffed in on top.

Finished eating, she set the empty plate and glass on the night table and tucked down under the covers. Joe watched her roll herself in the blankets, trembling with sobs, and pull one blanket over her head. The moon was starting to brighten the eastern treetops and the tops of the hills. He waited a long time until she swallowed back the last gulp of crying and began slowly, slowly to ease into the calmer breathing of sleep.

Only when he was sure she slept did he leave the cypress tree, moving away through its branches to the springy limbs of a small pine and across to his own roof, to his private tower. There he slid through its open window, looked out once more at Mindy, then burrowed among his scattered pillows where there was only peace: no crying, hurt child, no hateful human mothers. He could just see, in Mindy's shadowed room, the child cocooned in her blankets. Curling down among his cushions in his own safe place, Joe positioned himself so he could keep an eye on her. Yawning, he wondered what would happen at Zebulon Luther's house when Nevin slipped in—or marched boldly in—to retrieve his bank statements, wondered if Zeb would be there, if he'd gotten Mindy's message? Or had he left it unnoticed on the recorder?

If Nevin got there first, as mad as he was, how cruel

could he get with his own father? And Joe wondered if he should go down to Clyde's desk and call Harper.

Or was their argument only a family hassle that would end up amounting to nothing? Even if Nevin did leave, would he have cooled down before he got to Zeb's place? Joe avoided vague tips to the law that could turn into nothing. That would only make Harper unsure of the reliability of his snitch. Yawning, meaning to think about it for a minute as he watched Mindy, he was soon sound asleep.

He must have been asleep when she left, he woke to see the moon shining straight in onto her bed, onto a mound of covers thrown back. Her shoes and sweater were gone. Her school backpack that had been leaning against the bed was no longer there. That's when Joe leaped from his tower into the house onto his rafter, down to the king-sized bed, and pawed at Ryan's face.

"Mindy's gone. Run away . . . clothes, backpack."

But Clyde was already up and dressed. Ryan rolled out of bed, pulling on sweats. "Mindy's not the only one."

"What?" Joe said. "What else . . . ?"

"That woman," Clyde said, "who was nearly buried, the woman Max moved to the care home . . . she slipped out of the home when Buffin was asleep. Buffin woke and couldn't find her. He couldn't shout for the nurses. He leaped to the phone and called the Firettis then followed her trail straight out the front door. She must have known where they hid the keys. Mary and John and Buffin are out looking for her and so are the cops. We . . . But *no one's* looking for the kid. A child alone, right now she's more important." He grabbed his jacket. "Come on, Joe, get a move on before she hits the highway."

Dulcie and Courtney prowled the antiques shop touching a soft paw to the old, delicate pieces, guessing at their age and origin; though some were already tagged, telling which century each hand-shaped, hand-glazed porcelain piece came from, each hand-woven tapestry or rug. They curled up at last in a delicate Queen Anne love seat, on a cashmere throw. Mother and daughter were whispering to each other ancient tales when the door at the top of the stairs opened. Dulcie vanished behind an ancient cast-iron stove. Courtney pretended to be comfortably dozing, snoring just a little in a ladylike manner.

Two men came down the stairs, softly talking: Ulrich Seaver and, yes, Joe's new neighbor Nevin Luther. They turned right, toward the workroom and the outside door that led to the alley. The cats heard the soft *tick-tick* as Seaver turned the dial of a huge iron safe as tall as the men. Nevin handed him a package, a bulging brown envelope. Seaver pulled on a pair of cotton gloves, opened it, and removed a stack of money, fanning out hundred-dollar bills like shuffling decks of cards.

He didn't count it; maybe he could guess about how much. Closing the envelope, leaning deep into the safe, he concealed the money beneath a stack of envelopes and papers far at the back, and locked the safe again.

Nevin said, "I'll pick this up in a few days, once I have some accounts set up; maybe leave some of it here. What about that cat, what are you going to do with it now? They've put out a reward for it, there're signs all over the village, a thousand dollars. No cat is worth . . ."

Seaver said, "I'm getting it up to the city pronto. I have a fellow up there building a nice big cage, three stories, little beds so she can change around, a scratching post, everything fancy for the looks of it, and everything a cat would want. She'll be happy there. You can't train a cat that isn't happy. It's a nice enough cat—but its color and markings, that's what we've been searching for, you've seen the antique pictures, the old tapestries. The training, the tricks, that'll be the icing on the cake."

Courtney, pretending to sleep, thought she was going to throw up. *A three-story cage—everything a cat would want.* A cage, and he said she'd be happy there.

The hell she would. *And you, Seaver, you don't know the half of what we found, and saw, tonight.*

She and Dulcie had not only enjoyed the wonders of the gallery, they had searched behind furniture, searched the shop's hidden crevices, pried and prowled not knowing exactly what they were looking for—until they found a prize that had them both smiling; and Courtney meant to find more.

In an elegantly carved rolltop desk with dozens of little drawers inside, they had found one drawer which, when they pulled it all the way out, revealed an opening behind, a cherrywood cubicle filled with something furry and dark that made them draw back, claws raised.

But then they relaxed. Dulcie reached a paw in, and smiled. Courtney took a good sniff, and laughed softly.

The shelf held a man's neatly trimmed beard and mustache, all in one piece, with some sort of sticky stuff on the back. That didn't taste good when they licked it off their paws. Beneath this, neatly folded, was a navy blue cap and, when they pulled it out, long, dark hair hung down, shaggy hair the same color as the mustache. This was the library prowler's disguise.

This was a find they could take to Harper. But, "No, don't take it," Dulcie said, "to move it is to contaminate evidence. But we can tell him where it is. The disguise of the man in the library."

"And tomorrow," Courtney said, lashing her calico tail, "tomorrow I *really* start to search. First, *her* side of the bedroom, the missing woman. Tomorrow, while I'm alone upstairs, I'll find more clues for Max Harper, and then we'll call him. Tomorrow maybe I'll find out who this woman is who was almost buried alive."

"If it's the same woman," Dulcie said. "And pray to the great cat god you don't get yourself into big trouble." She licked her child's calico ear, reminding herself that Courtney was nearly grown and that she was strong and clever. They finished the shrimp and kibble that Seaver had put down for Courtney, and curled up for another little nap.

Lucinda and Pedric had finished supper, Lucinda setting aside an ample helping of hot beef stew for Kit and Pan. Its scent embraced the neighbors' yards and drifted across the rooftops as the two cats raced along the oak branch and in through the cat door in the dining room window, Kit already telling their housemates about finding Courtney; she was halfway through her story as she flew to the table so she had to start over again. "Slowly," said Pan and Lucinda and Pedric to-gether. She tried, she told the whole tale of Joe Grey finding Courtney, of their secret entry into the an-tiques store to get her out, jimmying the powder room window; but she forgot to tell it slowly, her monologue raced faster and faster . . . *"and Courtney was so will-ful and stubborn she wouldn't leave. After we all got out the window safely, she leaped back in and sassed Joe but refused to come out, she means to stay there until she finds out who that woman is, if she's his wife and if he tried to kill her and bury her alive and . . ."*

Lucinda and Pan both hushed her. Lucinda rose, turned on the phone's speaker, and began making calls to tell their closest friends that Courtney had been found—while Kit stuck her face in the phone's speaker, adding her own long comments. They called Wilma first, because Wilma had fretted so about the lost kitten. When they called the Damens, Ryan answered. "The victim—Joe thinks her name is Maurita, he heard it in the tearoom—she walked out of the care home. We're in the car, looking. And looking for Mindy Luther, she ran away, too. She—"

"Oh, my!" Kit didn't wait for the end of the call, she spun around crowding Pan as they bolted out the cat door to look for Maurita. Lucinda watched them vanish.

Ryan said, "Joe's with us. He told us about finding Courtney. Thank God for that—but how strange that Maurita disappears on the same night that Courtney is found, and then Mindy runs away."

"Where do you want us to look?" Lucinda said. "Who shall we search for? If you'll tell us where to start . . ."

"Why don't you wait, Lucinda. Wilma and half the department—patrol cars and foot officers—are out searching . . ."

Lucinda didn't want to wait at home feeling helpless. But for the moment she and Pedric settled back, building up the fire. While on the roofs, the cats ran, the bright night pulling at them, the moon making Kit so giddy she wanted to dance across the shingles except they were on more serious business. They peered down into every courtyard and alley, every garden, looking for the child who might still be nearby hiding—but always they moved toward Ocean Avenue. Maurita had a whole crew searching for her, while Mindy was alone and, most likely, was headed for the freeway, for Zeb's farm, for her own true home.

As Kit searched and scented out in the moonlit night, part of her was still filled with Courtney's ancient myths—until her dreams were jerked back. When, as they galloped up the roofs beside Ocean, they saw on the light-struck street below a little girl running. Red sweater, brown backpack. They scrambled down a camellia tree and ran silently behind her as she raced up the sidewalk's steep hill heading for the highway alone, in the middle of the night.

"Damn kid," Pan breathed. "Some no-good will have her. We need to turn her back before she hits the freeway."

"Or before her family finds her," Kit said. "Her father and uncles are as mean as hornets and her mother not much better."

He turned to look at her. "I'll catch up, I'm stronger, maybe I can stop her. The vet clinic is right over there, go ask for help."

And Kit was off, across Ocean Avenue among a tangle of cottages, past the automotive shop, through Mary Firetti's garden heading for the cat door when she stopped.

Neither car was in the drive. No porch light shining. She slipped into the house through the little door they had installed for Misto before he died.

The house was totally dark, only a few shrinking coals left in the fireplace, enclosed by its glass door. Only silence, no soft breathing from the bedroom. Where had they gone? They were not party people, Dr. Firetti got up early, and so did Mary. Were they out searching, too? Kit leaped to the living room desk and called Ryan's cell phone.

Ryan answered: "Mary? John?"

"It's Kit. The house is empty, both cars gone. Where are they? Where are you? Looking for Maurita? Mindy's run away, too, Pan's following her toward the highway, I came here for help but no one's home and . . ."

"She *has* run away," Ryan said, "we're looking for her. Mary and John are . . . oh, but that's a long story. Kit, you said Mindy's headed for the freeway? What's the child thinking! We'll be right there . . ."

Kit hung up and fled back through the cat door toward Ocean and the freeway watching for Mindy and Pan, looking around for Ryan's red truck, but the first car she saw was Clyde's dark green Jaguar gleaming in the moonlight. Clyde pulled over. Kit leaped in beside Ryan and Joe.

"There," Joe said, front paws on the dashboard, staring ahead where Mindy and Pan were almost to the highway, Pan pressing against her legs, rearing up, pushing her back. When Clyde pulled up just ahead of them Mindy looked shocked and turned to run, but not before Ryan bailed out, grabbed her, knelt and put her arms around the frightened child. "Were you going home, Mindy? To your grandpa?"

The child looked uncertain, and nodded.

"In the night? Alone? You don't know what kind of dangers . . ."

Mindy tried to break away. "Let me go. I won't go back, not to that apartment. My father's gone and good riddance. Now my uncle's gone, too, and anyway he's just as mean. So is my mother, most of the time. I don't want to live there, they argue about money and about stealing and . . . I *won't* go back."

"If you want to go to your grandpa, we'll take you there," Ryan said, looking at her deeply, stroking the child's mussed hair.

Mindy still looked uncertain.

Clyde said, "We trust your grandpa, and we trust you with him."

"We've heard your parents fighting," Ryan said. "We know how that must make you feel."

Mindy's look softened. Hesitantly she climbed in the front seat next to Joe Grey, putting her arms around him. Kit and Pan leaped in beside them, crowding onto her lap, while Ryan climbed in the back.

"Will you park away from the house, let me go in alone?"

"Yes," Ryan said. "But we'll wait, to make sure everything's all right." They were just passing the Harper ranch. All the lights were off except the outside yard lights. Cops got up early, Mindy guessed, and so did writers.

If anything happened at Grandpa's house, once they were alone, if tomorrow Mama came to get her she could run to the Harpers, and hide. If Charlie wasn't home, Billy would hide her, he took kind care of the horses and dogs and cats. For fourteen, he was responsible and smart, he'd know where she could be safe. Billy Young was an orphan, too. She wasn't an orphan, but she felt like one—except that she had Grandpa.

At the next road, Grandpa's house was dark, too, and tonight it looked coldly forbidding; they could see no movement within, beyond the moonstruck glass, no one looking out. Sometimes Zeb went to bed early, but sometimes he sat up watching old westerns. Clyde parked halfway up the gravel drive. Mindy flung the door open, untangled herself from the cats, and leaped out. "Will you wait for me? Until I make sure he's home? Everything's so still . . ."

"Of course we'll wait," Ryan said as Clyde turned off the engine.

But not everything was still. At the sound of the child's voice a nicker came from the far field, loud and eager in the night, and then the sound of hoofbeats.

"Tango," she cried, and a louder whinny reached

them and Mindy was racing across the moonlit yard past the house, dropping her backpack, her sweater flying, the child herself flying to the back fence and under it where the big buckskin pony came galloping, still whinnying, so excited he rushed the fence and rushed Mindy. He slid to a stop beside her as she ducked between the rails; her arms went around his neck, he nuzzled and pushed and mumbled the child's cheek, nosing at her tears, and that made her bawl the harder. Ryan had gotten out, and she was crying, too. And were those tears in Clyde's eyes? Kit wiped her black-and-brown face with a tortoiseshell paw. If Joe Grey and Pan turned away, it was only because tomcats weren't supposed to be softhearted. They all watched Mindy slide bareback onto the pony, without even a halter, and ride away into the moonlight.

13

When Mindy scrambled on Tango, she looked back toward the house, too, longing for her grandpa. But he would be asleep, and Grandpa was hard to wake—while Tango *was* wide awake, bright and sassy with the excitement of her return; he looked away through the pasture and beyond, ready to go anywhere; Tango loved the night; and when she leaned forward he broke into a canter. Her thrill of being home, of being on his back, of guiding the pony with no halter, with only her gentle movements; the thrill of his loving response filled her with the joy she had so longed for. They were together, free, with miles of country around them, just the two of them alone in the moonlight.

Far behind her at the house, Clyde tried the kitchen door, found it unlocked, and he and Ryan stepped in, the door squeaking, the three cats crowding against their ankles. Ryan found the wall switch and turned on the overhead bulb. Harsh light glared in their faces.

They stopped cold.

They stood looking, both guns drawn, as the cats slipped back silently into the shadows. They scanned the open doors and what they could see of the living room—then stared at the floor where the old man lay sprawled silent and unmoving, blood seeping from his torn arm. Blood flowed from his wounded head and face, running across the scarred linoleum. Clyde grabbed his phone and called the chief's house as Ryan called 911.

Max said, "On my way. Call the station, get a medic. Are you carrying?"

"Did that. Of course we are." Clyde grabbed the kitchen towels Ryan handed him, they both knelt trying to ease the bleeding but still watching the open doors to the bedrooms and the living room. The three cats slipped away staying to the shadows, meaning to inspect those rooms even before the cops arrived. Ryan couldn't tell if Zeb was conscious but when she took his hand, his eyes flashed open filled with rage and he came up swinging.

Then he saw who it was, and he lay back down;

gently she helped him, supporting his undamaged arm. Clyde said, "Lie still, it makes the bleeding worse. The medics are on the way." And in the silent night they heard a truck come barreling over the back road from the Harper place, soon they saw its lights out the kitchen window and saw, at the far end of the pasture, the pony veer away to safety, Mindy leaning over him. In minutes they heard the medics' sirens, too, from the highway, and could hear two cop cars, could see their flashing lights.

As the rescue team pulled into the drive, the kitchen door squeaked open and Mindy stood in the doorway staring down at her grandpa, her face white, the pony pushing through where she'd forgotten to latch the gate, pushing into the house behind her. Ryan put her hand on his nose and backed him out as the little girl knelt beside Zeb.

The next half hour was all confusion, front and back doors wide as the cops cleared the house, the four EMTs bringing in their equipment and a gurney. Ryan led the pony into the pasture and locked the gate properly. Max arrived in wrinkled jeans and a work shirt. He questioned the old man as much as he could, with the medics hushing him as they tried to do their work. Mindy tried to cling to Zeb, but a medic gently moved her away. When Zeb did talk, his speech was shaky, sometimes muddled. "It was the boys, fighting. Fighting bad . . ."

He spit up blood, then spoke more clearly. "I was in bed, I heard a car pull up, heard someone come in . . . I thought a burglar was in Nevin's bedroom . . . a light went on . . . I put on a robe and went out. It was Nevin . . . rummaging like he was packing some of the stuff he'd left . . ."

He was quiet for a while, then, "I sat down at the table . . . another car wheeled in . . . the kitchen door opened again, I'd forgot to lock it . . . Footsteps . . ."

A medic tried to hush him. "If you'll be still, maybe I can bring your blood pressure down."

Zeb paid no attention. "His white hair . . . It was DeWayne, he headed right to Nevin's bedroom, he must've seen his brother's car . . . maybe seen the light . . . They began talking real loud then yelling at each other. I got myself some crackers and a glass of milk . . . I sat listening to them fighting. I shouted, 'Keep it down.' I didn't give a damn what they were arguing about, I just wanted them out of there.

"Nevin yelled that DeWayne was into his bank statements, that they were all out of order. 'Or *you* were,' he shouted at me. He said he saw my horse one day over at the Harpers', said maybe I showed them to Harper.

He looked back at DeWayne, said, 'Either him or you were pawing through them.' They came reeling out to the kitchen stumbling and pounding each other . . . red faces . . . then stopped and stood staring at *me*."

Zeb was running out of steam, his voice dropped to a whisper, weak and angry. "I was afraid. Afraid of my own boys.

"Nevin grabbed me, shouted, 'You know, don't you, old man! You know about the money. And you know what happened at the bank. You say a word, and Thelma goes to jail right along with me—it was her car—there'll be no one left at home, and where does that leave your precious Mindy? Child welfare.'"

Mindy stood in the corner against the old refrigerator, stood straight and silent, her face white. She hurt for her grandpa and she prayed for him; but she knew the medics and the doctors would make him all right. And there was something else in her brown eyes besides her worry and pain for Zeb; there was a gleam of fear which, slowly, morphed into the hard look of fight.

This was *not* the end of her life as she knew it! This was *not* the beginning of something far worse, of years in child welfare! She'd run away, first, where they'd never find her.

But, watching Max Harper kneeling beside Zeb, she

knew that, despite what might happen to her thieving family, Max wouldn't let her be sent to welfare, that Max and Charlie would somehow see that she stayed with Grandpa; and she leaned down and kissed Zeb on his forehead.

The medic sighed, and grabbed fresh ice packs to ease the bleeding. He wished the child would back off, wished the old man would shut up. The old guy was hyped with anger, and if he had a concussion they couldn't give him a sedative. He wanted to get him on the gurney, get him to the emergency room.

Zeb took a sip of water from a straw the medic gave him. For an old man with a head injury he was talking too much. "Nevin shouted about some big jewel robbery then about murders and warrants . . . it didn't make sense. They were fighting so bad I swung up out of the chair . . ." He stopped to cough. "And all of a sudden they both laid into *me.* DeWayne shoved me and hit me real hard . . . Nevin yelled, '*You* were into my bank papers. What kind of father *are* you!' He grabbed DeWayne, said, 'You knew, too.' He hit DeWayne again, knocked him into the table . . . kicked him until he was down, until DeWayne's white hair was all bloody."

By this time the old man's voice was about gone.

The blond medic gave him a cool cloth. Joe could see, by the blood pressure gauge, that Zeb was pushing takeoff.

Zeb said, "DeWayne staggered up and out to his car, I heard the door slam, heard it race away, roaring rough up Highway One like it needed an engine job. Not one of those limos they drive but one of those old rough-running cars they brought with 'em, and I hope he doesn't come back."

Officer Crowley went outside, walked around the place; he came back in, avoiding others' footprints and tire tracks. "Both cars gone," he said needlessly. "What is this about bank statements?"

Max said, "Let him rest." Crowley nodded, said no more. A car pulled up out front, Charlie's SUV. She came in the front door, stood out of the medics' way watching, and then followed Max outside where they could talk; of course Joe Grey followed.

"He said it was about the statements," Max said. "What statements?"

"Zeb brought them to me," Charlie said. "Nevin's bank statements that Zeb copied, in town. He put the originals back in Nevin's dresser where he found them. He said to give you the copies when the time was right. He said he didn't want to be seen going in the station." She grinned at him. "Now, I guess the time is right."

"Statements from a Molena Point bank?"

"No. Santa Cruz and three others."

"And the originals? Zeb has them here?"

"That's what he said, that he'd put them back where Nevin hid them, folded in a gray sweater—but that he also found a stack of newspapers in the trash that gave the dates of the robberies. He compared them with the statements, cut them out and made copies. He gave those to me, too. It's all at home, in the safe." Charlie had never done anything like this, had never hidden evidence from Max or lied to him—except the one secret she had sworn to keep, about the speaking cats. Now, it took her a while to tell Max all that Zeb had told her. "But why is . . . ?"

"It's only corroborating evidence," Max said. "Might not mean much now. But it could mean a lot if Zeb knows even more than he's telling. The snitch's voice, the night of the murder and bank-money theft, pretty much matched Zebulon's. What else did he see, that he didn't tell you about? And why not?"

"Maybe because he wasn't sure?" Charlie said.

"Maybe because he *was* sure," said the chief. "Because he's scared as hell to lay out the truth."

They went back through the house to the front, watched the medics load the gurney into the emergency unit and strap it down. Detectives Kathleen Ray and Dallas Garza had arrived. Both were shooting pictures of the many tire marks, those that their own units had driven around trying to leave the suspect ones clear. Two officers were still searching the house, and taking pictures in Nevin's room. Kathleen smiled as she took shots of the pony's hoofmarks cutting over the tire prints they thought were DeWayne's and Nevin's, pony prints that went right into the house then out again.

Max went into the bedroom carrying the uniform Charlie had brought him. Mindy was crying again, she escaped outdoors, avoiding sympathetic looks for a few minutes. The cats followed her; Joe Grey, Pan, and Kit sat on the fence nuzzled by the pony, who in turn was hugged by Mindy, the child bawling into his buckskin neck. The pony was her comfort, but she wanted to hold Grandpa tight, too. The medics had three times chased her away. When Ryan came outside and put her arm around the child, Mindy cried against her, cried all the harder.

Joe could see Max in Nevin's bedroom hastily changing into the uniform. "To impress the hospital staff," Charlie had said. Hospital social workers, if they started asking questions, could be surly about Zeb's living arrangements when he was sent home, an injured old man living alone trying to take care of a little child. They would be asking questions like, Where is her mother? Where is her father? Why doesn't the child live with them? How can an old man who needs a nurse himself care for a child? Can he cook? How would he get her to school?

It would be easier for a chief in full uniform to subdue the complaints of those with an overblown sense of authority. Easier to drill into them that *he* had complete jurisdiction over Mindy. And, Joe thought, Max *did* have jurisdiction or might soon have it if Nevin *had* robbed and killed Jon Jaarel and if Thelma had contributed her car, making her an accomplice.

A breeze stirred Ryan's dark curly hair, tangling it with Mindy's brown hair and with the pony's black mane. "Your grandpa will get good care. Do you want to go to the hospital with us? You can be in his room with him at least part of the time. They'll wheel him away for X-rays and whatever else is needed, and bring him back to you."

Mindy nodded, very serious. She was filled with questions she didn't ask, the one big question she daren't ask.

"It's more than a shallow scalp wound," Ryan said, "but they don't think it's too deep. They won't know more until they've done the tests. Head wounds often look worse than they are, and they always bleed a lot."

Mindy hugged Ryan, pressing her face hard against her. "If he has to stay in the hospital I'm going to stay with him, I'm not leaving him alone." She studied Ryan's green eyes. "*Can* I do that?"

"I don't know, we won't know if he'll need to stay until the doctors are done. If he must stay, and they'll *let* you stay, I'll be there with you." Ryan pulled on her jacket. "Here comes Clyde."

The cats slipped down from the fence as the medics' van pulled away. When Clyde's Jaguar eased up, Kit and Pan jumped in the backseat with Mindy. Clyde idled the engine waiting for Joe. In the front seat Ryan leaned out her window. "You coming? What's the matter with you?"

Joe Grey stared back at her for only a moment then beat it for Charlie's SUV. She was going home, followed by Officers McFarland and Crowley to help her clear their house and the barn area. Joe wanted a look, too. The Harpers' was the closest ranch to the Luthers', in this open part of the hills. It wasn't likely, but if Nevin was hurt bad enough, he might think it a good place to lay up for a few hours, gather his strength until he felt like moving on; it probably wouldn't occur to him that he could weaken and get worse, that he might need a doctor.

They were halfway to the Harpers' place when Charlie's phone rang. She turned on the speaker. "Billy?"

Their young stable hand's voice was soft, as if someone might be listening. "There's an old gray car, maybe a Suzuki, parked back in the woods. Its lights woke me and then went dark. I can just pick out a shine of moonlight on the fenders."

Joe could picture the boy in his room above the barn, rising from bed to look out his windows into the woods, maybe a rifle already propped by his side, a gun that Max had trained him to use carefully and with skill.

Billy was fourteen, a member of Max's young police cadets. He had lived with the Harpers since he was twelve, since his grandmother died. He could use a firearm as well as Charlie. But just the two of them, on that large piece of land, might not be enough.

But, Joe thought, if that was Nevin there in the woods, if he was hurt bad enough to need to rest, maybe he'd soon be gone. He'd sure not stay around the chief's place long, not with possible murder and burglary raps hanging over him. Three hundred thousand dollars had vanished in that last robbery, and plenty more from earlier thefts. To say nothing of whatever Varney had stolen. Joe Grey didn't trust those Luther sons any more than Max did—he sure didn't trust them after they nearly killed their own father.

Still on the highway, far ahead they could hear the Harpers' two big dogs barking. Charlie dimmed their lights, as did the squad car behind them. She looked over at Joe. "Too bad you can't handle a shotgun."

"I never tried. But it's amazing what some cats can do . . . Wait, slow down . . ." She slowed. "There's the car, sticking out between the trees . . ."

She moved on. "Get in the backseat, on the floor." He did as he was told just as her phone rang again. She hit the speaker but kept moving.

Billy said, "He's in the stable, right below me." The dogs were barking so loud they could hardly hear Billy. They heard a horse scream. Billy said, "I'm going down." Before Charlie could stop him the phone went dead. She punched in the one digit for McFarland, and repeated Billy's message.

Joe said, "You still have that black stallion, that boarder? Isn't his stall back there?"

"We have, yes. Last stall. Max is sending him away in the morning, before he hurts someone. He was gentle as pie when the man's wife brought him in, they hauled him down from San Andreas so she could ride in the hunter trials at Pebble Beach, they're waiting for a stall there. I expect the folks at Pebble aren't anxious to have him, though they do have several women grooms. His owner said he hates men, that he can be vicious around men. Once he's moved over there, the woman is planning to take care of him herself." She looked over at Joe. "What's on your mind? What are you thinking?"

Joe looked at her innocently, gave her a sly tomcat smile, and said nothing.

She said, "He was barred from the racetrack because he bucked off the male jockeys. Max is sure that when they brought him in, they had him on drugs, to quiet him—so we wouldn't know how mean he can be. When the ACE or whatever it was wore off, that stud turned crazy. She showed me how to handle him. I laid down the law to Max and Billy: he's off limits to them both, and I'm real careful with him." She turned into the long drive slowly, as quietly as she could on the gravel. She pulled up to the stable, to the big, sliding front entry, which was closed tight. She parked in front of it; the squad car pulled up next to her.

At the sound of her car, the dogs in the barn had gone quiet. They heard a tortured moan, from a man, at the back of the stable. The stallion screamed, a startled, angry retort, and they could hear water running, the hard hissing of a hose. The dogs started barking again. Charlie got out and slid open the big front doors just enough for a person to slip through, the deputies behind her. She looked back at McFarland, he always made her feel more comfortable.

"Whatever happens in there, Jimmie, stay out of reach of that stallion, he's crazy mean, he'd kill a man." The two officers looked skeptical, then looked at each other with an amused hope. And they sure weren't bothered by the dogs, who were leaping at the stall and barking. The officers knew them and had played with them both. Charlie looked around for Joe Grey, who had already fled the car. She didn't see him but she knew he'd be watching. Her concerned and searching glance told him to keep out of the way—as if he needed telling.

At the far end of the stables, those sliding doors were closed, too. Along the alleyway, all the stall doors were closed, Dutch doors with heavy wood below, strong woven wire forming the upper half. The doors on the far side of the stalls stood open to paddocks, to vast fences seven feet tall with hotwire at the top to discourage the occasional cougar. The stallion was in the last stall, charging the closed door, fussing and screaming, snorting as if he were drowning. Billy stood at the closed stall door with a big, heavy hose, squirting a powerful stream through the screen into the horse's face. Nevin lay at the far end of the stall, curled up, bleeding and groaning and covering his head as if the stud were still attacking.

Billy wielded the hose like a rifle, making the stallion back away from the man.

Encouraged by Billy's attack, Joe Grey left the tack room where he'd taken refuge, crossed the wide alleyway, and jumped on McFarland's shoulder for a better view. Jimmie gave him a sidelong glance, half a stern cop look, half amusement as Joe sat working out the scenario of what had happened.

Nevin must have slipped in the back stable doors. The dogs were watching silently from the shadows, as they usually did. When he slid the doors closed thinking he was alone, they attacked him. He wrenched open the nearest stall door, squeezed through, and shut it in their faces. Maybe he didn't think a horse was in there, or think that it might be mean. He knew only the horses his father had had, and they'd all been gentle. Joe watched Billy wield the hose like a fireman until they could see he was getting tired.

Crowley moved up to take it from him, but Charlie slipped in past him. She took the hose from Billy, getting herself drenched, and held the power steady in the stallion's face. She heard Jimmie latch the gate behind her but she knew he was holding the lock for her quick escape. She drove the stallion back and back into the empty corner, working close to him, strong squirts in his nose and ears making him duck away. She reached and pushed open the paddock door, then changed position with the hose, driving him through the opening. "Get out," she yelled. "Get out now, you son of a bitch."

Hearing a woman's angry voice confused him, women didn't treat him like this; he stared at her, reared, struck at her twice but she backed away: he missed her and, avoiding the fury of the hose again, he spun and raced for the paddock. Charlie locked the door behind him. No one had paid any attention to Nevin. When the medics' van came screaming, Officer Crowley slid the front doors wide to let them in; and Joe Grey curled more comfortably across McFarland's shoulder; he watched Nevin look up in gratitude for medical help—and in cold fear at being surrounded, at being trapped by the law.

14

If those hours at the Harpers' ranch were terrifying to Nevin Luther, those same hours for Mindy, with Grandpa Zeb at the hospital, were nearly as frightening—as X-rays were done, and tests in strange machines, as some of the kinder technicians let her watch the scans; and later as diagnoses were pronounced by an array of doctors. Max Harper had given permission for her to stay through it all; Ryan sat with her, holding her close.

Kit and Pan had not, as they had planned, been allowed inside to watch the amazing details of hospital procedures that they could only imagine. Earlier, riding in the backseat of the Jaguar, Kit had said, "We're going in the hospital, too," thinking of the patients in their beds hooked up to all the fancy equipment, looking ahead as they approached the handsome white building. "We can go in the patients' rooms and look all around and see the huge waterfall like Joe did, we can beg bites in the cafeteria, we can stay with Zebulon all night, snuggle with him and keep him warm."

"I don't think so," Ryan had said, pushing back her short, dark hair as she suppressed a smile. "The nurses are more alert for a cat slipping around, since the time Joe Grey prowled the rooms and offices and upset half the staff, since he enraged the doctors—and the nurses thought he was trying to smother a patient. Since then, hospital policy has probably been changed to throw any cat they see out on its furry behind. I'm taking you two home."

Long before the sun came up, Kit and Pan *were* at home, asleep in their tree house; and long before the sun came up, Zebulon was pronounced out of immediate danger and was moved to Intensive Care. Mindy and Ryan were allowed to stay with him—in a room the size of a storage closet. The two had had little sleep; Ryan dozed on a cot crowded against Zebulon's bed, Mindy napped on pillows on the floor, the room so crowded that the nurses could hardly tend to Zebulon; some were amused, some highly annoyed. A nurse came in frequently, stepping around Mindy to wake Zeb. He accepted water and his medications willingly, he ate lightly. Each time he woke he reached down to take Mindy's hand, then soon he slept again.

In the dim environs of Seaver's Antiques, low moonlight shone soft through the west windows where Dulcie and Courtney dozed on a brocade settee after a long night of telling each other ancient tales, Courtney telling her own half-remembered stories of palaces, and repeating tales of the Netherworld that Kit and Pan had told her and Dulcie wished they hadn't. But now suddenly Courtney woke, she stood up on the settee, one paw in Dulcie's face. "Something's happening! Wake up! Oh, my!"

What woke her was a sense of her daddy and of danger and of men fighting, it was at the Luthers' place; but then she saw the Harper ranch, she felt a man's fear, and Charlie's anger and the hard wariness of cops; she saw a wild horse rearing up screaming and striking out, and it was the worst nightmare she'd ever imagined.

At nearly the same moment the upstairs door of the antiques shop opened. Footsteps were coming down, Seaver's steps. Dulcie ducked deep under the pillows out of sight while Courtney stretched out languidly on top as if she were sound asleep.

But Seaver barely looked their way. He went out the

first back door, through the workroom, through the second door to the garage. They heard its door slide up, and in a minute heard his car start, heard it back out. Where was he going this time of night?

When the garage door had gone down again Courtney said, "He goes out late sometimes. If his wife is dead, maybe there are other women."

Dulcie, squirming out from under the pillows, said, "Maybe there are other women anyway." Her daughter was growing up, she needed to know how humans led their lives. They were not the same as cats—as speaking cats. She crawled out from under, and licked Courtney's ears and face as if the calico were still a small kitten, and she cuddled Courtney as they settled down. "Come now, sleep. You can do nothing about Seaver—not just now. And your dream . . . It was only a dream, Courtney, and soon it will vanish," and she could only hope the source of the dream was like that, like steam from a kettle, that it would hang in her memory for a few moments, then dissolve into nothing and go away.

But Courtney's dream had been so real. She snuggled against Dulcie, trying to cling only to her mama's comforting ministrations; and at last, under Dulcie's mothering, the terror did begin to fade, the fear and the screaming horse to slide away, until she began to feel safe again, and she knew that her daddy was safe, that he was with Charlie, and safe; and she began to feel sleepy and soft once more. Dulcie watched her child until all the fear was gone, until she slept.

Earlier, when the medics had come for Nevin, he still lay hunched up, his leather jacket twisted around him—and Joe Grey slipped in through the open stall door for a look. Atop Nevin's earlier wounds, received in his father's kitchen, a bloody tattoo of hoofprints marked his neck, and his left cheek was already swelling. There was a long wound on his chest where the horse's shoe had torn down his shirt. His leather coat had a ripped side pocket with a pale cream envelope spilled out, hundred-dollar bills scattered thick across the straw bedding. Joe Grey's idea to trap Nevin had proceeded on its own, without his help; yet a sudden shame held the tomcat as his belated conscience kicked in: this might be the result he'd hoped for, but he hadn't planned on Nevin being hurt this bad—Joe really didn't care so much about Nevin's condition, he looked like he'd live to stand trial. But the way things had turned out could have gotten Charlie hurt, bad, and that did give the tomcat a guilt trip.

When the medics entered, the two big dogs dropped down at Charlie's command, and were quiet. They felt certain that it was their barking that had saved the day. At the far end of the paddock, the stud was nibbling grass. He'd worked off his rage, for the moment. But when he saw McFarland and Crowley enter the stall to photograph Nevin and collect evidence, his ears went flat and he headed fast for the closed paddock doors. When Charlie spoke to him, he quieted. She walked into the paddock carrying a small bucket of oats; a halter with a stud chain hung over her arm. The black horse put his ears up listening to the rattle of grain in the bucket, he gave Charlie a more kindly look and came right to her. Greedily he ate the oats, gave her a friendly nudge, and settled down again.

"That's better," she said. She shut the door to the paddock, locking him out of the stall as two of the same young medics who had rescued Zebulon hurried in, ragging Charlie for making a busy night; in fact it was nearly morning, the moon almost gone, its last gleam dull and fading to nothing out across the face of the sea.

Moonlight gleamed on the locked glass doors of Seaver's Antiques where Courtney had settled down, putting her fear away, feeling now that her daddy was safe; and her mama was right there cuddling and calming her. Dulcie did not say, *For a great big, grown kitten, you are as spooky as a wildcat.* Dulcie had no idea whether Courtney's sudden alarm had sprung from some keen feline telepathy—another wonder of the kitten's amazing nature; or only from too much storytelling. But all in all, good and bad, the sun would soon rise, and wherever Seaver had gone was his own business.

And if, Dulcie thought, the weeks to follow were filled with more puzzling situations than a cat wanted to deal with, if no two events seemed to fit together—and then if all of a sudden they all *did* fit, smooth as a paw in a mitten, wouldn't that be fine.

But who, she thought, would be responsible for that? The skill of the cats themselves and of the cops? Or, she wondered, a power greater than theirs?

15

On the night that Buffin's patient slipped away from the convalescent home, when the young cat woke to find Maurita gone, he was more than ashamed. He knew that she was healing, that the nurses had had her up during the day, walking with her. He felt so close to her, could feel her getting stronger. He could feel her needing him, could feel that she was happier. If she had seen the man again, why hadn't she rung the nurse?

She had a corner room, small but with heavily mirrored windows looking out on two sides, her own bathroom, a little desk and a phone. If she'd seen the prowler again—even if he couldn't see much through that heavy, prisonlike mirror—why *hadn't* she grabbed the phone and called the cops? She could speak that much, even if her voice was garbled.

On this night when he didn't appear, she had crept completely under the covers, and they slept peacefully. But even in sleep, something within Buffin remained focused on Maurita, stubbornly maintaining the mysterious strength that burned within him, to ease her, helping her to rest, to heal in ways that he did not understand. He was just a plain buff-colored kitten with nothing special about him, yet he could feel the sickness and pain in someone, in an animal, in a human, and soon, if he gave himself to them, if he put all his soul into them, he could feel the patient slowly, slowly growing stronger.

But now, tonight, when he came half awake, chilled, and heard no breathing beside him, felt no warmth there, he woke fully. Maurita was gone. The patient he had grown to love, with whom he had spent cozy days and nights, wasn't there. Maurita was not in the bed.

She was not in the bathroom, that door was open, the room dark, he could hear no sound from within.

But the door to the hall was open, and in the room across the way where a gleam of moonlight shone in, where the nurses and attendants hung their dark blue scrubs and extra sweaters, a closet door stood open. He could see where hangers had been pulled back, could see Maurita's nightgown lying on the closet floor—and he heard the front door open. The big, main door that led past the admitting desk and outdoors. At first he heard some scraping and rattling, then heard the lock give; she had found where they hid the key. He was out of bed on the nightstand reaching a paw to the phone. He started to punch 911, then instead called the Firettis. He had learned early from his parents how urgent it was to remember phone numbers—and had learned from Kit her tricks of concentration that set facts and imprinted stories and numbers forever in her head. Although she was fluffy brained sometimes in her wild conversations, the information she *meant* to remember was imprinted as solid as hieroglyphs carved in stone.

In the Firetti cottage, the phone rang only once, John answered half awake.

"Maurita's run away, out the front door. I'll follow her, but can you follow me?" Buffin dropped the phone and raced out the door tracking Maurita's scent.

Pausing in the shadows, he couldn't see her on the street. So slim and beautiful, with that long black hair, how could he miss her? He followed her trail mixed with the smell of the uniform she'd taken from the closet, and of the borrowed nurse's shoes. Followed her down the sidewalk clinging to the dark side of the convalescent home, clinging to the next building, then across a yard where she couldn't help but be seen in the moonlight—but she had already passed.

He followed her borrowed scents among the shadows of peaked roofs that further darkened the street—but here came a car driving slowly. Its lights picked her out, and Buffin raced after her. He wanted to shout that this was the Firettis' car, that they had come to help her. How many times, in Buffin's life to come, would he fight the terrible urge to yell out human words? To cry out, *Stop! Wait, please!* To yowl out an urgent message that he dare not utter?

And now, behind Buffin came Striker running and scenting out, both young cats wanting to jump on her shoulder, to tell her they came to help, tell her the Firettis wanted to help her escape the prowler. John pulled up beside her and got out, he reached kindly to stop her, taking her hand. "It's all right, Maurita, we'll take you where you want to go." But then here came the cops.

Maurita froze, surrounded by the Firettis' car and two patrol cars in the narrow street, the drivers jumping out facing her, their holstered guns in clear sight and John holding her, and she didn't know what to do. Her whole being was still traumatized by her near murder, and then her attacker prowling, trying to look in the windows. Now, she could only stand shivering.

The last of her bruises shone dark in the car lights. Her long black hair was tangled, covering her lumpy ear. The cats could see the stitched-up scar down the other ear where the one earring had been ripped away. John Firetti still held her hand but he was as gentle with Maurita as he would be with a tiny animal, gentle and kind; he put his other arm around her shoulder so she wouldn't run away.

Only slowly did her dark, frightened eyes look directly at the doctor and the two officers. Only reluctantly did she warm to the kindness in their faces. She watched Mary Firetti step out of the car, and Mary, too, drew her closer.

Leaning against Mary, Maurita said, "There was a man, looking in the windows. Back and forth, but I don't think he could see in. When, tonight, he wasn't there, I knew I had to get away . . . I know him . . . I need . . . I need to see Captain Harper."

The Firettis didn't know why she hadn't called the station, just as Buffin had wondered. Both young cats watched as plump Officer Green helped her into the backseat of his squad car. Buffin leaped in and she held him close. Green said, "Captain Harper's at the hospital, with a prisoner. Detective Davis will take good care of you, she's on her way to the station. I think Dr. Firetti had better take the cat, there could be a lot of turmoil, he might try to run away. The night clerk . . ."

John said, "Let me ride in back with Maurita and

the cat. Mary can follow us and then take the cat and me on home." Buffin scowled at him, he didn't like being called *the cat,* but when Green grinned and nodded and Dr. Firetti slid in beside Maurita, the tan cat didn't fuss.

Mary, in their own car, called Ryan on her cell phone to tell her that Maurita was all right and they were headed for the station.

In the squad car, Green glanced in the rearview mirror at Maurita. "This isn't exactly protocol, taking you to jail when you've committed no crime. But Davis will see that you're safe. You two will get along fine, Davis has cats, too, she loves them like babies." Green didn't look as if he was comfortable dealing with nervous women. Maurita *was* still shaking, she did want to get into the station with a female detective who would care for her, who would understand. Her trauma from the grave had not left her, she was not herself again, not yet.

"Except," she said, thinking of MPPD, "that man will find me here, the station's so open. The bars . . ." As if the stalker wanted so badly to finish the job. As if, if she were put behind bars, he could easily see her and shoot her there, would finish her before she was securely hidden. Cops had been shot in other PDs. Prisoners had been shot in front of police stations in sudden gun battles—had been sent to their demise by their enemies while being arrested and before they could talk.

She wanted to hide somewhere secret and unobserved. The information she had for Max Harper embraced more than one well-timed robbery that her attacker planned. He and his partners had talked over a number of break-ins, all lucrative, all clearly laid out. But Maurita had, as well, evidence on newsworthy robberies in other cities and other countries, cases that distant law enforcement agencies were already working; some spectacular thefts that she had participated in and about which she might offer additional facts.

Green pulled into a red zone before the station. Mary parked a few spaces away. Both John and Mary walked in with them, Mary hugging Maurita, who in turn hugged Buffin securely in her arms. She glanced over at Green, then looked down at Buffin.

Green winked at her. "It'll be all right." But, entering the station through the bulletproof glass doors, Officer Green and the Firettis paused.

EvaJean was at the desk, finishing her temporary assignment of night duty. As Green guided them past her, she snapped, "Wait there, Green. What are you doing? You can't bring a *cat* in here. And you have to book your prisoners in, you know that. How long have you worked for this department! Fingerprints, forms to fill out. You know the routine," she said coldly.

Green kept walking, past the desk and down the hall, one hand lightly on Maurita's shoulder.

"You can't take a prisoner back there, Green. You have to have identification, fingerprints. *Officer Green . . .*"

Green continued to ignore her, his short brown hair catching the overhead light; his uniform had been recently getting too tight. He said it was his age, not the lunches he ate. Never glancing at EvaJean, he guided Maurita down the hall to the third door on the left.

Alerted by EvaJean, Juana Davis stepped out of her office. Her black Latin eyes were like Maurita's. But Juana was shorter, more squarely built; black uniform, black skirt and hose, black regulation shoes. Davis seldom took liberties like the other three detectives, who might come to work in jeans and a sweatshirt. Why would Max Harper care, when he preferred jeans to his own uniform. Davis's square face softened as she smiled at Maurita and petted Buffin. Mary, turning to leave, started to take Buffin from Maurita but the tan cat put his paws tighter around Maurita's neck. She held him close and kissed the kitten on the head.

"Let him stay," Juana said, "she needs him."

Maurita looked gratefully at Davis as Officer Green and the Firettis headed out. Green, glaring at EvaJean, paused long enough to put a guard in place by Juana's door.

In her office, when the Firettis and Green had left, Davis took a look at the thin blue scrubs Maurita was wearing, and pulled a blanket from the closet. She found a pillow, and got woman and cat settled on the love seat. "You've been lying in that bed a long time, and then the stress of the escape. A little more rest won't hurt."

Maurita was embarrassed at being so raggedly dressed in the company of a uniformed detective. She pulled the warm blanket over her as Buffin snuggled into it, and she felt a tear come. She was being treated not as some kind of abandoned refugee, but only with thoughtfulness.

Juana cracked open the door, asked the armed officer who was sitting outside if he would have someone bring them a cup of tea, then she looked back at Maurita. "Do you feel like answering some questions? You've told no one who attacked you?"

"No, I haven't."

"Do you know him?"

Maurita nodded.

"And do you know who found you?"

There was a knock on the door, and a young officer poked his head in, offering two cups of tea and a sweet roll.

"That's the strange thing," Maurita said, accepting the tea and roll gratefully. "I was hurting so bad, and bleeding, I felt like all my insides were broken. I must have passed out. I woke so dizzy. It was dark but when I looked up I saw the moon, then I went dizzy again. I heard a little noise like a branch snapping then heard the man who hurt me running away, I heard a car start and recognized the sound. I tried to look around toward the street but he was gone, I didn't see anyone."

"You knew your attacker. Was it the same man as outside your window, the man you ran from tonight?"

"Yes. Oh, please. He's known in the village. He has a record, enough to send him up for life. If he finds out you're looking for him, with what I know about him, he'll kill me before you catch him, he'll keep looking until I'm dead."

"He almost did kill you! How can we stop him if you won't help us? We've combed the whole crime scene, not a hair, not a thread or button. His footprints all scuffed in dry grass and sand. It looked like he was wearing some kind of cloth booties over his shoes." Juana looked at her for a long time. "You know him but you won't tell me his name—a man who almost buried you alive. What did you do, to put him in such a rage?"

The young woman was silent. Then, "It's what I *wouldn't* do, that's why he wanted to kill me. That, and what I *know*. He'll kill me because of what I could tell. Don't be hurt, or angry, but . . . I have to tell Captain Harper first. Do you understand that?"

"I understand," Juana said gently. Then, "You said someone else was there, whoever found you. The crack of a branch. You heard someone else, then heard your attacker running. But you saw no one else, no one chasing him?"

"No one; and that was odd. Maybe someone heard him digging and came to look, and he saw them and ran, but I didn't see anyone, not from down in the ditch— from in that grave," she said, shivering. "I heard little sounds but no one was there. How can that be?"

Juana lifted a second blanket from the closet, and covered her more warmly. She turned off the overhead lights, leaving only her desk light burning. "Rest a little while, until I finish up some work. There's a guard sitting outside the door. He can call more officers if we need to. Someone will bring fresh clothes for you, and we have a secure place for you to stay."

Maurita nodded gratefully; she sipped her tea, set the cup down, closed her eyes and, already half asleep, pulled Buffin close against her cheek.

She had no idea how long she slept. It was daylight through the office window. She sat up, swallowed down her cold tea and ate the breakfast roll, ate the still warm breakfast that sat on the table, a pancake, bacon, and scrambled eggs, sharing them with Buffin. Were they treating her so well only to get the information about the attacker, or were these cops really that kind? She'd known others that weren't. Latin American cops that treated you like dirt. She looked up at Juana's back, her face reflected in the computer screen.

"Feel better?"

"Yes, thank you." Maurita yawned, hugged Buffin, and sat up. "Much better." Did Detective Davis know how soothing her treatment was? And this little cat, he was amazing, healing in a different way.

There was a light knock, and the door opened. Another detective entered, a tall woman, as slim as a model in her uniform, and beautiful, long black hair shining down her back, as sleek as Maurita's should be when she took care of it. She carried a black camera bag open at the top with a dark garment sticking out, perhaps a jacket.

"I'm Detective Ray. Kathleen." She put out her hand, shook Maurita's bruised hand carefully, and sat down beside her. "I brought you some clothes." She opened the camera bag, took out a folded suit coat, nearly black but not quite. Police blue. Maurita glanced at Juana, frowning.

Davis said, "See what you think of our plan."

In the dim shadows of Seaver's Antiques, Courtney, in sleep, had slipped away from her nightmares about the dangers to her daddy, into softer dreams. Dulcie continued to talk to her, reminding her how bold and strong Joe Grey was, trying to ease her into happier environs, to help the soft night soothe the young calico until she was peaceful once more. As the moon sank lower toward the sea, Courtney and her mother dozed.

But soon Courtney woke again and sat up, her mind full of the sharpest dream yet, a spark of gold shining among ragged logs, blood on the sand and on the grass. She couldn't make out the golden spark, but she saw moonlight touch a woman's face, her delicate earlobe ripped and bleeding, torn in half as if by a scythe from some medieval tale, rough steel through tender skin. She saw the vision for only an instant, then it was gone—and that's when she heard the sound. The same sound she'd heard days before, the faint hum of a car stopping behind the building, a ring of the upstairs phone, Ulrich's voice as he answered, and then Ulrich padding down the stairs barefoot or in slippers, quietly opening the inside door to the storage room, closing it behind him. She heard the outside door open to the driveway; it didn't close.

Ulrich's voice and that of another man. Brief words. The sound of the safe being dialed. She heard it open and then close again. The back door closed. She heard Ulrich lock it, and the car pulled away.

Before the sounds and voices, *had* she been dreaming? That shifting ray of moonlight among blood and sand. *Had* she glimpsed the torn-away earring? No one knew what it looked like, Courtney thought. Joe Grey hadn't seen it, he'd seen only the torn ear and the flowing blood. He had told her what he heard at MPPD, that when the coroner and Detective Kathleen Ray examined the other earring, the crushed gold wires embedded in Maurita's other lobe, no one could be sure what shape it might have been; that puzzle was now at the jewelers, to see what they could make of it. Her daddy said it might mean nothing at all, but the earrings were part of the case and should not be overlooked.

As the moon eased lower, its glow touched Kit and Pan where they slept in their tree house. It touched

Joe Grey in his tower. All had arrived back in the village, Ryan taking Kit and Pan home from the hospital, where the two quietly snuggled down in their tree house. They didn't go inside to wake Lucinda and Pedric, to launch into a long tale at this late hour.

Charlie had brought Joe Grey home, leaving Officers McFarland and Crowley still at the ranch working the scene, photographing and printing Nevin's car, photographing the stall, taking blood samples. The three cats were still edgy with the emotions of the night, unease born of the storm of human anger at the Luther house, the smell of human blood, the rage of shouting and hard-hitting fists—and for Joe the thud of the stallion's hooves striking human flesh, nightmare images that, even in sleep, made him growl and made his ears go flat, made his fur stand stiff.

But Courtney and Dulcie slept peacefully now, feeling sheltered and safe, mother and daughter snuggled together, Courtney willing herself to forget the ugly dream of the woman in the grave, forget the hate that lay beyond her cloistered world of velvet and carved rosewood. They slept soothed by the magic of the tales they had told each other, Dulcie's dreamy fairy tales, and Courtney's sharp images from her past and then from the underground that Kit and Pan had described. On that journey into the Netherworld, her two friends had seen wonders beyond most cats' imagining. Wonders that Dulcie wished Courtney didn't know. When Kit started telling an adventure, it was nearly impossible to stop her.

That evening, listening to Courtney's retelling of Kit's tales, Dulcie had found it hard to quiet her own distress. Courtney relished those stories; she was so intense with longing to see those wonders that Dulcie didn't like to think where this might lead.

But maybe it was better that Courtney's thoughts were trapped, for a little while, in the Netherworld's wild and impossible lands, than trapped in the dreams of fame and stardom that Ulrich Seaver fed her— visions that might lead to far more misery than any Netherworld haunts.

16

It was earlier when Joe Grey woke in his tower, listening. Downstairs, the phone had rung once, in the master bedroom. It hadn't awakened Clyde, Joe could hear him still snoring; but he could hear clearly Ryan's sleepy voice as she picked up. Outside Joe's windows, clouds had gathered so thickly that there were only occasional smears of moonlight. When Charlie had brought him home, he had leaped out of her SUV, had gone straight up to the roof, to his tower, and collapsed among his pillows yawning hugely.

"They did?" Ryan was saying. "She's coming there with you? Well, that's good news." She sat up in bed holding the phone, pushing back her dark, rumpled hair. "She managed to unlock the front door? But she's all right, Juana? She didn't mind being brought into the station?"

She listened, then, "Trying to look in the windows. *Was* that her attacker? After all your trouble to hide her, the guy tracked her there? But why did she run? Why didn't she call the station?"

Another silence, then, "Maybe the patrols will corner him." Then, "You do?" She smiled. "Sure you can. That will be a blast. Let us know when." They talked for a few minutes more. Ryan said, "I will," then a little click as she put the phone back in its cradle. Joe peered down over the edge of his cat door, watched her stretch out again and pull the covers up as if to catch another few winks. Clyde was still snoring.

All over the village, Joe thought, while night patrols searched for Maurita's stalker—and *had* searched for Maurita—other officers would soon be getting ready for first watch. The tomcat felt smug that he didn't have to answer to MPPD hours and rules, *and* that he didn't have to shave, shower, and put on a uniform.

But, too curious about Maurita to stay in his warm nest for long, Joe Grey gave his sleek coat a couple of licks, skipped breakfast, and headed for the station.

He had known that Maurita was getting better in the nursing home, word passed quickly from John Firetti among their friends. But to know that a man, likely the same man who nearly killed her, had found where she was, must have triggered her fear all over again—frightening her enough to run.

Well, she was with the cops now, and safe.

Making straight for MPPD, Joe hit the roofs running—hoping that Mabel Farthy, their motherly desk clerk, was back at work after her flu and had brought something good to slake his hunger. Sugar doughnuts? Oatmeal cookies? Fried chicken? Hoped he could get at the goodies before the guys in the department scoffed them all up.

Leaping to the courthouse roof, racing for the oak tree at the far end, he was backing down its rough bark when he paused, clinging among the branches. He didn't need to peer inside to know that Mabel wasn't at her desk; even through the bulletproof glass doors, EvaJean Simpson's scolding voice made his fur crawl. The temp he hated, whom they all hated. If *she* ever brought him breakfast, it would be laced with strychnine.

A squad car stood in front, beside the Firettis' car. Officer Green, Maurita, and the Firettis were just headed in through the glass doors. Maurita *was* beautiful, even in cotton scrubs, her bruises nearly gone, the thin woman looking far better than she had lying half dead and nearly buried in the sand. She was carrying

Buffin close against her shoulder. Only the young cat spotted Joe Grey, or caught his scent. His ears went up, he gave his daddy a silly cat grin, then turned innocently away. Joe wanted to slip in, too, but one look at EvaJean, and he stayed where he was. She was in a hell of a temper. He backed down the tree and peered in through the glass, cringing at the clerk's bossy voice. He watched Officer Green urge Maurita and the Firettis on down the hall, saw Juana's door open and they all disappeared inside, EvaJean still fussing. The door had already closed as she shouted, "And get that cat out of there or I'll call an officer who will."

That made Joe laugh. Anyone in the department would offer ear rubs and back scratches, but no one would toss a cat out, certainly not one of Joe Grey's own kittens.

Joe backed into the bushes when a squad car pulled up in the red zone. Officers Carlos and Haley opened its back door and ushered out a tattooed prisoner, at least six feet four and hard muscled. They had him in handcuffs and leg irons but he was still fighting them, he was so angry he was probably on drugs, which would make him harder than hell to handle. Joe knew better than to try to slip past this bunch, which might explode despite the chains—but against better judgment he was through the door behind them anyway and into the holding cell hoping they wouldn't put the guy in there with him.

It took a long time to book the prisoner, he wouldn't answer questions without being strong-armed. They should have been booking him in the back by the jail. He fought the fingerprint routine, he swore he didn't have a driver's license, they had to frisk him for it. Twice Joe pushed out through the bars and started to make a dash down the hall, but the guy began to fight again, and the tomcat drew back. He could have made it fine, he thought, but a cop had set up a folding chair outside Juana's office to guard Maurita, and how could a cat eavesdrop now?

He waited forever until the prisoner was dragged away down the hall to the jail, and until Maurita's guard rose as Davis's door opened, and moved away as if on an errand. In that moment Joe fled down the hall and in through the crack in Max's door. He had slid deep under the console into the shadows when he heard a knock on Juana's door and could smell tea and sweet rolls. He heard the guard sit down again. The best he could do, to eavesdrop, was catch every third or fourth word, he couldn't make much of it. Someone else went in and out, he could smell bacon and eggs, which didn't help his hungry mood much. Two women talking. Then someone left heading down the hall, then silence for a little while, so quiet that Joe dozed, jerked awake now and then by the creak of the guard's metal chair. He woke fully when he heard the steps of two women leave the office. He watched Detectives Juana Davis and Kathleen Ray head down the hall and out the rear door. He could just see them through the bars as they crossed the back street toward Juana's condo. He slipped out of Max's office, following them, ignoring the guard. Kathleen was carrying a camera case, slightly open. As they started up the condo steps they were joined by two fellow officers. They'd left Maurita alone in Davis's office? But the deputy was guarding her.

Curious, Joe eased behind the officer's back and into Davis's office, listening to the faint click of computer keys.

He faced Kathleen's back where she worked at Juana's computer, her long black hair hanging over the chair. Officer Bonner sat on the couch reading aloud a report as if Kathleen was typing it for him—but Kathleen couldn't be here. By this time she'd be in Juana Davis's condo. No way she could be here, working at Davis's desk.

With Kathleen sitting right here, who the hell *was* with Davis? No one in the office looked like Kathleen, tall and as slim as a model, long black hair like Maurita's, like . . .

Joe Grey's eyes widened. He leaped to the desk, stepped around behind the computer monitor and stared into the woman's face.

Kathleen looked back at him, startled. "What? What, Joe Grey? What's that expression, what's the matter with you?"

He slipped around the monitor and rubbed his face against hers, comforted by her familiar scent. The computer itself and the desk still smelled as they should, smelled like Juana Davis. When he leaped to the couch beside Bonner, the scent at the other end of the cushions took Joe a minute to sort out: yes, it smelled pleasantly of Maurita. A pair of blue scrubs lay over a chair, a pair of white nurse's shoes were pushed underneath. He looked up when Davis entered alone. Kathleen looked around at her. "All settled?"

"Clean sheets," Juana said. "Maurita has the other twin bed in my room, two officers to rotate in my office-guest-room. That'll be pretty crowded. I'm sending my two cats to board with the Firettis, Ryan's picking them up. And she's dropping Rock off at my place. He might lack a little in some finer points of training, but he's a good guard dog. And a good loud alarm," she said with a warm Latino smile. "And he likes cats just fine. But my two cats' view of dogs . . . they don't like them so much. They'll be better with John and Mary.

Ryan's bringing Rock's special diet and a leash and choke chain. She'll teach Maurita Rock's commands, which she and our officers will need to know."

Joe Grey didn't think much of the condo as Maurita's hiding place. Two walls of second-floor windows with easy locks, the windows on the north open to a small rooftop surrounded by staggered walls and crannies and taller roofs, a little retreat where anyone could stand, looking in.

Between the condo's front door and the side windows, glass sliders opened to a wide deck, from which Juana could see the back of MPPD. That, at least, was screened and roofed with wire mesh so Juana's two cats could play outside. A straggly young bougainvillea vine led up to it. A cat could bypass the deck and slip right up onto the open roof beneath the side windows.

Could a prowler do the same, crawl up that flimsy vine and over? They would have to be lightweight, and agile.

But when he thought of sharp Weimaraner teeth and of well-used service revolvers resting in the officers' holsters, he guessed that would be a hazardous climb, even if Maurita's stalker *was* superathletic. Smiling, he hoped Rock and the cops got a good bloody crack at him.

17

Early sun shone in through the display windows and big glass doors of Seaver's Antiques. The store wasn't yet open but passersby, glancing in, could see Bert, in his brown store smock, vacuuming the ornate rugs and carefully dusting the intricately carved furniture and brightly glazed porcelain. Bert was quiet and shy but he was a good assistant, he knew his antiques, and he had a businesslike and friendly way with the clients; he wasn't reluctant to shop the auctions for a special piece for a customer, or to call around the country for an item a client wanted. Now as he did the daily cleaning he paid no attention to Courtney; he knew where she was, could see her sleeping in a stack of pillows. The doors were all locked, and he had strict instructions to keep her inside. He did not see Dulcie beneath the pillows, he had no idea she was in the building. When he heard the garage doors slide open he turned, smiling. Ulrich was back. Courtney raised her head to look, then tucked her nose into her paws again as if she were asleep.

Where, she thought, had Ulrich been all night? *Did* he have a girlfriend on the side, besides his supposed wife? She felt Dulcie wriggle deeper under the pillows and slip to the floor, heard her brush against the furniture looking for a way to escape. Courtney belonged here. Dulcie didn't. Her presence would stir questions as fierce as nesting hornets.

They heard the outer door open and close, footsteps coming through the workroom then the inner door opened and they heard voices, two people coming in, and one was a woman. That made the cats stiffen with alarm. Bert kept vacuuming but gave the arrivals a smile and a wave—while behind the couch Dulcie vanished, racing for the powder room. Praying she was unheard over the continuing sound of the vacuum, she pushed open the powder room door and was on the counter at the window. Fighting it open a few inches, with fierce claws she ripped the corner of the new screen. Made a hole big enough to slide through, the rough edges tearing at her tabby fur. She pushed the window closed behind her but not enough to lock.

She hit the crate below, leaped soundlessly onto the sand and kept running, into the weedy, tree-shaded park.

Courtney lay listening to the couple. Was this Ulrich's wife, did he have a wife after all? Or was this his lover, visiting while his wife was absent?

Absent for good? Courtney thought. Or could *this* be the victim from the grave, healed and able to move about once more? That didn't seem likely, as badly as Joe said she was hurt. And why would she be here with Seaver, if he had attacked her so cruelly? So many questions. If she was his girlfriend, if he *had* nearly killed her, she couldn't be dumb enough to let him lure her to him again.

And if this was his wife, returned from some trip, Courtney didn't know whether to hide from the woman or play "loving kitty," and pretend to like her.

When Ulrich switched on the hall light and Courtney got a look at her, she was so elegant and neat, and with no scars or wounds, that Courtney was sure this wasn't the injured woman.

Wife, Courtney thought, and she even smelled like the lavender scent in their bedroom. Wife or not, this was the woman who lived with him and who talked to him on the phone—he called her Fay. Fay Seaver? They talked about their grand plans for "the calico," about exhibits and crowds and flights to New York, causing her shivers of excitement, but then of fear. With the two of them together keeping her captive, maybe she should escape right now, chase after Dulcie—if Dulcie had gotten out.

Yet if she ran away, how could she find out any more about Fay, any more than she'd learned from prowling her closet and her dresser drawers? How could she find out the rest of their plan? Because there *was* more. Little innuendos on the phone—she thought that was the word—that she didn't understand, but things that Ulrich didn't want the cops to know.

But now, when Seaver switched on the desk light, too, so it shone across directly on Courtney, Fay stood looking at her, smiling with delight. "Oh, my, she's beautiful! She's elegant, with those striking bracelets, and that wonderful mix of colors down her back—like the queen's robes. She outshines all the photos you sent me."

Fay was nearly as tall as Ulrich, slim and sleekly dressed in a tailored suit as handsome as the others in her closet. She was wearing expensive hose and low leather shoes that looked hand-stitched, striking but comfortable. Courtney was surprised at how much she'd learned about people's clothes and the habits of humans in the short time she'd been on this earth—or maybe she'd known from lives already past, and was just beginning to remember. Or maybe, she thought, amused, she had learned from watching those mind-numbing TV shows?

Seaver set Fay's small suitcase and leather overnight bag down by the stairs. Her luggage had carry-on tags. Her hair was the color of deep maple, sleekly styled, with a bun in the back, a gold pin through it. Her eyes were brown. She watched Courtney sit up taller between the pillows. She took a step toward the calico and gently put out her hand.

"You're lovely, my dear." She said nothing more, she didn't gush; but her eyes were bright with pleasure, and only softly did she move closer, as if wondering whether Courtney would tolerate being petted or stroked on their first meeting; as if Courtney might be too shy, or too austere, and would need to be courted, like the real queen she was. "And you're smart," she said, "I can tell by your looks; you'll learn your tricks in no time."

Courtney went very still. *Tricks.* She considered Fay for some time, then decided to play Fay's game, for a little while. She lifted her right foot prettily, her three black bracelets bright in the lamplight. Fay looked and looked at the calico's vivid markings. "So perfect," she said, and gently she sat down near her.

Courtney eased closer, sniffing her scent, admiring

the looks of this finely turned-out woman who intended to make her famous . . .

This woman, a little voice in Courtney's head whispered, this woman who means to keep me captive just as Seaver is doing? This woman who, no matter how nice she seems, means to teach me tricks and show me off to crowds of strangers and make lots of money on me?

Sitting close to Fay and enjoying her petting, or pretending to, pretending to be a loving kitty, Courtney was all mixed up. Was she, all her life, going to be so excited by fame one minute, but as confused as a trapped mouse the next?

While Bert put away his vacuum and opened the shop, the three of them went upstairs, Fay carrying Courtney tenderly over her shoulder—a tender but very firm grip that offered little chance of escape. Upstairs in the little kitchen, Ulrich made a cup of tea for Fay, while Fay opened her overnight bag and spread out a stack of oversized photographs across the coffee table. He set her tea on an end table, and they sat on the couch, Fay shuffling the pictures as they looked. "All taken at the museum gallery," she said, "a preview of the show, though the finished exhibit will be far more wonderful."

Ulrich exclaimed and admired, and Courtney couldn't help purring as she was held across Fay's shoulder. Some were of Courtney herself that Ulrich had sent Fay. Some were of tapestries of her. All were framed, and some already hung on the gallery walls; some were of the museum building itself, so elegant that the calico was wide-eyed with pride.

"You see how much she likes the pictures," Fay said inanely. "And she's already cuddling up to me. Oh, she'll love her new home, and she'll love learning her new tricks—she'll love the audiences' applause, she'll be so happy in her new life." She turned to rub her face against Courtney's. "Oh, you'll be such a wealthy cat, my dear," but her glance at Ulrich held a twisted smile that turned Courtney cold; it might be a very long time before Joe Grey's daughter learned to trust this woman.

18

While Joe Grey watched Maurita's drama play out at MPPD and considered her new hiding place, Dulcie, on the rooftop outside Seaver's second-floor apartment, having scrambled out through the powder room window, climbed up a spindly tree to join Kit and Pan. Where the draperies were partially open, the golden tom and his fluffy tortoiseshell lady were crouched beneath the sill peering into the living room. Dulcie joined them; all three cats were impressed by the elegant woman who sat at the oversized coffee table with Ulrich, holding Courtney on her shoulder. They had spread out a stack of enlarged color photographs; most were pictures of Courtney herself, flattering her little cat ego. Some were of a museum gallery, its high ceiling lighted through an impressive glass dome, the walls hung with framed pictures and tapestries of cats exactly like her, each within an ornate gold frame. The works were from many centuries and many lands. Each piece had a printed card on the wall beside it telling the story of its history.

One oversized, bright photograph showed a velvet-draped corner of the gallery where a queen's throne might stand. Here rose the calico queen's aerie, a satin bed within a tall cage rising up, hand carved of what might be rosewood, a bright, three-tiered structure big enough for a dozen cats, its many nooks and shelves embellished with embroidered pillows and handwoven throws. This was Courtney's home-to-be. But this enclosure, instead of impressing her, totally undid the young calico. When she looked past Fay, out the window at the three cats, her amber eyes were big and frightened. Suddenly she wanted out—out of the apartment, out of the antiques store, outside on the far rooftops, and free.

Yet her look was determined, too. Dulcie could read her calico kitten's intent: she did not mean to leave this place until she knew what final fate these two meant for her.

When Seaver rose, the three cats dropped flat and backed away on their bellies, sickened by the kitten's fear and uncertainty. She might revel in thoughts of fame for a while, and then in fame itself. But what next? Would she live all her life as a captive, a caged show cat? When the woman rose and closed the draperies, they could still see beneath, through a tiny space. They looked at each other, and backed away. They hated leaving Courtney but at that moment there was nothing they could do to free her, even if she *had* been ready to escape.

All these windows were beyond opening, and the door to the stairs seemed always to be closed tight. They wished Joe Grey were there. Watching Courtney, they knew that deep in her calico soul she was as conflicted as a kitten ever could be. One minute happily purring with thoughts of a life as glamorous as a movie star's, the next minute her eyes wide with fear, imagining herself forever locked in a cage stared at by strangers while the Seavers' gold-framed tapestries of her raked in the money—and who knew how many of those beautiful pieces were even authentic?

The three cats left Seaver's feeling grim, trying every way they could to work out a plan, to get Courtney out of there. At least the Seavers seemed to be treating her well, cushions strewn around, a soft blanket, and they were feeding her lovely delicacies—though they didn't know much about cats. If she were an ordinary feline, she'd be sick as hell from that diet, and soon she'd be dead. Speaking cats did fine on human food, but ordinary cats did not. With all Dr. Firetti's tedious research, with all his blood tests, he had never found the answer as to why.

As they prowled the rooftops, Dulcie's mind on Courtney and on the fancy promises that the Seavers had laid out, shame touched her—how could a kitten of hers, certainly not one with Courtney's beauty and intelligence, stupidly hand over her life to captivity, how could she sell out cheap to this shoddy deception?

Heading over the shingles for MPPD, they stayed close together, each trying to think of a plan to free her and wondering if one of them, in the role of snitch, should report to the cops that they knew where the lost cat was, and that she had been stolen. Was there a law against stealing cats?

Or they could capture Courtney themselves. If they could still get out the window. If they could, but she refused to go with them, their claws and teeth might force her out of the shop.

But how do you imprison your own kitten? Maybe they could lock her up at home with Wilma until she found her senses. Dulcie could imagine her tall, gray-haired housemate, her retired parole officer housemate, nailing the guest-room windows shut and standing guard at the door, and that made her roll over laughing.

They had reached the roof of the station and were about to drop down the oak tree when a sheriff's car pulled up, a deputy got out, opened the back door, and hauled out two young boys handcuffed together.

"We didn't *do* anything, that's my uncle's house, we were only—"

The deputy laughed. "With three broken windows, and a pile of jewelry and electronics already in your car . . . ?" He marched them into the station fighting and kicking. The three cats slid in behind them, Kit trying so hard not to laugh that she almost got kicked, herself, by the little varmints. The cats fled down the hall past the young officer at the desk who was standing in for EvaJean; he glanced down at them and smiled. The deputy from the sheriff's department, unfamiliar with MPPD's casual routine, grinned broadly. Usually the cats were more careful around officers from other departments. Now they sped past the counter as fast as they could run. Behind them the desk clerk started to book the boys while the sheriff's deputy called their parents.

On down the hall, Kit and Pan and Dulcie sniffed at Max's door, listened, then peered in. They did the same at Davis's office and then Kathleen's. Not a sign of anyone. Joe Grey's scent lingered at all three doors. They found the back door closed, both the barred door and the heavy wooden one. They waited in the shadows for some time until the boys were booked and led back to a cell. As the two angry youngsters were pushed into their cage, the cats were through, too, between the bars behind them. They leaped up through the open, barred window as the boys jumped at them and shouted, and they hightailed it across the police lot between parked black-and-whites, following Joe's scent.

Crossing the street avoiding slow-moving cars that had dutifully lowered their speed when passing the PD, they were soon up a small vine to the roof that joined Juana Davis's condo; her second-floor retreat was one of two dozen, worked into a design as complicated as a three-dimensional chessboard. Climbing the bougainvillea to the low roof, they crouched low beneath Juana's side window.

Juana had drawn the draperies against any glimpse within. Though with the roofs tilted and angled all around, it would be hard for a prowler to gain that flat area and see in—except for the three cats, crouched below the sill; even with sharp reflections of rising sun from the other, distant apartments, they could peer up below the drape for an occasional look. Now, they pressed their ears to the wall.

They could hear Chief Harper, Juana Davis, Detective Dallas Garza, and Kathleen. And the low, unfamiliar voice of a woman they didn't know—then they caught the scent of Joe Grey and heard a short purr behind them. The next instant he was crouched below the sill beside Dulcie, his ears flat, his short tail down, leaving no eye-catching appendage sticking up. Juana had left the drapery slightly open but as the sun moved higher sending a bright gleam off the tangle of roofs, she rose and pulled them fully closed; the dazzle ended. The cats could see only by crowding at a tiny crack in the corner—but they had gotten a glimpse of Maurita. "That," Joe said, "is the lady of the grave."

She lay on the couch, a blanket around her, talking with Captain Harper; her scars and bruises were fading, there were still bandages on her face and ears, and one large scar wrapping her throat. She was nearly as pale as the room itself, which Juana had recently redone. Clear white walls, soft white furniture, stainproof but decorated with a number of multicolored cat hairs, an expensive sisal rug that showed only a few kitty claw marks. It wasn't a large room, the five officers and Maurita took up all the furniture. Rock's blanket was folded in the corner where the big silver dog, scenting the cats, was intently sniffing. Dallas told him to be still, then looked again at Maurita.

"How long have they been at this? You had nothing to do with the first robberies?"

"I was with him maybe five years. Enough to be part of the last seven thefts . . . Brazil, Colombia, Panama, New York, but every one of them frightened me more. I wanted out. I didn't know how long they'd been pulling these jobs, but I didn't like it.

"With each one he got less loving, soon he was treating me like a slave. He made me dress real refined to do the shopping—pretend-shopping while I made the jewelry inventory. He always had to be sure I had it right, the prices, the value of the gems, always asking questions, when I knew more than he did. I managed a jewelry store for ten years in Panama City.

"That's why he wanted me. He'd be nervous, but real loving, until a job was over, until I'd done my part and we'd gotten away clean. Then he'd forget me, treat me like mud. Like a trick dog that, after its act, got put in a kennel and forgotten."

Like Courtney will be, Dulcie thought. And Joe and Kit and Pan thought the same.

"When I got up the nerve to tell him I didn't want to do the robberies anymore, he blew up. I knew he would, but I wanted out real bad. I had a bag packed. I didn't like the danger, the tight planning, avoiding cops all the time, watching for store detectives. I didn't like any of it. We fought a lot between jobs. The other guys didn't care when he hit me. I was his woman, he could do what he wanted, it was none of their affair.

"That night when I told him I was leaving him, he beat me really hard." Her eyes teared up. "I was half unconscious when he dragged me into one of the older cars. I tried to fight but I was already hurt pretty bad. I remember the smell of dirt. I don't know, maybe I fainted. I was lying on the dirt, I could see fallen trees, night-dark clouds and a smear of moonlight. I heard him digging. I was dizzy, sticky with blood. When he pulled me into the grave I fought him harder. He clutched at my throat, I couldn't breathe, I was thrashing and kicking him. When I kneed him, he grunted and let go. And then the real pain . . ." She caught her breath. "Pain like knives when he ripped off my earring."

At the mention of the earring, tears came to her eyes again, as if the lost piece of jewelry meant far more to her than a mere earring.

It was then that Kit, listening at the window, sneezed. Rock heard her, and saw a small movement beyond the crack of drapery; he let out a bark and leaped for the window. All four cats reared up, they didn't realize until too late that their shadows showed through the draperies. Seeing the faint shapes, every-one but Maurita stood up to look. Dulcie, Kit, and Pan fled the scene fast, down the bougainvillea to the sidewalk and they were gone, into the early sun and the fog that crept after it.

Joe Grey stayed where he was. He strolled to the center of the window and stood tall, scratching at the glass, yowling at Rock's leaping shadow; the excited Weimaraner could see Joe's silhouette and could clearly smell him. Dallas rose and took Rock by the collar. His vocabulary, at Rock's bad manners, was the law's finest.

But he wasn't going to shut the dog up until he let Joe Grey in—the two were pals, housemates, sometime fellow guardians. The detective opened the drapery and the glass and slid back the screen. "What the hell do you want?"

Joe came flying in, leaping at Rock as if he hadn't seen him in months; the two wrestled, banging against furniture and uniformed legs until Max and Dallas settled them with a few sharp words and Rock lay down, pressing his head against Max for sympathy. Juana and Kathleen were bent over laughing. Maurita only looked startled, then turned away from where the low rays of the sun shone directly at her, sharpening the scars on her face.

As Juana rose to more securely draw the draperies, Joe glimpsed Dulcie and Kit and Pan fleeing across the courthouse roof, flipping their tails with annoyance. They'd be thinking, *Too many cats converging all at once, too many cops wondering why, too many cops asking questions.*

Max petted Rock, then sat looking at Maurita. "Can we get to the logistics, to just how he laid out these jobs?"

He, who? Joe thought, watching the chief. *She must have told Max who her attacker was before I got here. If the guy thinks she's still alive, he'll keep looking until he finishes her*—and Maurita mirrored his thought. "If DeWayne sees me in here he'll find some way in, and he'll kill me."

DeWayne Luther! Joe thought, sitting up to stare at her, then hastily rolling over. *DeWayne Luther!* A sharp picture in his mind of Maurita lying battered in that damp and moonlit grave, and now he could see Zeb's white-haired son bending over her . . . A vision he hadn't seen but felt as if he had, as if he had seen the killer as well as his victim. On the couch, he stretched out innocently pretending to nap while Maurita gave Max and the detectives details of every crime that she and DeWayne and his partners had committed.

"And the earring," Max said. "He must have been really in a rage to rip it off like that."

"Those earrings were the only gift he ever gave

me, part of our first burglary, from the museum of Panama. They were ancient Peruvian, and valuable. They were among the few pieces that remained when the Spaniards melted down all that beautiful work just for the gold. Did they even know what a real fortune they destroyed? It was the only sign, right at first, that he loved me—or, I thought he did."

She said, "A locksmith with an electrician's skills traveled with us. He quietly cased the lock mechanisms while I assessed the jewelry and handbags and luxury items. Every job went down without a hitch." She twisted her long black hair. "At least, every robbery since we became a twosome. A twosome," she said, laughing. "Such as it was. The bastard."

She looked at Max. "My blood should be on the earring, but I guess no prints, he was wearing gloves. I suppose it's not much use as evidence, now that you know who he is."

"With your blood and flesh on it, it could corroborate your testimony."

She said, "It's silly, but I want the earring back. If anyone ever finds it, and when the police are done with it, I want it."

It was late afternoon, nearly dusk when Max, Kathleen, and Dallas left the condo, crossing the back street hastily to the department—three uniforms: the chief and two of his detectives. Juana stayed with Maurita until Officers McFarland and Crowley arrived through the back door, the two officers dressed in jeans, sport shirts, and loose vests. Young McFarland was neatly shaven, hair trimmed short; tall, big-boned Crowley with such large hands that Joe always thought he should be farming or felling timber. Both were armed, both carried black camera bags, which Joe and Rock immediately inspected. It took only one sniff to know that these were packed with a few clothes and with a supply of groceries. Juana busied herself making sandwiches until Clyde arrived to show them Rock's commands, and to give the big dog a last run for the night. When they returned, McFarland, Crowley, and Juana, and Maurita wearing Juana's blue robe, had settled in for their supper. As Clyde headed home, Joe Grey followed him, leaped in through the Jaguar's open driver's door, and lay down on Clyde's smoothly folded sport coat.

Clyde scowled down at him. "I just had that coat cleaned. I suppose you think you're going home to pig out as usual on our dinner. Why didn't you eat with Maurita and the cops? You too good to beg?"

"I'm going with you because you smell like lasagna, that's why."

19

Clyde turned the corner on the green light. "So you've been spying on the law, watching Maurita dress up like Detective Ray."

"Not a bad likeness. If Max would let her carry, just in case . . ."

"That's not up to Max. That's the governor's call. Max has *given* her two guards."

"And for how long will that condo be safe?"

"A long time with two or three cops and Rock. I wouldn't want to tangle with them. But I don't think Max will keep her in one place very long. Every time I think of that grave I wonder all over again, what kind of society has this turned into?"

Joe sighed. "A culture of kidnappers, rapists, killers, and druggies."

"And porn addicts," Clyde added, "their minds gone. And the meth kids, if the users *have* kids, born already twisted or half crazy." He slowed at a light. Joe looked over at him. "You missed the part about the grave digger. It was DeWayne Luther."

The light changed. Clyde didn't move, he sat staring at Joe. "*DeWayne Luther? DeWayne* beat up Maurita, tried to bury her alive? My God, Joe."

"Well, the guy *is* mean as hell, he half killed his own father. I hope Max doesn't let the hospital discharge the grandfather to Thelma. No telling what more those boys would do to him."

Car horns started to honk, and Clyde moved on.

"At least Nevin's locked up in a prison hospital," Joe said. "Thelma didn't seem so broken up over her husband being injured so bad and arraigned for murder and attempted murders. Mindy didn't seem very upset, either. Maybe he'll end his days right there in prison."

Clyde turned into their driveway beside Ryan's truck; they could smell the lasagna, a breath from heaven. He said, "Thelma told Zeb's doctor she's taking him to her place, that she's going to take care of him, not take him back to that dirty farm, as she put it. She takes him back to that apartment, Varney will be all over him."

Joe scratched his ear and turned to hop out of the Jaguar. "She won't. She'll find out differently when Max gets hold of her. He's not letting Zeb stay there. Even with Nevin gone, Varney has a long record, all small arrests but enough that I don't trust him, enough he should be off the streets. And Thelma herself is ripe for accessory to murder," the tomcat said, leaping out of the car between Clyde's feet and racing for his cat door.

"Accessory," Clyde said, opening the front door and wiping his feet on the mat. "If it *was* her car that Nevin used." He looked down at Joe, shrugged, and headed for the kitchen; he kissed Ryan, her dark, bouncy hair freshly brushed, her flowered apron tied prettily over her black work jeans, which were streaked with caulking, and a clean blue denim shirt. Her bare feet were snug in bunny slippers, her boots stood on the front porch. Joe leaped to the table, onto his place mat, and sat eyeing her impatiently.

"DeWayne Luther," Clyde told her. "It was De-Wayne Luther who tried to do in Maurita, and who dug the grave."

"Oh my God," Ryan said, sitting down. "Is there a warrant?"

Clyde nodded. "So far, five stops, heading east. All the wrong guy. Two of the officers swore he looked exactly like DeWayne's picture, but his driver's license, name, everything was different, so they let them go—and those could all be fake."

"What about prints? On the . . . on Maurita, on her throat . . . ?"

"He was wearing gloves."

Joe said, "Poor Mindy. Her dad in county prison hospital, her grandfather beaten up and mad as hell. And a warrant out on her uncle DeWayne. Varney's at home, maybe he'll take pity and decide to be a good uncle."

Ryan and Clyde looked at him as if he'd lost his reason.

Joe said, "So far, is Mindy all right?"

"From what I've seen of her today," Ryan said, pouring olive oil on the salad. "I don't think she wastes much love on that family, except for her grandpa. She wants . . ." She looked up at Clyde. "She wants Zeb to come stay with us, she says she can take care of him here. I told her it's too close. But she knows that—right across the street. Thelma would be all over her, telling her what to do—unless Thelma goes to jail as an accessory to Jon Jaarel's murder. It was her car that Nevin used to kill him. I talked with Charlie about Mindy and Zeb staying there. She said she'd talk with Max."

Clyde raised an eyebrow. "Wouldn't that make Max look bad, his protecting a witness at his home . . . ?"

"He'd be under guard, for his safety. Mindy under police protection, to get her out of that family. That's just good law enforcement."

Clyde didn't look convinced.

She lifted a hand, smeared lasagna sauce smartly on his cheek and turned away before he could smear it back. "The Harpers have the Luthers' two horses at their place, so why not the child and the old man?"

"Max can't afford any more men on guard duty twenty-four-seven. And a child living with the chief? No department in the country could operate under such casual rules—except maybe Max Harper's shop."

As Ryan put supper on the table, the little white cat came yawning down the stairs, looking for Rock. When Snowball didn't see the big dog or smell him, didn't hear him, she rubbed lovingly against Joe Grey . . . but Rock was her real protector, she needed his company. Ryan picked her up, petted and cuddled her, then settled her in the overstuffed chair at the end of the kitchen and set her dish of cat food and pumpkin beside her. They had learned, several years back, that a little pumpkin was good for aging cats, along with a saucer of chicken broth, to keep their tummies clear. Despite her nice supper, Snowball looked up at them forlornly, missing Rock.

Ryan set the salad on the table. "I was in the bank this morning making a deposit. Fay Seaver got home this morning. Ulrich was in there. We talked a little while. That made me feel weird, to be talking to the person who kidnapped Courtney—I wanted to punch him out.

"He said Fay would be back at work tomorrow. You'd think she'd want a day or two off. He said they were taking a vacation together soon. He looked at me with that amused, sarcastic expression and turned away. It was all I could do not to snatch him up, march him home, and make him give Courtney to me; we don't know half of what goes on in there."

"So far," Joe said, "they're treating her all right, spoiling her. She seems happy, most of the time."

Clyde's face was frozen. "I told you, Joe, if we don't get her out of there soon, it'll be too late, she'll be on a plane for New York."

"She won't *come* out," Joe said. "When we got her out the window, she dove right back in. She's scared of Seaver one minute and wants to get out. The next minute she's giddy with vanity at being in such a fine place, filled with big dreams from the stories he tells her. We should have forced her back out that window even if it meant a cat fight."

Ryan said, "Now that Fay's home, I'm really afraid for Courtney. That woman gives me the shivers, I can hardly stand her. For one thing, she smiles too much, fake smiles. Doesn't Courtney notice?"

Clyde said, "You cats got in after they closed, you could have let us in."

"Those locks on the big doors, you'd need a locksmith and an electrician. And that bathroom window," he said, looking keenly at Clyde, "you'd have a hard time getting in there, with those bars on the outside."

Clyde sighed. Ryan thought of the many times one or another of their friends had walked by the open shop and glanced in knowing Courtney was shut in upstairs, wanting to race up and grab her but afraid Ulrich would follow, that he would snatch her away and hurt her. She felt like there was nothing they could do—nothing Clyde *said* they could do. He said to wait for the right chance and until Courtney really wanted out.

"I still say . . ." Clyde began.

Ryan gave him another small serving of lasagna to shut him up and stop the argument, and opened a second beer for him. Clyde shook his head at the beer, glanced at Joe, and pushed his plate away. Joe demolished the several bites of extra supper thinking that, with Fay home, they had to do something *now*, despite what Courtney wanted.

Giving Ryan a lick on the cheek, Joe hissed smartly at Clyde and headed away up the stairs. Up onto Clyde's desk. A leap to the rafter. Out his cat door and across the darkening roofs to the Seavers' where he had a feeling that, with Fay home, some kind of change was about to begin. He felt that time was running short, that they had to find a way out for Courtney even if their humans *had* to storm the place, even if they had to call 911 and claim the building was on fire. Galloping over redwood shingles to the Seavers', he wondered if Dulcie and Kit and Pan had returned and were once more clawing at that small bathroom window, fighting for a way in . . . To do what, when his daughter was so damn stubborn?

20

Peering over from Seaver's roof, Joe looked down at Dulcie, working away at the powder room window. She should have been inside, this was her night to stay with Courtney. When he hissed softly, she looked up. She was standing on the tallest crate digging away at the window screen—even as he watched, the screen flew to the ground ripped aside, lay tilted atop the fallen dead branches and tall grass.

The evening was nearly dark, the antiques shop had been closed for some time. At this angle, from the shop's roof, Joe could see only the softly lit sidewalk, a reflection from the display windows; he couldn't see into the windows themselves, not without hanging by his hind feet. As Kit and Pan appeared, from the higher roof of the apartment, Joe leaped into a shaggy stone pine and to the ground, the golden tom and Kit behind him. They stood looking at the screen and at Dulcie.

"*I* pulled the screen off," Dulcie said proudly. "That woman is back, her name is Fay. I think she's his wife, the way she acts. Courtney's upstairs with them. When Fay and Ulrich came in, with her suitcases, Courtney and I were asleep. Courtney didn't stir, she just slit her eyes open. She belongs here, or they think she does. The minute I heard them I flew into the powder room, pulled the window open a few inches, dove through so fast the whole screen went flying. I'd closed the glass and I'm sure I left it unlocked but I was in such a fright. Bert was still in the back. I guess he heard me, he looked out, saw the screen off but didn't see me. Maybe he thought it just fell off, it was that old. He put it back. Maybe he found the window cracked open and locked it." She looked at Joe and Pan. "I came back when he left and listened at the glass, that's how I know her name. If we can open the window again, just a crack, maybe he won't notice when he puts a screen up?"

And maybe he will, Joe thought. Pan thought the same. They could see inside where already a box of tools sat on the tile counter.

For a while, all claws dug fiercely at the window

latch. If they could only open the glass, they could get in and Courtney could get out, and this time they'd make her come with them. Pan had a dry stick in his mouth, he was forcing at the edge of the latch. They had loosened it before, but now it had been made tighter. Pan looked at Joe, looked down at the towel they had left behind the crate. Wrapping it around the outside of the latch, they tried again. It took a long while before they knew they couldn't open it. Together, the three of them headed for the roof, to make sure Courtney was all right and to get a look at Fay Seaver.

One would think that all the times they'd passed this shop, and the few times Dulcie and Kit had slipped in to admire the lovely relics, they would remember seeing Fay. The tomcats weren't big on antiques; and all Kit had remembered was Ulrich Seaver, and the clerk. Maybe she'd thought Fay was one of the customers, or an interior designer; they came in here often, bringing their clients; the cats, staying in the shadows, had paid no attention to them; most interior designers were hand-some, well-turned-out women.

Climbing the stone pine to the roof again, they made their way across the roof of the shop to the upstairs apartment. On the other side of that smaller structure they eased down onto the fancily sculpted edge of the overhang, its pie-crust décor iced with pigeon drop-pings. They arrived just as a woman was closing the draperies.

Was this Fay Seaver or someone else, maybe his lover? A handsome, auburn-haired woman about Ul-rich's age. As the draperies closed they left a little tiny slit at the end where a bookcase jutted out. The cats, crowding close, could just see through—and Joe Grey swallowed back a hiss.

Just look how Courtney had taken to this woman. Fay was gently holding his grown kitten, sweet-talking and cuddling her. Neither Dulcie nor Joe could bear to see Courtney smile up at her, they could both see that the calico was purring and they watched her lift a paw with delight. Joe was so disgusted he nearly bailed over the edge and left the scene.

When Fay turned to speak to Ulrich, he nodded and left the room. With both preoccupied, Courtney looked from Fay's shoulder directly across to the slit in the draperies. From out on the ledge, four pairs of eyes looked in at her. Courtney, draped over Fay's back, let her claws come out in fighting mode, long and sharp, not touching Fay but catching the light like rapiers, and she gave her family a wicked cat laugh. But when Ulrich returned with a large hoop such as a child would play with, and with a ball and a box, her expression changed to one of dismay.

Fay hugged her and set her down by the hoop. "Let's start our training, shall we?"

Courtney didn't run off, she waited patiently, but as Joe watched Fay try to manipulate his grown kitten, rage flared deep within him. He tried to think, *What harm can a few tricks do?* But the idea sickened him, to make his beautiful child into a slave cat. He wanted his girl out of there, and when he looked at Dulcie, she had a cold snarl on her tabby face—but now, as Fay tried to get her to jump through the hoop, the calico looked across into her daddy's eyes with sly cunning.

It wasn't easy to watch Fay try to teach Courtney, at this first lesson. The cats could see, from across the room and into the bedroom, Fay's unpacked suitcase open on the bed; she seemed so eager to get started that she hadn't even taken time to unpack. She called Courtney her "little prize," her "shining star." Courtney, seeming not to get the hang of this, again peered behind Fay not only scowling but sticking out her tongue, showing her hidden audience her real feelings.

Fay put Courtney down on the carpet in a better position and held the upright hoop at floor level. She held a little treat on the other side to get Courtney to walk through. Such a simple beginning; but Courtney seemed not to get it. She walked around the hoop to Fay's side and tried to accept the bit of salmon from her hand. Fay withdrew it.

Fay tried again, and again, until at last she had Courtney stepping through. But when she lifted the hoop four inches, she never did get Courtney to hop or even step through. All four cats knew Courtney could have leaped to the ceiling, could have done all Fay's tricks as slick as a circus tiger. Fay, frowning more and more, at last turned away looking as sour as spoiled pickles. "Is this what you brought me? Your famous exhibition cat?"

"She's afraid, it's something new for her, give her time. Or," he said, looking intently at Courtney, "she's bluffing, she doesn't want to do tricks. Maybe . . ."

"Well, she's not going downstairs to entertain herself, with that attitude. She can sleep up here." Turning, she marched away to the bedroom. Ulrich joined her, just as annoyed, shutting the door behind them.

Courtney sat in the middle of the room looking at both doors. She turned to look at her cat family. She was half laughing, half weeping with frustration.

When the four cats could hear Ulrich snoring, Courtney began to leap at the door that led downstairs, wrapping her paws around the knob and swinging her hind legs. No matter how she swung, it was impossible to gain enough leverage. Was it locked? She couldn't turn the bolt above the knob, either. She tried until Ulrich quit snoring. At once she went quiet, dropped softly down and came to the corner of the window. She touched noses through the glass with her daddy and her tabby mama, with Kit and Pan. Though barely whispering, they could hear one another well enough; but their ears were cocked for any more sound from the bedroom.

"You're getting out of here," Joe said through the corner of the window. "Now. No arguments. No matter what dreams they've sold you, you're out of here as soon as we can get you out. We may have to ask Clyde's help but I don't like the idea, I don't want him arrested for break and enter." He looked hard at Courtney. "No more changing your mind. No more wild visions that could lead to a cage, for the rest of your life!" He glanced at his mate. "If Dulcie hadn't accidentally locked that window . . ."

"I didn't," Dulcie hissed. "Burt did!"

"If I go now," Courtney said, "if we can get me out,

I'll never know what else is going on here. Those Luthers coming in the back, opening the safe . . . counting all that money, so much money . . . things Ulrich and Fay said on the phone . . . Things I want to know and Max Harper will want to know . . ."

Her great adventure was now only ugly. Her dreams of living as a beautiful princess—*a beautiful show-off,* she thought, ashamed—were no more. She'd stay until she knew all the story, then she was out of there, away from this trap, free of the Seavers' control. She needed only one more chance, and this time nothing would stop her. She'd be fast and sly and she would absolutely make her escape.

Outside the glass the four cats looked at each other. "Until we get her out," Dulcie said, "we take turns watching, upstairs and down. Whoever's on duty, if something bad happens we'll get help somehow. But right now," she said, yawning, "I'm going home for a nap." She was so angry at Courtney she almost didn't care—almost.

At home, once she'd had a little snack, she curled up on the couch so as not to bother Wilma. She slept deeply, escaping her anger and frustration—slept far longer than she meant to and woke awash with guilt for her anger at Courtney. She leaped up and raced straight out of the house, out her cat door, longing, now, only for her dear, headstrong youngster.

When Joe and Dulcie and Kit left Courtney locked in the apartment, Pan remained outside the window. He would stay until the store opened in the morning, then Kit would come back to switch places. That would give his lady some rest at home snuggled by the fire with her old couple; Pan knew they missed one another, these three who were so close—he knew the Greenlaws missed him, too, that they were family. But the relationship Lucinda and Pedric and Kit had wasn't the same, Kit had been the wonder of their lives long before Pan came to them, long before Pan and the lovely tortoiseshell became a pair.

Kit was to the Greenlaws a magical creature; she had found them and they had found her as if by some mystical charm, found one another out on the empty green hills high above the village.

Kit had been watching the old couple for some days, hiding from them. She had never in her life been around humans. She was amazed at the tales that Pedric told Lucinda, many of the same stories she'd learned as a kitten tagging along with the wild clowder. Those speaking cats had let the starving kitten follow, but they were never fond of her. When they had set out to travel north along the green and empty hills, she had wanted to break away from them but she didn't know if she could live on her own yet, and she kept following.

But then, above Molena Point, slipping off by herself among the boulders, she had heard Pedric talking. Startled by human voices, she had crept up to listen. She had found the tall, elderly couple sitting among the great rocks having a picnic. She had padded closer, had sat listening to Pedric's stories for a long time. Then, boldly, she had stepped through the tall grass and onto their picnic blanket. Just like that, the little cat was suddenly with them. Pedric and Lucinda almost felt she had appeared out of nowhere, and it was love at first sight. From the first moment they saw her, Pedric, with his Scots-Irish background, knew that shaggy little kitten had been listening, that she could understand them, that she was different, and had the true Celtic spirit. Her delight in finding them and in listening to his stories had made her golden eyes gleam with joy.

And, Pan thought now, watching through the window as Courtney curled up on a blanket on the Seavers' couch, Courtney has magic, too. But it is a different magic. Like my father had—like Misto still has now, living a mysterious new life in another dimension.

I know Misto remembers his past lives and everyone he loved—and Courtney remembers her past lives just as he did, she can tell them just as if she sees them again, and that is the greatest wonder of all.

Sitting close to the corner of the window trying to keep warm, intending to watch Courtney the rest of the night but tired and hungry and cold, the orange tomcat, despite all attempts at vigilance, was soon sound asleep. He didn't hear the apartment phone ring. He didn't see Courtney wake suddenly and sit up, listening.

21

Joe Grey arrived home to a dark house. From the roof, slipping in through a window of his tall glass tower, he waded through his pillows and nudged open his cat door to the inner rafters of the master bedroom. He could hear from just below the comforting rhythm of Clyde's snoring, and that eased his nerves. It had seemed a bitter night, Courtney being prodded to do tricks that she refused to do, his young calico so distressed that Joe could see tears in her amber eyes; and on his way home it had started to rain, hard little drops piercing his coat and driving into his ears—the whole night seemed to have turned sour. Even the Luther apartment across the street looked grim, dark, and silent. The wet street below was deserted, both Thelma's and Varney's cars gone. All the house windows were black except for one tiny, blurred light behind Mindy's curtain; a sheltered glow as if, left alone, she didn't want to be noticed from outside. Looked like she had turned on a flashlight beneath her quilt and was reading, pushing away her loneliness.

How long had they left the house empty, Mindy vulnerable to whoever might want to break in, no one to watch over her? He wondered if they had even locked the front door? Did either one of them *care* what happened to the child? And where the hell were they at this hour?

Into some kind of trouble, you could bet. At least Varney would be. Likely out robbing some poor citizen or knocking around a pair of lovers in a parked car, taking their petty cash and cell phones.

It wouldn't surprise him if all the scattered robberies that had occurred on the outskirts of the village over the last months were Varney's doing, or Nevin's. Maybe even DeWayne, maybe he'd been in town longer than anyone knew. If so, he'd been slick, to evade Harper and his men.

Joe was used to Varney being gone all hours of the night. As for Thelma, she was no better, likely up to the same thefts as the Luther brothers—scattered crimes at the edges of the village that had gone on for months: assaults totally different from the slick and professional daytime thefts right in town: fast, well-planned heists and the thief gone so quickly that no one but the victim knew anything had happened—then suddenly, those snatch-and-grabs had ceased altogether, and that was puzzling.

As he settled among his pillows licking his fur dry and watching Mindy across the way, she sat up sleepily, pushed back her quilt, and peered out through the curtain. The rain had eased. Could she see him watching her? She was staring straight at him. Rain-smeared moonlight shifted across his face, maybe causing his eyes to flash yellow, maybe that had drawn her attention. He turned away and curled down deeper. Was she wishing, all alone, that she could be in his cozy tower with him cuddled close and warm, soothed by his welcoming purrs? Wishing she wasn't shut up by herself in that dark and empty apartment?

So many souls closed up alone tonight. Mindy. Courtney locked upstairs after her disgraceful performance. Maurita huddled inside Juana's condo, although at least her guards were friends.

Someday, the way the world seemed to be traveling—more crime, more fear, less joy—would everyone isolate themselves alone? No more friends or groups of friends, no more loving families? Was that what life would be like in the future, a multiplicity of electronic horrors to run what was left; living creatures cast aside, abandoned as afterthoughts? Was that how the world would end?

Well, hell, didn't that make him feel great! Angry at his own stupid ideas, he pushed deeper into the pillows and turned his mind to how to free his own young captive, how to help Courtney escape, how to spring her without human help.

He and Clyde had argued more than once about that. Clyde wanted to barge in when the store was open, charge up the stairs, bust through the door and grab her—or wait until midnight, break out a showroom window with a sledgehammer and order her straight out of there.

"Sure," Joe had said, "you can do that, and have the Seavers after you, maybe with a gun. And what if she runs from you, if she doesn't want to come? They call the cops, you'd be hauled into the station, you'd have Harper, your best friend, in a hell of a mess. The judges . . ."

This had gone on with increasing heat, over several uncomfortable meals and in between, until Ryan put a stop to it, read them both off with amazingly colorful language. She told Clyde that Joe was right, that human interference would put Clyde *and* the department in trouble, and could get Courtney hurt. She had left the table, Clyde glaring after her as snarly as a mad possum, only Joe Grey hiding a smile.

Now, from under her quilt, Mindy peered out at Joe again. A little earlier, she had watched the gray tomcat come across the rooftops nearly invisible in the rain and moving fast, his white paws, the white strip of nose and chest like pale moths winging above the shingles. The Damens' cat heading home for his tower.

Slipping back beneath her covers, still she looked out admiring the tomcat, wishing that she, like that free soul, were out in the small hours, free and on her own.

But more than admiring Joe Grey's freedom, she coveted the tomcat's tower. She wished that was *her* elegant little house, she knew she would feel safer there, with Ryan and Clyde present in the room below. Two people and the gray cat whom she was sure cared for her and would love her. She'd like to crawl across to Joe's roof and in through his window and snuggle up against his soft gray fur. The tower would be plenty big enough for her and Joe if she curled up just right among the pillows. It had glass windows all around, at least one unlocked, she'd seen him go through. Her mother always closed Mindy's bedroom windows at night even when it was too hot, she said it was dangerous to leave them open, that someone might break in. So why was it all right to leave her alone and leave the downstairs windows and doors unlocked?

She watched Joe Grey turn over yawning. She got out of bed and looked up and down the street below. Empty, no cars. She pulled on a dark sweater over her pajamas and put on her slippers. She unlocked and opened her window, unlatched the screen and stepped out onto the wet roof.

The big pine tree that she remembered being there when she was younger was gone now, it had blown down in the last storm. She could easily have gotten across on its heavy branches. Instead, she headed for a smaller and spindly pine down at the end of her house near the Damens' driveway.

Its branches swayed unsteadily when she put her weight on them. She worked slowly across toward their living room, swinging like a monkey from branch to branch, getting soaked and soon full of scratches. She clung finally to their living room roof, scrambling precariously until she was safely on top of it. There she crawled along the wet shingles to Joe Grey's tower and looked in at him asleep, his paws limp over his belly, his eyes closed. She eased a window open and slipped in, closed it, and curled down around the tomcat among the pillows. Joe Grey didn't move. She smiled, getting him damp again after he'd dried himself, but also getting herself warm against his thick fur. She was almost asleep when suddenly his yellow eyes were open looking directly into hers. A knowing look that told her he'd been aware of her all along.

She stared back uncertainly. Was he angry at her coming in here, was he about to scratch her? But Joe Grey wouldn't do that. Was that piercing look only a sly smile? *Did* cats smile? When he didn't seem disturbed at her presence she pressed closer against him. He eased closer, too, and began to purr, and Mindy felt safe and peaceful. Even if she was hogging his space, he was kind and caring and there *was* goodness in the world. Here was someone, here was a whole family, cat and humans, that she could trust and love, with whom she was safe. She drifted off, secure and warm.

She didn't know how long she slept; seemed like hours but it was still dark when lights woke her and woke Joe Grey. He sat up and slipped out of the tower to the edge of the roof as car lights came along the street, two sets of lights, one from either direction. Thelma's car, and Varney's.

They pulled up next to each other in the middle of the street, their engines idling, the drivers sitting face-to-face where they could speak softly through their open windows:

Varney handed his sister-in-law a package, which

Thelma shoved deep in her jacket pocket. They talked for a minute, mumbling so softly that neither Joe nor Mindy could understand much; Joe thought they were talking about money. It sounded like hundreds of thousands, like something you'd hear in a movie or on the news.

Thelma said, "Of course I know the combination. Anyway, it doesn't matter, he's there, I called him." They closed their windows and Thelma headed away into the center of the village. Varney parked in his usual place in front of the apartment, Mindy watched him get out and go in the front door. She waited, looking across, but no lights came on in the living room or kitchen. In a moment the light in Varney's room shone. He hadn't bothered to stop and check on her, hadn't had time to see if she was all right after being left alone, to maybe pull up her covers and tuck her in, the tender things that Grandpa or Grandma had done. What if he *had* gone in her room and found her gone? Would he even care? She was glad to be out of there, to not be alone in the house with Varney.

When she turned to look at Joe Grey he was wide awake, alert and poised for flight, watching where Thelma's taillights vanished around the corner turning left—and suddenly he fled away over the slick rooftops, following her.

Why would a cat care where Thelma was going? Mindy herself didn't care. All she cared about was getting Grandpa home from the hospital. Until then she wouldn't think about her mother's nighttime prowling, she'd think only about Grandpa.

Earlier in the evening, after Dulcie and Joe and Kit had left the Seavers' roof, and golden Pan curled up outside the Seavers' upstairs window intending to watch Courtney for the rest of the night, a fitful rain blew then eased. He pushed closer under the window's ledge. Tired and hungry and cold, trying to keep dry against the plaster wall, the orange tomcat did indeed fall asleep, didn't hear the phone ring, didn't see Courtney wake and rise—the phone had startled her from her warm spot on the couch. She felt grouchy anyway from being shut upstairs all night—retribution for her stubborn response to Fay's lessons. She listened to the second ring and to Ulrich's low, gruff answer; she heard him get out of bed.

She rose and shook herself and changed position to make sure she *was* awake, that this wasn't another dream. Ulrich said something she couldn't understand, she heard him moving around then the bedroom door opened and he headed, in his robe, through the living room straight for the door to the stairs. He looked over at her where she'd curled up again, her eyes closed as if asleep. Did he expect her to wake up and watch him, expect her to know or care what he was doing?

Maybe, she thought, if she had done the tricks tonight, if she had made the Seavers proud of her cleverness, if she showed them how she really could perform, it might be easier to escape; they would be more loving again and less bossy. Maybe if she were more obedient she'd earn more freedom, maybe find a careless moment when she could pull off a fast vanishing act.

Yes, and maybe not.

Ulrich, turning the upper knob for the bolt, then the doorknob below it, glanced over at her then eased the door open and shut it quickly behind him. For an instant she considered darting through between his feet and leaping to freedom, but she thought better of that. She looked at the door with interest. He hadn't locked it behind him, there was just the knob to deal with.

Slipping from the couch, she listened through the door as his slippers padded down the stairs, the back door opened, and he scuffed across the storeroom toward the outer door to the alley. Trotting into the kitchen, she put her ear to the floor just above where he had stopped. The outside door opened and there were low voices.

She approached the door again, at the head of the stairs. Leaping, she swung on the knob. She worked at it with all her might, swinging, swinging harder. She felt the knob turn, she was almost out when she caught her pad on a screw and blood ran down, soon making her paws so slippery that the knob wouldn't turn at all. Leaping to the kitchen sink, she took the dishcloth in her teeth.

After what seemed hours, swinging with the cloth wrapped around the knob, pushing with her hind feet against the molding, she was able to turn the knob far enough so she could force the door open. She wiped blood from her paws on the cloth, slipped through, pulled the door softly closed behind her, and hurried down the stairs where she stuffed the cloth under an Egyptian dresser. She paused, listening.

Two voices coming from the storeroom, Ulrich and a woman. Was that Thelma Luther? The inner door stood half open. Peering through, she saw the door to the alley open, too. Thelma's car stood there. Ulrich must be certain that his "little cat" couldn't get out the upstairs door, that she wouldn't know how to open the knob. In the workroom itself, the big door to the safe hung open. *Now!* She thought. *Do it now!*

She crawled beneath a carved armoire, deciding. She'd have only a second—could she pull this off? Joe

Grey had told and told her, it was time to get out. She could imagine her daddy's voice echoing, *"Get the hell out, Courtney! Now! Do it now! What are you, a sissy little housecat? Do it now! Right now!"*

Ulrich and Thelma had removed the safe's contents, they were laying out thick envelopes and packets on the worktable. Thelma was removing packs of money from each, counting it on a little hand computer, recording it in a ledger and putting it back in the envelope. At first Courtney hardly knew Thelma, she was dressed like a man, dark jeans, black shirt, heavy-shouldered black jacket, her hair tucked under a black knitted cap pulled low in front, even a man's thick shoes. She had removed her thin black gloves to be able to count the cash. Adding up each packet, she wrote the total on a list with a name written at the top, and put the envelope back in the safe. When they were turned away Courtney crept closer, under a buffet carved in gold and red. A cloth lay beneath, a dust cloth that Bert must have dropped. Using one front paw, then the other, she managed to drape it over her back and shoulders, covering her bright colors, all but a few smears of blood on her paws.

With the two thus occupied jotting down numbers she ducked her head, tucked her tail under her belly, and crept behind their backs through the workroom like a pale ghost; there she eased among some packing boxes into a draft of cold air coming from the open door—but just as she started to dart out, a small noise from above, a creak in the upstairs floor, made Thelma glance around the storeroom then look up at the top of the stairs. But that door was shut tight. Maybe Fay had gotten up for a moment.

"No worries," Ulrich said. "It's just the cat." He laughed. "It can't get out, no cat would think to turn a doorknob, not when she couldn't even jump through a hoop last night." Then in low voices, they began arguing.

In that instant the dust rag flew behind the two of them like a gray ghost and Courtney was gone into the alley. The two thieves were after her as she headed for the street, racing through the shadows into the bushes, losing her dusty cloth on thorns and tangles, panting at the sound of their pounding footsteps. She didn't hear Joe Grey bolting over the rooftops, she didn't hear Pan leap from his cold nest against the apartment wall and race to join him, she only ran.

22

Shortly before Courtney fought the apartment door open and followed Ulrich down the stairs and across the shop to the storeroom, across the village Joe Grey leaped from his tower racing after Thelma's car. A cold flash of fear had awakened him, almost a vision—though he'd never believed in visions. He had imagined bloody pawprints going down the Seavers' stairs, more bloody prints leading behind the fancy furniture, then a gray rag draped over Courtney. What the hell was the matter with him, what was he seeing? Back there in the tower, had he had some crazy premonition? The scene was still with him as he raced across the wet shingles and peaks following Thelma, he was so uneasy he could feel his belly churn. He'd heard enough of Thelma's ". . . I won't need the safe number," Varney's indecipherable mumble then Thelma's "I already called . . ."

Now, not seeing Thelma's car parked before the antiques shop he galloped along the front and side looking in through the big display windows. He didn't see Courtney. When he climbed to the roof and padded along the edge peering into the second-floor apartment, into the bedroom and living room, he didn't find her. Fay was sound asleep. He crossed the roof and looked down, and there was Thelma's car backed into the alley; leaning down right over it, he could feel the engine still breathing warm air. Why had she backed in? Lying flat on his belly just above the outer door to the storeroom, his head cocked over the edge, he saw that the alley door was open—and the inner door open wider. Had Ulrich shut Courtney upstairs knowing she couldn't get out, that she wouldn't know how to turn the knob?

Right. His vision, that impossible dream-picture that only Kit might have seen, had shown him bloody pawprints on the knob and on the stairs. *Well, she's sure as hell out now,* he thought, smiling. *At least she's out of the apartment.*

He heard Thelma Luther's voice from the workroom beneath him, and then Ulrich; sounded like they were counting money. He could just see the door to the safe standing open. "Nine hundred and eighty-two," she said. "That's a total." Then the faint sound of clicking, like an adding machine. "Five thousand, ninety-six. Next column?" It was then that he saw the faintest movement among the shadows behind the two figures.

Leaning so far over the gutter he had to claw hard not to fall, he prayed that was Courtney, that she was positioning herself for escape. Even from the roof he caught a whiff of her, faint but fresh. Was she waiting for a chance to bolt into the alley and be gone?

Maybe he should climb down the ivy vine to the alley and make a great yowling and scuffling like a giant cat fight, bring the two crooks racing out to see what was going on, and Courtney could dart away behind them?

Would that work, or would it only screw up her own plan? He almost jumped out of his skin when Pan, making no sound, appeared out of nowhere pushing against him. The yellow tom must have dozed on his watch at the window where he was supposed to be alert. Had he seen or heard any of what went on? Pan eased down beside Joe. It had started to rain again, a shower of small, sharp needles. Below them, Thelma and Ulrich were arguing, Thelma's voice coldly angry. "Nevin was stupid to do that! Stupid and just asking for prison—and putting me in a hell of a fix." The outside door opened wider, the tomcats ducked back, and Thelma hurried out, angrily pulling on her jacket against the blowing shower . . .

In that instant, the dust rag flew out the door behind her and Courtney fled for the alley, followed by her bloody pawprints, a streak vanishing in the rain, Ulrich and Thelma after her at a dead run. Ulrich grabbed at her, missed her, grabbed again and caught her tail. She swung around slashing him, she raked down his arm and leaped into the ivy vine; she was halfway up when Ulrich jumped, reaching for her—and Joe and Pan exploded onto him from the roof so hard they knocked him to the asphalt; the tomcats were all over him scratching his head and shoulders, he tried to get up and they knocked him hard against the alley wall— while Courtney flew to the top of Thelma's car and from there to the stone pine that crept up the neighboring building.

She leaped from the pine to the next-door roof and ran, she vanished among the peaks that rose around her. Ulrich ran along the alley looking up where Courtney had disappeared. From the shadows the calico heard Ulrich swearing, calling her names she had never heard before. She knew that if she moved again, they would hear her running on the wet gravel. Ulrich paused frequently, listening for the sound of scrabbling paws or the occasional flip of tiny pebbles. Courtney crept along as quiet as a frightened rabbit until her footfalls grew silent on the wet wood shingles of the steeper roofs.

When they couldn't hear her anymore, Thelma returned for her car; but even circling the block peering up at the rooftops, circling the next block and the next, she could see nothing, no distant flash of bright calico, no flying streak of color. Neither Thelma nor Ulrich glimpsed the racing tomcats following Courtney at a distance, hidden in shadows or around corners so as not to lead her pursuers to her. It had stopped raining but the air was heavy and damp.

Just once did the tomcats catch up with Courtney, deep between two peaks. "The PD," Joe whispered, "they won't come there." Courtney gave him a bright and devilish look. As if this were a game, and not a race for her life. Swerving into the shelter of a stone chimney, she spun backward when she saw Ulrich straight ahead. He was racing up the stairway between two apartments. Courtney leaped to the adjoining roof, vanished beneath a steep overhang, bellying down beneath a heap of rotting leaves.

There she crouched shivering—until Ulrich saw her. He came right at her, reaching. She flew out past him scattering leaves, she was gone between chimneys and ledges, her heart thundering so loud she couldn't hear her own footfalls. She leaped to a steep dormer where Ulrich had to scramble to get up. She could sense Joe and Pan behind them, she knew they were gaining; she thought they'd jump him again. Ulrich Seaver, so kind and sweet-talking—plunging after her now with rage enough to kill her.

Thelma's car was still cruising the streets, maybe she was afraid, in the dark and wet, to climb to the roofs. Ahead, across the street, was the courthouse and its big parking area, she was near the north end where its tower rose up. Police cars were parked at the other end, in front of the station, and more black-and-whites were lined up in the back. Oh, Courtney ran for the PD, her breath nearly gone. She dove into a giant pine that spanned the street to the court building, and crossed the heavy branches onto the courthouse roof. As she looked ahead to the police station, she heard Joe and Pan scramble across and they were beside her. She heard Ulrich behind them crawling clumsily across the biggest limb, and the three cats flew up the tower's steps, six feet, ten feet, Ulrich close behind them. He was up the stairs reaching for Courtney when she clawed his hand and leaped away. She flew straight down to the courthouse roof again, the tomcats guarding her, rearing up snarling at Ulrich, their claws flashing until Ulrich drew back, he'd had enough of cat scratches.

Nor did he like being this close to the station and the cops. He started down the stairs scanning the roofs and streets, but the cats had vanished. Thelma's car had drawn up below him. He swung down the last steps and into the front seat. "Get out of here, they're gone. Where the hell did they go?" He touched a contact on his phone. "Send the men up by the courthouse. Damn cat is out, running across the roofs. See if you can catch it. Search the whole damn town until you find it."

Thelma said, "When Fay wakes, when she gets up to get ready for work, when she can't find the cat, what will you tell her? And what will she say when she sees the safe and the back door open?"

"Oh, the damn safe."

She glanced at him and put her foot to the pedal, more anxious about the money than the cat. If that money was gone, nearly a fourth of it belonging to her, she swore she'd kill Ulrich.

They skidded into the alley, found the door and safe open as they'd left them. That was a load of luck. Making sure the money was all there, and that the way the envelopes were arranged was the same, they locked up and took off again. They didn't see small, wizened Officer Bean standing deep in the shadows of the workroom among crates and stored furniture, a camera in his hand.

Bean had shot the envelopes in the safe without moving anything. He *had* slipped out one envelope, opened it, and photographed and fingerprinted the money, but so carefully that Ulrich would never know. When he heard no one coming, he had been able to fingerprint several envelopes and their contents without leaving a trace of his own prints. And Bean, with what amounted to a criminal's degree in safecracking, now had the combination to the safe. He prowled the office as well, took some additional pictures, let himself out, pocketed the key that had hung on the inside of the open door, and he was gone into the night.

As Thelma and Ulrich left the antiques store, headed back for the courthouse, three of DeWayne's men appeared behind them in a small gray Audi. The two cars parked behind the courthouse on a narrow side street. The men climbed out, pulled a ladder from a rack on top of the Audi, and they hit the roofs. Seaver had pulled on a cap from among the junk on Thelma's backseat and had wrapped a scarf around his neck. He looked as much like his companions as DeWayne did, where he watched, wrapped in darkness.

23

The courthouse roof didn't thunder under their paws like the gravel had; they fled along the sloping far side, out of sight of Thelma and, hopefully, of the men racing the roofs behind them. But when the cats dropped down to the lower roof of MPPD, praying the window of the holding cell was open, their pursuers saw them and saw the barred window and they fled, evading the nearby cops. Bailing over the side of the building, swinging down clutching the window moldings and dropping to the sidewalk, they piled into the two cars and were gone. The cats crouched in the shadows smiling, watching them race away.

The high window was wide open to dispel the ripe scent of the holding cell, of the occasional drunken detainee—but tonight, when they looked in, the cell was empty. Though if the rain increased, some homeless people might come in trying to haggle for a bed. Quickly the cats slipped through the small window between the bars, dropped down six feet onto the thin mattress of the narrow bunk and dove under, Courtney pale with fear, her pink nose and ears nearly white.

Even before they could huddle together in the darkest corner, so the young officer at the desk might not see them, a squad car pulled up in the red zone. Peering out, they could see Max Harper at the wheel looking in through the bulletproof glass doors and through the cell bars straight at them, straight into the shadows beneath the cot. Had he seen them racing across the roof, had he seen the men chasing them?

Max sat a minute, frowning. Well, hell, there was the lost calico everyone had made such a fuss over, and Joe Grey and Pan were with her. All three cats were scared as hell! The calico was trembling, the look on her face one of icy fear. Joe Grey and the orange tomcat looked nearly as frightened.

He'd seen those guys chasing them across the roofs, seen the four figures get in their cars and take off. One could be a woman, it was hard to tell, the way the person was dressed. Thelma Luther? He recognized Ulrich Seaver, but he didn't get a good look at the other two sleazebags; both looked like limo drivers for De-

Wayne Luther. Why would they be interested in a lost cat? And other men had run, into the night. Max could have followed any of them; but he knew Thelma's car. *Was* that Thelma, bundled up like a man? His thoughts about following them were mixed.

For days, everything had been crazy. Everything that happened seemed to rotate around cats. Posters all over the village and in nearly every shop. His friends and all the folks from CatRescue combing the neighborhood searching for the calico, for Joe Grey's grown kitten. While all that time, a few people knew very well where she was, and had said nothing. Not even Charlie, and he trusted her with his life. Ryan and Clyde, Wilma and the Greenlaws had been just as secretive, not a word. Those five, and Kate Osborne and Scott Flannery. He knew and loved them all, he trusted them all, but they too often made him wonder.

Whatever, it looked like the calico herself had finally made the decision. Max guessed that when she did escape, Seaver had seen her and given chase. He must have called DeWayne's drivers to help him—his fellow thieves. But he couldn't call DeWayne himself, he was long gone, by the reports they were getting from across the country. Those departments would keep looking until they had DeWayne locked up. He was wanted locally for assault and attempted murder, they had three more warrants for murder out of state, more than a dozen warrants for big-time robbery, to say nothing of the out-of-the-country extradition papers for his return.

Before Max left the squad car he called the desk, sent three officers to work the streets for the men who had run. There was more to this than just a cat. He didn't know what they'd arrest them for . . . Making a disturbance . . . Trespassing on the roofs? They'd think of something. He told the young clerk to put the coffee on for roll call. "And lay out the doughnuts Kathleen brought in last night." That got the young man out of the front office for a few minutes. When he was gone, Max stepped from the squad car, stood at its open back door rearranging something inside. He returned with a small and ancient suitcase the cats knew well. It was the shape of a two-centuries-old carpetbag, soft leather, a solid bottom, a clasp and two handles together at the top. Joe Grey imagined him emptying the bag in the car, pulling out his neatly folded uniform, his regulation cap and black shoes, and setting them on the seat. These were the spares he carried in case he had to go to court or see the judge or the mayor unexpectedly. For serious occasions, Max didn't often wear jeans and a western shirt as he was wearing now. Before he left the car he made one more call. Then, moving in through the glass doors, he knelt before the holding-cell bars adjusting his boot, his back to the desk, hiding the cats, looking down at the fear on their faces—but not fear of Max.

Joe Grey had no reason to fear the chief, the tomcat slept all over Max's reports, he practically lived at the station—despite Harper's crankiness when he couldn't find a document, Joe and Max were pals. The thought did cross Max's mind that Joe Grey himself might somehow have found and released the young calico, but that idea was beyond bizarre, cats weren't that clever or that handy; and the tall, tanned chief didn't like fantasies muddling his reason. Courtney looked up at him, frightened and pleading. The chase, those men pounding across the roofs grabbing for her, had left her rigid with fear.

Courtney was indeed shaking so badly her stomach felt sick. She wanted to curl up in the darkest corner and vanish. Watching Max, she didn't know what he'd do. When she looked at Joe and Pan, both tomcats looked unwell, themselves; too much running, too much fear—and Max had never caught them being chased into the station, hiding from crooks in the station. This would not look good for the department, men chasing cats all over the rooftops and then the chief finding them hiding in the holding cell. Max knelt by the bars, looking in at them, looking as distressed as she'd ever seen him.

A hurt or frightened animal got to Max, where a defiant felon only made him mad. He glanced toward the desk but the clerk was still in the conference room. He opened the bag he had emptied. "Inside, Joe. Quick." Reaching through the bars he pulled Joe unceremoniously into the bag, picked up Courtney more gently and settled her beside him. "Pan, get in here."

Within seconds the cats were being carried down the hall, peering out the thin crack that Max had left in the nearly closed suitcase. Past the conference room where Jerry was laying out paper plates and they could smell the coffee start to brew. Past the closed doors of the other offices and out the back door beside the jail. Crossing the police parking lot, Max swung into a decrepit old Ford, one of the shabby cars the department kept for when officers didn't want to be spotted. Pulling into the street, he turned left. Then a right, and two more rights into a shadowed space tucked between two condos.

Joe couldn't see much from the bag, but they had to be behind Juana's condo where, upstairs, Maurita was hidden. What was this, a group shelter? Max carried them up the back steps, and knocked softly. Juana let them in at once, shut the door behind them and opened the bag. Reaching in, she stroked the three huddled felines, seeking to calm them. The dark-haired Latina cop looked nearly as square in her pale blue sweats as she did in uniform. Seeing the distress in Courtney's eyes, she took the calico in her arms. Courtney purred and rubbed against her—but when she saw Buffin snuggled on the couch in Maurita's lap, she was so glad to see her brother she leaped straight for him, burrowing on the blanket between them, smearing blood across them from her injured paw. Maurita, in her scrubs and a robe, ignored the blood and snuggled Courtney close.

Juana brought salve and bandages; she knelt and began to help Maurita doctor Courtney's white and calico paws, examining each tiny bone. No shrieks, nothing seemed broken. Maurita found a tissue in her pocket and wiped the heaviest blood from her calico coat, then gently she ran her hands over the rest of Courtney, flexing her legs for injuries, running her hands down her sides while watching the calico's face for any sign of pain. Maurita's black hair was tied back in a knot, her bruises and scars were fading. When she looked into the calico's frightened eyes, she saw the same fear as her own—they stared at each other, the look between them filled with their mutual need for comforting, sharing the distress that would take a long time to heal. Courtney put a gentle, carefully wrapped paw on Maurita's arm, and the young woman held the calico tighter; she could feel her shivering; they clung close to Buffin, too, his curing strength warming them both.

When Juana turned away to join Max and the two deputies, the men were smiling, watching the warm scene, and then watching Rock and Joe Grey. The minute Joe bellied out of the leather bag, the big silver dog had been all over his housemate, licking and nibbling at him while Joe slapped at Rock playfully and purred against his sleek coat. Such warm, innocent moments were all too rare in the life of a cop. Tall, big-boned Officer Crowley, looking very tender, rose to stack the breakfast dishes and carry them into the kitchen. Jimmie McFarland gathered up the cups and cream and sugar, still watching the two animals. His short brown hair was neatly trimmed and he was clean shaven, his uniform sharply pressed. "So the lost cat is found," he said, grinning.

Max said, "Someone chased the hell out of them."

"No wonder they're scared. I've never seen Joe Grey frightened—but where are Dulcie and Kit? Did those guys catch them or did they escape? And what the hell do they want with cats?"

Max said, "I hope they escaped, and are unhurt. These three got away with a lot of fight, from the amount of blood on them. All the posters about her being lost, everyone searching for her, all that time someone had her locked up, maybe in a cage."

Juana said, "What kind of person would do that, yet apparently not harm her? What *do* they want . . . ?" She paused, staring at the window. They all turned to look. Rock and Joe Grey abandoned their tussle and leaped on a chair nosing at the drawn drapery, at the open corner where, in the soft lamplight, a pair of green eyes shone and a dark tabby face looked in. When Dulcie saw Courtney inside she rose up, meowed softly, and scratched frantically at the glass. As Juana opened the window, Rock stuck his nose in the tabby's face; gently she nipped the big gray dog and pushed past him, leaping to join her escaped kitten. She wanted to cry, she wanted to praise Courtney. All she could do was meow.

"Come up," Maurita said.

Dulcie landed softly on the blanket between her two kittens and curled down, licking Courtney's ears. Her child was free. They couldn't talk, she'd hear the story of Courtney's escape later. Right now all that mattered was that her child was safe. Buffin put a paw on Dulcie's face and licked her nose, and she could almost feel him healing her, as he seemed to be soothing Courtney and Maurita; and Dulcie sighed. They were all together, and they were safe. They were secure under the protection of the cops, of friends they could count on and trust.

Jimmie McFarland watched them with interest, this close and loving cat family. He watched Maurita, her own eyes damp. When she looked up, he handed her a tissue, watched her wipe her tears then wipe remaining blood from Courtney. He hoped most of it was human blood. The way she held and stroked the cats touched Jimmie deep down. This was not the hard-cop part of him, as he thought he should behave. Their eyes met for a moment, Maurita's dark eyes wide with a sudden surprise as well as with tenderness. McFarland blushed and looked away.

Earlier, when Kit awakened from her nap in her tree house, she hadn't gone along the branch that led in through the dining room window, she hadn't wanted to wake Lucinda and Pedric and get caught up in a long explanation; that could come later. She had left the tree house backing down the broad trunk of her oak tree, racing through the rain, across the yards to where the village roofs would take her to Seaver's Antiques, on her way to relieve Pan at his watch; it would be dawn soon, the sky in the east was barely turning light.

But when she got there, she couldn't find Pan. Dropping down to the sidewalk by way of a potted bush, she peered in the windows of the closed store looking for Courtney. Not finding her, she climbed the tall pine at the side of the building and went across the flat roof, looking in the second-floor apartment. No sign of her kitten. Circling the apartment on the window ledge, she didn't find Pan crouched outside in the sheltered corner where he had chosen to keep watch. But when she padded along the ledge back to the alley, she smelled blood. Human blood and cat blood. *Courtney's blood?*

She could see no one. Scrambling down the ivy vine to the alley she found spots of Courtney's blood glistening on the wet macadam. She could smell both the calico's and Pan's fresh scents, and the trail of Ulrich and Thelma. But the smells that alarmed her were where they were all mixed together: Courtney's blood, Joe Grey's and Pan's scents and the two humans, tangled with the lingering smell of fear and of rage, a fighting stink that sent Kit racing away to the rooftops again following where the three cats had fled, and Thelma and Ulrich had climbed after them.

Earlier, looking down from the roofs, she'd thought she glimpsed DeWayne Luther for an instant. A tall man with a touch of white hair under a floppy cap—but no, this man smelled like a gas station. He had a mustache, his service jacket was stained with grease, and his shoes were filthy. Anyway, DeWayne wouldn't be here in the village when there was a warrant out on him. And why would he care about Seaver's crazy plan? DeWayne Luther ran to high-toned robberies, to the most exclusive stores, to jewelry worth millions, not to stealing cats; and why would he care about ancient, ragged tapestries and old fairy tales surrounding a stolen cat?

Had that been DeWayne back there despite his looks and smell? *Had* he been part of the chase? Pan said she had too much imagination, that her wild ideas sent her flying off into tangents.

But right now she wanted to know if the three cats *had* escaped, and where they had gone, she had to find them. Following their scents over the roofs to the station, she could smell several men's, and Thelma's, trails along the shingles, they crossed back and forth then separated. Thelma and Ulrich had gone down some steps to the street. But Kit followed the path of Courtney and Joe and Pan past where the humans had turned away, followed them toward the PD. When she found the cats' scents strong on the bars of the holding-cell window, she sighed with relief.

But when she looked down into the cell, no one was there. Not even a drunken prisoner—then, looking across the roofs, she saw Joe Grey at Juana's condo, leaping out a slightly open window. Juana and two officers stood behind him. For an instant, Joe turned back to rub his face against Juana's hand then he was gone, heading over the rooftops toward home looking very happy. As if, for the moment, his job was done. Kit raced over the roofs and branches for the window, mewling and mewling at Juana before she closed the glass. She burst into the room, into the detective's arms, and was amazed at the gathering.

She looked shyly at the chief and the two deputies, flicking her tail in a demure greeting. She thought at first the dark-haired woman on the couch was Detective Kathleen Ray snuggled with Courtney, Buffin, and Dulcie; then she saw the woman's scars, the bruises, the stitched-up ear: the lady from the grave. And Kit found it hard not to speak right out, to shout out her surprise and her joy.

24

The rain had eased. Low in the east, thin, orange streaks of dawn shone into Joe Grey's tower, waking Mindy. She felt around among his pillows and found she was alone, Joe was gone. She pushed up and looked out the open window. Yes, earlier in the night the tomcat had raced away chasing her mother's car, heading into the village.

Why would a *cat* want to follow Thelma? Why would a cat *care* where she was going? When she looked across toward her room and down at the street, she eased back deeper among the pillows out of sight. Her mother was home. Even in the first whisper of dawn, Thelma might glimpse her dark silhouette up here in the tower.

How would she explain how she'd gotten over here on the Damens' roof and why? Thelma's Volvo was parked behind Varney's Toyota. She didn't want to go home; if Thelma caught her coming in she'd fuss and haggle at her for being outside and she'd ask a hundred questions.

But maybe her mother would go right up to bed and wouldn't know she was gone, wouldn't bother to check on her. Varney hadn't, when he came in. It would be nice to have a mother who looked in on her after she'd been left alone all night, someone to just glance in and see if she was okay, if she hadn't been abducted or murdered.

But why should Thelma care, any more than Varney did? Or than her own father had cared, after *he'd* been out all night, stealing? He'd never checked on her, never pulled up her covers like fathers in movies did.

Well, her father wasn't out stealing now, Nevin was in county prison in a barred hospital room, maybe never to get out again. Never to rob again, never to steal anymore. And why did she care what he did with his life?

All she *did* care about was Grandpa in the hospital. He was coming home today, she thought with excitement. He'd be here by noon, home with her, and she could take care of him because Mama sure as hell wouldn't.

So he'd demand to go to his own house. So he'd

make a big scene. So what? Maybe she could figure out a way the two of them could go home. She could order groceries delivered, they had chickens and eggs at home, they had flour and cornmeal; she could cook as good as Grandma—well, the simple things Gram had taught her.

A streak of moonlight shone low in the west as the clouds shifted away. And in the east the touch of dawn returned, so light shone within the tower. If Thelma looked out and saw her, there'd be trouble. Slipping out the tower window, she didn't head for the wobbly over-hanging branch to sneak back home as if she'd never been gone. She crawled along the Damens' roof to the far end, above their driveway where Ryan parked her truck.

Yes, the big red truck was there, ladders chained on top, locked cupboards along the sides for building tools. It was pulled up close to the house to make room for Clyde's two cars, his Jaguar and an old car he was working on. She pulled off her slippers, tossed them down to the driveway. She slid down to the top of the truck's cab, from there to the hood and then to the ground next to the Jaguar.

The truck's hood was warm, so the engine would be, too. It wasn't really light yet, and she wondered where they had been.

When she looked up, Ryan was standing in her open front door, a soft light behind her, her short, dark hair curlier than usual from the damp air. Her work boots stood by the door. She was wearing worn jeans, a gray sweatshirt, pink fuzzy slippers, and a flowery ruffled apron. She looked drawn, as if maybe she hadn't slept; or as if something was wrong. Mindy would wait to ask. She could smell coffee, hot syrup, pancakes and bacon. She looked down at her thin pajamas and realized how cold she was without the warmth of Joe Grey and his pillows.

"Mindy, it's wet and freezing. Come in, I'll get you something dry." Ryan picked up Mindy's slippers and the child followed her inside. Ryan got her a long T-shirt, a pair of her own wool socks, then wrapped her in a long, fuzzy sweater.

The kitchen was warm and homey, with a flowered, overstuffed chair at the far end beside some inviting shelves of books. Clyde was already eating. They both looked worried, and as if they had been up most of the night. But Clyde was freshly shaven, she could barely smell his aftershave, and was dressed in sharply pressed chinos and a pale blue shirt. Ryan poured pancake batter for Mindy, and a cup half of coffee and half of creamy milk. Mindy added sugar. Clyde didn't ask why she was up before dawn or what she had been doing on the roof. After three pancakes and two slices of bacon she sighed, her hunger slaked; she looked at the handsome couple who made her feel so welcome. "I slept with Joe Grey in his tower. I was scared in the house alone. Mama and Uncle Varney were both gone. Usually I push the dresser against the door but I fell asleep and then something woke me. I thought it was Varney or Mama getting home but it wasn't and I wanted out of there.

"When the noise stopped, a kind of creaking wooden sound, I looked across at Joe Grey's tower and he was there; the rain was mistier and a little moonlight shone through. Joe Grey was sitting up among the pillows looking across right at me. Could a cat *see* me, in the dark bedroom? He looked so warm and cozy I climbed out my window into the oak tree and up to our roof. I crossed over the street on that spindly pine tree to your roof and into Joe's tower and cuddled up with him. We were nice and warm and I felt safe. Until later, when lights in the street woke us, and the sound of cars.

"Mama and Varney were parked in the middle of the street in opposite directions, their engines running, their windows open so they could talk. Varney handed her a thick package. She said something about going to Seaver's, something about a locked safe . . ."

A noise from upstairs stopped her; it sounded like

the flap of the cat door that led inside from Joe Grey's tower. Last night she had looked through it down into the master bedroom. Now she imagined Joe stepping inside onto a bedroom rafter, maybe dropping to the desk below. She had seen a stairway leading down, and the next instant they heard him pounding down the steps, racing for the kitchen. Who knew a cat could make so much noise just coming downstairs, even a heavy tomcat?

Joe flew through the kitchen door, took one look at Mindy, and landed on the table beside her empty plate. He was frowning, too. Mindy looked at him, puzzled. Who knew a cat could frown so hard? They all three looked miserable. What had happened? Ryan was pouring pancakes for Joe, and she looked a question at Mindy. "More?"

"Maybe two," she said, fascinated that they let a cat on the table, even this very nice tomcat. She *had* begun to think of Joe Grey as a special cat, the way he'd looked across at her last night, his yellow eyes wide, the way he'd welcomed her into his tower among his warm pillows, and then later his strange behavior when he raced off following her mother. That was a puzzle: why *would* he care where Thelma went? And now, whatever worried the Damens worried Joe Grey, and how could that be? When Ryan put a place mat down for

Joe, Mindy had a hard time not laughing—and Ryan and Clyde had a hard time, with Mindy present, not to ask Joe a hundred questions they hadn't asked when they were out looking for Maurita.

Joe, too, needed badly to ask questions. *Could* he keep quiet until Mindy left? When across the street a car door slammed, and another opened, Mindy stepped to the living room window, standing out of sight.

A light was on in the apartment kitchen, the front door was open, and Thelma was outside looking in Varney's car and then again in her own car, searching among a tangle of sweaters and jackets.

"Looking for me," Mindy said. "Can I go out the back door? Maybe I can slip in behind her, get back in bed before she searches the house. If she finds me over here, she'll throw a fit." She grinned at Ryan. "Thanks for the pancakes." She petted Joe Grey, gave Clyde a loving look as he walked her to the door—but Thelma heard the door open and came flying across the street, her hair a tangle, her black shirt torn, her heavy jacket gone. Her arms and face were scratched, the wounds long and deep like cat scratches. Ryan and Clyde looked at Joe, and at the disarray of his own fur; Joe Grey looked back at them with a studiously blank expression. Clyde took Mindy's hand and stepped out into the street. The child followed reluctantly. He pulled her close to him and, on her other side, Ryan put a protective arm around her.

Thelma was in such a temper they didn't know what she would do. She was reaching for Mindy when a car came down the street, a squad car, its headlights on though the morning was beginning to grow light. Max Harper stopped and got out, looking at the little scene, looking Thelma over. He looked at the two parked cars. He got out and felt their hoods. Joe Grey followed him, no more nosy than usual. Both cars were warm and still smelled of exhaust. Max looked at Mindy, at her solemn, frightened face.

"Were you alone in the house all night?"

She looked at the chief. She couldn't be afraid of Max Harper but she could be plenty afraid of what Thelma would do if she admitted she had been alone there. Even when Harper looked angry, somehow she wanted to hug him. "Yes," she said softly. "I got scared and I came here. I slept in Joe Grey's tower. He didn't mind. When Ryan got up, I came downstairs. She made pancakes."

Max's eyes held Mindy's, amused and caring; but not caring when he turned on Thelma. "Where's Varney?"

"In the house, probably already asleep," Thelma said, having watched Max check the heat of both car engines.

"Was he out all night? Where was he?"

"I have no idea."

As the two faced each other, both angry, Joe Grey slipped behind Ryan and Clyde into his own yard, behind the bushes.

"Of course you know where Varney was," Max said. "I know where you both were, and the other three."

Thelma suddenly looked like she wanted to run.

"I'm not going to cite you," Max said. "I could arrest you, take you in on several charges. Child neglect. Robbery, several counts. I could leave you in jail, or the judge could put you under house arrest. For now, I want to see how you two respond to a serious warning. And how you do when we bring Zebulon home, how well you take care of him."

"We'll do just fine. I'm to pick him up this morning."

"You and I will pick him up together. I signed him in. I sign him out. They'll be sending a physical therapist for a few days, and a visiting nurse. While Zebulon's here, I want at least one adult with him and Mindy. You are not to leave either one alone," Max said. "The hospital has him ready and waiting. Are you ready? Do you have a bed made up for him?"

"He's well enough now to be up and around."

"Do you have a comfortable bedroom for him?"

"He'll sleep in Mindy's bed. I have a cot for her. I'll wake Varney, tell him to change the sheets. I'll only be a minute." She was a little more diffident now. Despite his usually easy ways, Max Harper could be frightening.

Max and the Damens sat on the Damens' front porch, out of the thin rain, waiting for Thelma. Joe always felt irritable when he could listen to his friends talking but could say nothing, not the smallest comment. When Ryan brought Max a cup of coffee, Joe wondered if he'd like some pancakes but, again, there was no way he could offer. At last he watched the two cars leave, Max's squad car following Thelma and Mindy.

A cop car following her made Thelma decidedly nervous. She made sure to come to a full stop at every signal, to watch if a tourist even set foot off the sidewalk, to follow every traffic rule. Don't tailgate, stay in the proper lane. The fact that the chief followed behind her was the same principle as, at the station, a cop always walked behind his visitor or detainee, never in front. Thelma had changed clothes and combed her hair, which was an improvement, and she had dug out a pair of pants and a shirt for Zebulon.

Joe Grey knew that Zeb would refuse to go to the apartment. That he'd pitch a fit all the way, that he would remain cranky until Thelma took him back to the ranch, to his own home. And Thelma wasn't about to do that.

Restless, Joe galloped up to his tower where he could look down into Mindy's window as Varney moved the child's bed to the back of the room and set up the cot by her own night table and dresser. Varney was tousled from sleep, was wearing an old corduroy robe over bare, hairy legs, and he was still yawning. He made up both beds with clean sheets, but making a mess of it. Even a cat could do better. He found an old tattered quilt for Mindy, and gave Zeb her warm covers. Yawning again, he wandered off toward his room; Joe watched him crawl back into his tangled bed, watched with disgust as Varney drifted off, snoring with his mouth open. The tomcat had the feeling that this last distasteful hour marked the tone of the days ahead, that whatever happened next would be ugly. He felt as if the whole village had fallen into a tangle of confusion. Yet there was no way, he told himself, that a simple cat could right all the wrongs in the world.

25

It was shortly before Fay Seaver arrived home, and before Courtney escaped, that the usual scattered crimes on the outskirts of the village began to decrease. A few break-ins, a missing billfold slyly slipped from someone's back pocket by a young entrepreneur, the annoying offenses that a small town might experience. The snatching of a purse in the late evening, a briefcase missing from an unlocked car. Max's crew patrolled the streets, answered routine calls, made a few arrests for break-ins, but his officers were beginning to grow bored; though they were always on alert for any domestic battle that could turn into murder as sudden and volatile as a lit cigarette thrown on gasoline. And still the crime numbers dropped—but then a new round of serious thefts jarred the department's attention.

Several quick daylight attacks on empty streets, the robber escaping with a thick pack of fresh new bills. Slick, midday snatches and the thief gone with an impressively large sum of cash as the lone victim left the village bank walking swiftly toward their car or their home or shop. This brought out the foot patrols dressed in civilian clothes wandering innocently among local shoppers, new hires that most village folks didn't recognize.

But younger men and boys wandered the streets, too, fellows who weren't hunting bank customers but were still looking for the lost cat. Looking for the nice reward if they found her, an incentive that Seaver had offered on the new posters he'd put up over the older, ragged signs. He had no idea at all where the calico was hidden, nor, he thought, did his accomplices. All over the village folks wandered casually, women and girls seeming preoccupied with clothes shopping while searching for the bright calico with the striped leg, thinking what they'd do with five thousand dollars. Even on the roofs, more cats than usual were seen boldly prowling, not hunting birds and rats among overhanging branches but slyly spying on the village humans.

Some of the cats, the villagers knew well: dark gray tomcat. Dark, striped tabby. Yellow tomcat. Windblown tortoiseshell, all appearing for a moment, moving from roof to roof, disappearing into the trees watching the seeking pedestrians. Other cats, just as quick and wary, were from the wild feral band, coaxed down by Joe Grey from their hidden clowder in the hills among the ruined mansion to help alert Courtney if they were needed; cats come to help because their human friends had helped them many times, wild, speaking cats generally afraid of humans. Cats who had sometimes looked to Joe Grey for their own protection. Cats who knew, better than any, the rare and intrinsic value of young Courtney, of the bracelet calico with the long and amazing lives.

This late afternoon Joe Grey prowled a roof near the village bank, not looking for Courtney—he knew where she was—but looking for a connection, for a link, for a key to the disappearing bank money. Now as he leaped to a building next to the bank, the drizzle increased. He found shelter against a second-floor wall behind a lacy acacia tree where he could look down into the bank windows. He felt the rain decrease; the low sun slipped out over the sea, the rain clouds driven back to lie dark and heavy among the far eastern hills. He could see through the big glass windows into the tellers' cages where Fay Seaver was back at work in her fancy cashier's cage, wearing, of course, one of her neat little suits and nice jewelry.

She was watching the streets as much as Joe was, glancing up frequently as she counted out money, peering under parked cars for Courtney, under stair steps and into the niches of alleys. Looking for the damned cat, for the headstrong, willful calico that had escaped them. She watched the cats on the rooftops, but Courtney wouldn't be there in plain sight. She looked, as well, for the cats that had run away with Courtney, the ones that had, earlier, hung around the antiques shop looking in, the ones that had clawed Ulrich.

Sometimes Fay would see a cat down on the street sniffing at the open cans of cat food that Ulrich had set out under steps and behind potted trees. No cat would touch it, though the air was rank with its smell. Ulrich, and DeWayne's drivers, had waited for hours near the cans, well before daylight, carrying heavy canvas bags; Courtney hadn't shown, and they were all tired and cranky. As excited as Fay had been about the museum, as hard as she had worked putting the project together, she'd known all along, somewhere down inside, the folly of the endeavor. Maybe they could have made money from it. Or maybe they would have gone under, ended up selling the tapestries for little more than they had in them, selling the cat to some breeder, or for a few dollars as a cured cat skin.

Joe Grey, looking boldly down from the shingles, watched wandering men, some of them DeWayne's drivers carrying rolled-up canvas bags. Young boys carried bags, too, stuffed in their back pockets, the kids scattered out searching, each with a look of greed wanting to be the one to find the stripe-legged calico for which Ulrich Seaver had offered five thousand dollars. Who knew, he might even increase the rich incentive. Pacing, Joe stopped beside Dulcie in the shade of a roof's low overhang. Together they watched Fay as she straightened her hair clip: at once they came alert as Varney Luther watched her and then wandered off following a customer who was just leaving the bank, a tall, bent man. When a patrol car appeared moving slowly by the bank between pedestrians, Varney turned away into a camera shop and vanished.

Fay had done that little gesture twice before at intervals, that tweaking of her hair clip, each time as a patron departed stuffing a heavy envelope in his pocket. Each time, as the patron walked briskly away, he was followed.

The first time, Joe Grey had watched Fay say goodbye to the customer, brushing at her hair, the tomcat had paid little attention. The second time she fiddled with her hair clip, the departing customer was clearly followed—and this time Joe followed, too, fast across the shingles, while Dulcie continued to stand watch.

When Joe found the victim two blocks away, the little, pale-haired man stood in the middle of the street looking perplexed, his cell phone dangling in his hand as he talked to an officer in a squad car.

"I don't know how he knew," the little man said. "It was just a plain bank envelope, like they give everyone. I put it right in my pocket. I had my back to the windows when the teller counted it. How could he know how much was in it? Teller was very careful, counting it below the counter, slipping the envelope across. How could anyone know I withdrew that kind of money?"

"Which teller did you go to?"

"Well, I . . . a woman. I . . . dark hair, I think." He looked back toward the bank, but he couldn't see in from there.

"You want to come on into the station, give us a formal report?"

The little man nodded.

"Slow down when we pass the bank, take a good look, see if you recognize her."

In front of the bank, the little man stopped his Prius and stared in through the big glass window; but Joe Grey, even from the roof, could see that Fay had left her station and a young blonde had taken her place. The Prius moved on, turning the corner toward the station, the squad car behind it.

"That's it," Joe said. "I'm calling Harper."

Dulcie said, "That rookie's already figured it out."

"Maybe. But I'm calling anyway." He gave her a whisker kiss and took off for home, for the nearest phone. The rain had gone, the daylight was softening, the bank was just closing, the last customers, most of them unaware of any robberies, were hurrying away to supper. That day, five arrests had been made. No one on the street had paid much attention, squad cars were common in the village. The thieves who were caught had been marched to a small, deserted alley, were locked in a paddy wagon and were now on their way to jail. But maybe someone else had seen Fay's signal, Joe thought with interest. Maybe some citizen had seen the clue repeated earlier, had figured it out, and had already called the station.

If EvaJean took the call, she'd likely laugh and hang up.

Dulcie, watching Joe race away, knowing that Harper would soon have the message—and knowing that Courtney was safe—left the scene herself, striking across the rooftops for home and supper and to tell Wilma what was happening. Kit and Pan, taking her cue, flew up the rising roofs streaking for home, too, wanting their own suppers and maybe a little nap. They would tell Lucinda and Pedric about the bank robberies later. Now that Courtney was secure, their heads were, for the moment, filled with Fay and the robberies; and somehow they could sense more excitement building with the coming evening.

Kit could almost feel cop anger, almost hear gunshots, could feel danger coming as the rain increased for a moment and then drew back, as a streak of moonlight shone behind the east hills then vanished like some kind of celestial prophecy. Pan looked at her and knew that something was brewing. The fluffy tortoiseshell had that talent sometimes, to sense danger, and Pan never doubted her.

And Kit was right; Fay and her little game were only a part of the action.

Even as Joe headed home, making a detour around MPPD, he wished he could just run in and *tell* Max about Fay's signal. He drew back into the shadows as a figure moved deep under the awnings and overhangs, a man walking along watching Juana's condo, a white-haired figure who, even as Joe himself ducked out of the fitful gust, pulled down the hood of his dark slicker over that glimpse of snowy hair—Joe watched him, shivering, then raced for home and a phone.

Max was in his office when a call came through that, because of the robberies, Max thought might be the snitch. He and Detective Garza were interviewing the third bank thief, bringing them up from the jail one at a time, all duly handcuffed and in leg irons, a precaution Max had learned long ago as a young officer after losing an escaped arrestee. So far, information from the robbery victims had given the total cash lost as some two hundred and seventy-five thousand dollars. Now, when the phone rang and Max picked up, Garza caught the chief's look, and called two deputies to usher the arrestee back to the jail.

On the other end of the line was a sheriff in Texas, Luke Wilson, whom Max knew well. He liked hearing Luke's Texas drawl. "All useless information, Max, but I thought I'd call anyway. DeWayne Luther was spotted outside Houston, taken in to a substation. One more fiasco. They printed him, did a DNA. They had to release him, they had the wrong man. You picked a good one, a BOL with a hundred doubles."

"I'd like to lock up all the doubles until we catch this guy." How could there be so many tall, white-haired younger men in the world that people would mistake for one wanted felon.

They talked for a while about old times, about their

ranches, their horses. Max enjoyed the contact with his old friend, but he wasn't happy. These misguided identifications put him in such a bad temper that when he got home, when he and Charlie sat down to supper and the phone rang, even if the voice was that of his favorite snitch, he almost banged down the phone.

26

eWayne Luther's back," the caller said. "Spotted him outside Juana Davis's condo." Max snorted with disbelief. One more damned double. But this *was* his regular snitch, there was no mistaking his voice, even over the sudden gusts of rain pounding against the roof.

"He was there in front of the condo, wearing a slicker open over ragged clothes. He looked like he meant to go on up the steps but then a light went on inside. He swung into the dark between two condos, stood there waiting. Maybe," the snitch said, "our luck is changing. You do have those five bank withdrawal thieves locked up, you have the money they stole. You've checked out the cash in Seaver's safe, and that should bring up plenty of prints." The snitch was talkative tonight, Max had never heard him go on like this.

"All that stolen cash that Davis and Garza locked in the evidence room, it has to be a fortune. And with plenty of prints and photos," the snitch said.

Max was silent. The snitch's comments made him more than edgy. How did he know this stuff? How did he know that one of his officers had slipped into the antiques workroom? That Bean had opened the safe, photographed the money, memorized the safe's combination and locked it up again, leaving the cash for the detectives to bag as evidence?

Max hadn't made any arrests. He had his reasons. He'd seen the Luther boys hanging around Seaver's alley. He didn't want to make waves until the next big move went down, most likely the Seavers and Luthers together. He didn't know how the two families had made a connection, but they'd both been in town for years—crook drawn to crook.

The phone had gone dead. Max was about to call the department, send a couple of men to nail DeWayne, when his phone rang again.

But this was a woman, one he'd never heard—until she identified herself, and then he knew Maurita's whisper, shy and hesitant, still hoarse from her injuries.

"DeWayne is back. He's just outside Juana's living

room window, in the rain. I'm standing in the shadows in the hall. I guess he woke me working on the window lock, he has some kind of tool, I can see it flash but now I can't hear a sound, over the rain.

"Juana's asleep. So is Jimmie. Crowley was standing guard but fell asleep in his chair. The rain's so loud that even Rock is snoring. When I came down the hall, DeWayne was at the window. Dark slicker, hood pulled down. I don't think he saw me. I've got to get out of here."

"Wake Juana, put her on the line."

But Juana had heard, and was up, she had pulled on jeans and a sweatshirt. She and the two officers stood by Maurita's side, out of sight from the window as the hooded figure worked on the lock. When Maurita shivered, Juana put her arm around the frightened girl, and took the phone from her; she turned on the speaker so softly they had to press their heads together, listening to Max order his men out on the street and to the roof. He said, "Juana, get a squad car, pull up front.

"Tell Jimmie and Crowley to take Maurita up to the ruins. Kate and Scotty will hide her. Take the calico, too, where Seaver won't find her—though I still don't get what that's about, stealing a cat, all the chase and fuss."

The lock clicked. The window slid open.

"He's in the house," Juana whispered as DeWayne swung in over the sill—swung straight into Jimmie's and Crowley's fists.

But this wasn't DeWayne.

Jimmie had the man down punching him hard, then jerked him up, swinging him around, twisting his arm behind him so hard he yelped. Crowley grabbed him, threw him to the floor facedown, and handcuffed him. And the real DeWayne was gone, speeding away across the roofs, hood blown back, a flash of white hair, heading for the far end of the condo building, dodging its tangle of patios and jutting walls—and Juana was gone, racing across the street, using the numbers lock to retrieve one of the squad cars. Wheeling it out of the lot and across, she parked in front of her steps—while inside her apartment, Crowley rolled the man over.

DeWayne's driver, Stope, scowled up at Crowley, his cap knocked off, revealing tangled auburn hair running into liver-colored freckles; he was drenched with rain, soaking Juana's carpet; he twisted, fighting and swearing, as the big officer flipped him again, bent him backward, and cuffed his ankles to his wrists.

Outside in the blowing rain, cops were spilling out of the station searching the streets. Three officers, catching a glimpse of white hair, headed fast for the man racing across the far roofs. Crowley saw DeWayne double back, and was out the window chasing him—but Rock leaped past him. Racing, flying, the big dog nailed DeWayne, too, and knocked him down, his teeth in the man's throat. Fighting and twisting, DeWayne grabbed the Weimaraner's jaws, was just able to pull them apart so he could breathe; with one hand he managed to draw his gun. McFarland was on him, kicking him in the stomach, wrenching away the automatic—while across the roof, among the far peaks and out of sight, Joe Grey raced, searching for DeWayne, missing all the real action.

Just outside the condo in the easing rain, Rock sat as he was told but was still primed to attack as Crowley fitted DeWayne with leg irons, locked his hands and feet together, then made the emergency call for the medics. Jimmie put pressure on the bleeding, but Rock had not cut a vein. Hastily Jimmie bound DeWayne's wound and then ignored him as they examined Rock, making sure this fine dog was all right.

Maurita wished Rock had killed DeWayne, that he lay, now, deep in the grave that he had dug for her.

Buffin hopped out the window, stood looking with disgust at the two captives, then turned away to lick Rock's face. The medics' van arrived as Juana called Clyde then called the vet clinic. Four medics came up the front stairs and out through the window. They examined Stope first, lifted him onto a stretcher and carried him down to the van. Before they finished with DeWayne, Maurita and her two guards were out the back door racing for the squad left parked, piling in, getting Maurita and Courtney settled. Crowley driving as they sped through the back streets heading for the Pamillon ruins.

Joe Grey saw them as he returned to the condo. He was tempted to leap down into the cop car and ride along, but somehow this moment belonged to Maurita and Courtney. He paused on the condo's window ledge, nuzzled Davis, and he was gone, heading home. Behind him, Juana closed the window watching the squad car disappear, hugging Buffin against her and holding Rock's collar as he fussed, wanting to follow.

In the squad car, Jimmie sat in the back, Maurita hunched down on the seat beside him out of sight, cuddling Courtney. Before they left the condo she had returned to the bedroom, pulled on a warm coat, and opened the lock of Juana's dresser drawer that she had jimmied earlier. She reached back beneath a stack of papers, removed a small revolver, checked the load and slipped it in her pocket; it must be a spare that Juana seldom used, but it was kept clean and loaded.

If she got caught, she would put Juana in big trouble. But if she swore in court that she'd jimmied the lock and stolen it, that she'd sniffed at the dresser and smelled gun oil . . . would that clear the detective?

But if they found DeWayne and if she could kill him, she'd be the one in trouble.

She didn't care, she wanted him dead.

When Crowley turned sharply up a narrow street, the careening car threw her against Jimmie's shoulder, he put his arm around her to support her. He had to smile at the way the calico cat clutched her paws around the young woman's neck, clinging to her fellow escapee.

They came out of the village through a tangle of twisted roads and small cottages onto Highway One and turned north, in the direction of the old Pamillon estate. The rain, which had come and gone all day, now had nearly stopped again, had turned into a drizzle and soon to a mist. High up, wind must be blowing hard, driving the clouds away. Soon they could see hints of moonlight and then a glimpse of the full moon.

The moon, Courtney thought, *the full moon means good fortune.* She glanced up at Maurita and hoped it shone for them both. And now they could see the mansion rising higher up the hills. Even the two cops admired the sudden view as they watched, as well, for anyone following them.

The stone of the ancient mansion shone pale in the moonlight. The once-neglected dwelling was very different from when Kate first bought it and began to remodel it, dreaming of the museum she hoped it would one day become. Glass had been restored in the front windows of the jutting front wing that had stood open to the weather for so many years. The feral cats had often hung out there, watching to leap down on the small game below, enjoying the view of village and sea, sleeping on an ancient, moldering sofa. Now there was a new ceiling, new rafters, fresh white paint; but mostly glass to enhance the interior. The far wings of the compound were still in ruins; the feral cats thrived there, dining on rats and field mice. The wild little cats had made friends with Kate and Scotty, and Kate knew they would be kind to Courtney. Redheaded, red-bearded Scott Flannery was Kate's new husband; they had been friends for years, their romance had been sudden and surprising. Scotty was Ryan Damen's uncle and was, as well, her building foreman.

The upstairs and downstairs of the large front wing would be the main art galleries. The one-story wing on the far side had been rebuilt into an airy but cozy apartment. The remaining rooms, as they were finished, would offer more space for special exhibits—but an environment nothing like the Seavers' too-fancy plan.

They pulled up beside the cat shelter, which now had a tall stone wall between it and the mansion, perhaps to give it privacy from the galleries. This, plus another stone wall on the land below, partially concealing a little wooden house, made the property seem drawn together into a more handsome unit, made it blend more cozily among the hills. Jimmie glanced at Maurita, imagining her living in the empty house; he wondered what she *would* do if she escaped DeWayne, if he were locked in prison for a long stretch, leaving her free to make a new life.

Kate came out to greet them. Levi's, work boots, she was all carpenter today—some carpenter with that strikingly beautiful face and tousled blond hair. Scotty came to join them. They'd had a short honeymoon, then had gotten back to work on their apartment and on the cat shelter.

Kate looked into the car, greeting Maurita gently, then studying Courtney's amber eyes. "So you escaped, too. What could be so valuable," she said slyly, "about an ordinary calico cat?"

Courtney looked back at her, equally sly and amused. Not everyone present knew that certain cats could speak. Kate said, "What crazy plan could Seaver have had for her, that made him and those thugs chase her all over the village? He has to be insane."

Earlier, in the squad car, before Crowley turned onto the narrow road that led up to the mansion, Maurita had said, "Kate will hide the little calico where Seaver will never find her, she'll take good care of her. But I'm coming back with you."

"The hell you are," Jimmie said. "Why do you think we brought you out here? Not to hide just the cat but to hide you! What the hell, Maurita. Max wants you away from DeWayne, not there in town with him. You want to end up in another grave, a permanent one?"

She went pale and very still—and beautiful, Jimmie thought, despite the fading bruises. The look she gave him was unreadable. "They're getting ready to pull off the Saks job, you knew it would be soon. On our way out of the village, didn't you see those old gray cars pulled in behind the motel, the cars they use for robberies, the ones they usually leave scattered around town? This has to be the night."

Jimmie glanced up at Crowley, who was looking back at him in the mirror. Of course they had seen them. Crowley had already made the call so Maurita wouldn't hear, texting skillfully with his big farmer's hands, a talent that always amazed Jimmie. By dark tonight Max would have their units in place, far better hidden than DeWayne's crew would be.

"That's why he kept me around in the first place, to

make sure they didn't miss the best jewelry, the finest designs and highest quality stones. The best antiques, that he stole on the East Coast and sent to his brothers, the Luther boys passed them on to Seaver. I had to pick them out, do the shipping to a storage unit. De-Wayne has no taste, no training. He always made me stay with him, there was no way I could shake them, there was always one of the drivers or DeWayne practically on top of me, even outside a restroom door. He kept me like a slave, made me do all the estimates and inventories—until the night they finished casing the village, settled on Saks, and sat around the motel drinking beer, planning their moves. Suddenly I'd had enough. I got up, I told him I was finished, and ran out. Didn't stop to pack anything or even grab my purse, I just got out."

"He comes after you and nearly kills you," Jimmie snapped. "So now you want to go back and help him rob Saks. You help him pull off this heist, and then he kills you."

"No. I thought . . . I know all their moves, their exact plans. I thought I could *help* you, that I could watch, maybe slip inside if you'd give me a phone . . ."

"You already told Harper every detail. What else do we need? What do you . . . ?"

She was crying. When she fished in her pocket for

a tissue, holding Courtney close and drawing her jacket around them, that was when Jimmie saw the outline of the gun. She saw him looking.

He studied her for a long time. "I won't ask any questions. If you meant to slip in among them as they loot the place, if you meant to kill DeWayne in there, you're putting yourself in big trouble." He reached to touch her face. Even crying, her dark eyes were beautiful. "Maurita, I want you to promise to stay up here at the mansion and do as we say. As Kate and Scotty say. Will you show it to me?"

Frowning, she removed the revolver carefully, aiming it away from Jimmie and the cat.

"Juana's Smith and Wesson."

"I took it from the dresser. I thought . . . I wanted . . ."

"Are you going to give it to me willingly, or do I have to take it from you and maybe get one of us shot?" He looked at her tenderly. "Maurita, I'll have to take the gun eventually. Juana will have to know, you'll have to give it back to her." She could feel Courtney stiffen, ready to break from her grasp. Jimmie said, "We have to tell Max. I don't keep secrets from the chief or from anyone in the department—except EvaJean," he said, grinning.

He touched her face. "Before this is over, if you don't mess it up, we'll have DeWayne in jail and then federal prison. With his rap sheet, count the years. He might never get out, you'll be free of him. You shoot him now, you'll find *yourself* in a cell for a long time."

She looked at him stubbornly. She wanted to kill DeWayne herself, she wanted to hurt DeWayne, hurt him bad. She started to slip the gun back in her pocket.

Jimmie had it before she could blink, her wrist bent back, her other arm twisted and helpless. Courtney had fled under the seat.

Jimmie opened the revolver's cylinder and removed the bullets. He dropped the gun in an evidence bag, the bullets in another, and put both in his pocket. "Scotty and Kate will keep you safe, they're both armed— legally," he said wryly. "Keep you safe so you can testify in court. That should damage DeWayne more than shooting him." When he gently turned her face toward him and kissed her on the forehead, Courtney crept out and sat at her feet, watching. Thinking about the ways of humans. Were they so different from the ways of cats? What would it be like to be human? What would it be like to feel the power of that tender look?

27

Zeb Luther was home from the hospital by mid-afternoon—*if you could call that fusty apartment home.* Hospitals were so damn slow, with all their paperwork. Riding in the backseat of Thelma's Volvo with Mindy beside him, he had his walker folded in the trunk; not that he intended to use it. "I'm not crippled. Ain't no broken leg, no need for that contraption."

Joe Grey sat across the street in his tower watching Mindy help the old man to the curb and Thelma wrestle out the walker as if it weighed a ton; he watched Zebulon manage the four front steps just fine without any hospital equipment, leaving the walker propped against the rail.

Thelma scowled at Mindy. "You can get him some lunch or an early supper. Both of you better eat, there's peanut butter and jelly, and milk if it hasn't gone sour. Then Grandpa might want to lie down."

"I had peanut butter and jelly in the hospital until it's running out my ears. And why would I want to lay down, I've been in that damned bed for three days. Mindy and I will take a walk."

Thelma made a rude comment and left the house saying something about groceries.

Thus the neighborhood disturbances began again, bursting forth from within, quite audible at all hours as Grandpa argued that he was going home—to his *own* home—as Thelma and Varney shouted at him, and as neighbors walked the street staring in, then began calling the station; as the dispatcher sent out an officer on a domestic that ended in nothing but a warning. Zebulon was so loud, and Varney's language so vile that, after the second domestic call, the responding officer threatened to take them in. Thelma managed to talk him out of it because Grandpa was just home from the hospital and how could she take care of him in jail?

Officer Wrigley frowned. "One more complaint, Grandpa goes back to the hospital and the rest of you to jail."

"Not my little girl," Thelma howled. "You can't put . . ."

"She goes to Children's Services," Wrigley said. As

he left, Thelma swore and slammed the door behind him. When she headed for her bedroom, Varney came down the hall wearing wrinkled jeans and an old jacket and stomped out of the house; who knew where he went? Joe didn't hear his car start.

Mindy and Zeb didn't hear it, either, but they heard Varney go out the front door. He did that sometimes, left his car at home. Mindy looked out the window, saw him walking away, up the hill toward the freeway.

When the house was quiet, when they knew Varney was gone, and thought that Thelma slept, Grandpa and Mindy, alone in Mindy's room, packed a few necessities in a small duffel and hid it under his bed. They went up the hall to the kitchen and as Zeb listened for Thelma, Mindy hastily packed some food in two grocery bags. She made some canned-ham sandwiches, taking two back to her room for their supper. They went to bed fully dressed. Whether or not they slept, Joe Grey himself dozed off.

Around midnight, Mindy put her ear to Thelma's door making sure her mother still slept; she slipped into the room as silent as a mouse and lifted Thelma's car keys from the dresser. Zebulon fetched the grocery bags from the kitchen broom closet and they fled the house.

The sound of a car starting woke Joe, he rose up among the pillows to see Thelma's parking lights on, and Zeb at the wheel. He watched Mindy hop in with an armload of blankets. The two grocery bags were already on the backseat, with the duffel, and Joe Grey smiled. Zeb Luther was having his way, he and Mindy were going home. Oh, wouldn't Thelma pitch a fit!

The rain was gone but the clouds still hung thick covering the moon, the night so black he could hardly see where street and parked cars met. Only up the block past a few dark cottages and shops did faint lights shine where the shopping plaza stretched away behind his own house: softly illuminated courtyard, subtly lit first-floor display windows. And on the dark street, only the trail of Zebulon's taillights headed toward the freeway. His dashboard lights were off, and he must be driving with only his parking lights. He'd be lucky not to crash into a parked car before he reached traffic and *had* to turn the headlamps higher. The village was so still, the only movement Joe could see was Thelma's "borrowed" car creeping along . . .

But when he looked again he saw movement at the front of the plaza, faint lights moving inside Saks's elegant second floor.

Leaving his warm cushions, Joe leaped up onto the top of his tower. From that height, perched on its slanted shingles, he could easily see past the roof of his own house. Yes, faint lights moving deep within Saks's second-floor display windows, the faintest of soft blue lights. Deeper in, black shadows moved behind the fashionably posed models. And in front of Saks, on Ocean Avenue, three old gray cars were parked half on the sidewalk with their backs to Saks's front door. Tonight *was* the night.

Dropping down from the top of his tower, Joe galloped across the bedroom roof and dropped to the kitchen roof; he jumped down to the barbecue counter and around the patio wall that Ryan had designed and built. Here he made a long leap to the top of the higher wall that separated the back of their property, and the entire residential block, from the plaza.

From that wall he could see behind the plaza buildings to the wide strip where buses and trucks could pull off the side street and park during the day. Four tour buses were parked there now, effectively concealing the back of Saks from the street, their occupants most likely tucked in for the night at the several motels that stood among the trees and village shops. Between the buses and Saks, two large black limos had been squeezed in close to the store's delivery doors, their lights out, nearly invisible in the blackness. Was this a new twist, DeWayne had split up the cars and the retreat routes? Maybe thinking that Maurita had told the department how he usually operated: all out at once, through one door, loaded down with their loot, gone before the cops had a clue?

Now, there was not a cop in sight, in front or in back of Saks. Not a squad car, not a single foot patrol that Joe could see standing in the shadows. He was about to spin around and head home to the phone when, through the upstairs store windows, lights flashed and the shadows moved fast in one direction, converging at the back, hauling cumbersome bags. They disappeared downward as if on service stairs. Where the hell were the cops? The men came out the back of the building, piled their black plastic bags into the limos, swung in themselves and were gone, turning left to Ocean Avenue then right, heading up the hill for the freeway. He heard the cars in front start up and follow them, those figures so stealthy he hadn't seen them. And still not a cop anywhere. He watched the line of cars turn south onto the freeway, and Joe Grey sped for home.

Bursting into the kitchen through Rock's dog door and leaping to the counter, he had knocked off the phone's speaker, forgetting that this call would be ID'd, when up on the freeway he heard tires squeal and sirens scream. He pushed the phone back in place, realizing only then how close the snitch had come to getting caught.

Just ahead of the mixed entourage of crooks, Zeb and Mindy, still driving slowly, saw the pack of cars bearing down behind them. They saw and heard the scream of squad cars, saw their lights flashing, coming fast, and they made a sharp skid onto the right shoulder; they were almost scraped over by the speeding limos. Zeb pulled over farther onto an embankment, tilting the Volvo nearly beyond recovery.

"Get out, Mindy, before we go over."

"You get out," she said, grabbing her cell phone and opening her door, watching Zebulon slide out to safety; and they both scrambled down the ditch.

"No point to call 911, the cops are here." Zeb smiled when he caught a glimpse of white hair among the escaping limos. When the chase had passed, they climbed the bank again and walked along the highway, then sat with their backs against a tree, watching. It was there that Joe Grey found them.

Ahead, the limos and gray cars had slammed on their brakes, skidding and sliding into each other as cop cars circled them, cops appearing out of nowhere hazing them together like sharks closing in on their prey. Gray cars, black limos, black-and-white patrol cars all in a tangle, cops with short-barrel shotguns stepping out, ordering drivers out of their cars and facedown on the ground. A shot was fired, and another. And Zebulon ran, back along the berm. He piled into his car and took off rocking along the berm until he was steady again, turning his lights high, reaching over to open the passenger door as Mindy and Joe Grey jumped in. Praying for the first time since Nell died, Zeb fled along the highway as a shot blasted too close to their back window. So far, the cops had paid no attention to them. He floorboarded the car up the road half a mile past the Harper ranch, he was sweating; he swerved into his own turnoff and it was then he realized there was a cat in the car, sitting calmly on Mindy's lap.

She said, "You saw him when he found us, back there on the berm. You *saw* him jump in the car, Grandpa." Zeb glanced at the cat and at Mindy, and said nothing. They heard the distant scream of sirens as CHP officers joined MPPD, speeding down the freeway from the north, these blending with the howl of medics' units from the village. Zeb skidded up his own drive, around the outside of the fenced house and pasture, and straight for the woods.

"The horses . . ." He spun around in the seat, looking. "Where are the horses?"

"At the Harpers'. I told you."

"Oh, yes, that was nice of them. Of course I remember." But in truth, he hadn't, no more than he'd remembered the cat. Since DeWayne beat on him, things had seemed to get a little mixed up. He turned onto the narrow path through the woods, scraping the top of Thelma's car against the hanging branches. A quarter mile, and he parked behind the Harpers' barn, out of sight from the highway. They didn't need Thelma or Varney coming after them.

Where was Varney? Had he joined DeWayne and his pack of thieves? Zeb had looked for him down on the highway, but in that mess of course he hadn't seen him.

They got out of the car and headed around the Harpers' barn and down the long drive. At the gate, halfway to the highway, Charlie Harper and their young hand, Billy, were standing watch in case one of those guys got loose, in case there was a chase. Both of them had shotguns. That much vigilance might seem amusing to Mindy, but Zeb and Joe Grey knew better—and it was Joe Grey, rearing up beside Charlie, looking down at the confusion of cars and cops, of medics and injured men, who saw DeWayne Luther, his white hair catching car lights where he lay on a stretcher, the coroner leaning over him. DeWayne lying death still beside the hearse, pale face caught in a squad car's headlights. Zeb let out a gasp, and turned away.

But what turned Joe Grey's stomach was not this dead man, but two police officers on stretchers, new young men that Joe hardly knew. They were being worked on by medics: tourniquets, oxygen tanks, emergency wrappings. Both were already secured in an ambulance, ready to head for the hospital. To see a cop who had been shot upset Joe so badly that he threw up, retching, in the tall grass.

Charlie handed Billy her shotgun, picked Joe up, wiped his mouth with a tissue and kissed him on top of his head, her red hair falling over his eyes. She gave him a gentle hug, put him down again, and reached to Billy for her weapon. They watched the coroner start to wrap DeWayne in a body bag. Zebulon stood looking with no expression on his face. Looking at his oldest son, dead. His son who had beaten him so badly and who had tried to kill that woman he ran with. Zeb opened the gate and started down toward the hearse, down the rest of the long drive, Charlie and Billy walking beside him gently supporting him. Mindy followed, her own face white, as Max Harper started up the drive to them. Down by the hearse the coroner had stopped working, he stood looking up to Max for a sign to proceed or to back off.

Max paused, looking up at Zeb. "Do you want to come down?"

Zeb was silent. He looked at Max for a long time, then shook his head. "After all these years, he deserved what he got. Now, I don't need to see him chewed up with bullets." He turned away in the direction of the barn. But then he paused, turned back, took a key from his pocket and handed it to Max.

"Thelma's Volvo. It's behind the hay barn, we borrowed it. Shall I take it back?"

"She won't need it, she'll be in jail with the rest of them, at least for a while." Max accepted the key. "We'll see that it's impounded." He looked down at Mindy. "You were headed home, to Zeb's place?"

She and Zeb nodded.

"Children's Services gets a whiff of that, you two alone there, and Zeb just out of the hospital, they won't like it. Thelma may try for dismissal or maybe home confinement on the excuse that she needs to take care of you."

Mindy looked stricken.

"Do you have anyone?" Max said. "Someone, maybe a relative who can live in, to get the welfare people off your back?"

"We don't need . . ." Mindy began.

Charlie shook back her red hair, and looked a question at Max. He nodded. She said, "You can stay here, until you find someone."

Max said, "Varney will be locked up, too. There'll be no one in that apartment, welfare would be all over you. But if you could be in your own place . . . what about your daughter-in-law?"

Zeb frowned. "You said Thelma was going to jail."

"Your *other* daughter-in-law," Max said. "Maurita told me DeWayne demanded they get married, several years ago. A mark of ownership, she told me bitterly. To keep his partners off her."

Even Joe Grey didn't know that. He was so surprised he reared up in the bushes, startling Max. When the chief looked at him, the tomcat could almost read what he was thinking: *How did that damn cat get up here in the middle of another crime scene? Why did he rear up just now? Why the hell does he always . . . ?*

Charlie said, "The Damens live right behind the plaza, that could certainly explain his presence: the cat hears sounds, car doors closing. He jumped on the wall and saw the limos take off, saw them hit the freeway. He heard the crash and sirens and, with that cat's annoying curiosity, he raced along the highway, to have a look."

She looked back at Mindy and Zeb. "I think you two *should* stay with us until Children's Services stops nosing around. And," she said, looking at Max, "do you think Zeb should meet the daughter-in-law he's never known? That Zeb and Mindy and I should take a run up to . . . where Maurita is staying?"

Max scowled at her. "It's the middle of the night, Charlie."

"While we're gone, Billy can make up their beds."

Billy nodded, and grinned at Mindy. "And set out some pie and milk?"

The chief gave Charlie that sly, sideways look. "So just why are you going up to see Maurita, at midnight?"

"Someone has to tell her about DeWayne. And you have your hands full. Don't you think she'll want to know that DeWayne is no longer a threat? That she's free, that she doesn't have to fear him anymore? And that his crew, with this burglary and their long records, will be on their way to prison where they can't get at her?"

Max considered her with a steady half frown. "You know that's my job, Charlie. To inform the wife of the deceased."

"This one time, Max? It'll be hours before you can tear yourself away from this mess, with officers all over Saks taking pictures, gathering evidence, lifting prints, and with two cops in the hospital. You'll be up all night."

They could see, even from the distance where they stood, that all the interior lights in Saks burned brightly, shining out over the village as MPPD went about its work. "Don't you think, this once . . . ?" Charlie said. "Don't you think she'll be anxious?"

"How would she know this was coming down?"

"You all guessed it would be tonight, or soon. When McFarland and Crowley took her to Kate's, while De-Wayne was still hunting for her, and they saw the gray cars all lined up as if DeWayne was ready to pull a job, and Crowley texted you . . ." Charlie shrugged. "Or maybe she heard it on the police radio," she said non-committally.

Joe Grey moved away, smiling. Harper's favorite snitch hadn't made the call on this one. But, except for their two young cops getting shot, it was turning out all right. So far. He wanted to ask Max how bad the officers were hurt, but there was no way he could do that.

28

Joe watched Zeb and Mindy move their meager belongings from Thelma's Volvo into the Harpers' barn. Zeb still looked shocked. Perhaps not so much that DeWayne was dead, but that the woman DeWayne had run with all those years was his own daughter-in-law. That made Maurita family, and to Zeb Luther, family was important. *Maybe,* Joe thought, *because his own children hadn't turned out so great?*

Would this woman be any different, this female jewel thief?

Thinking more about Maurita and Zeb than about the Saks burglary, Joe watched Max take Thelma's car on down to the highway, parking it among the limos. Some were shot up, some dented, all under police custody and filled with hundreds of thousands of dollars' worth of stolen property. Already officers were starting them up, driving them back to the station to unload. An armored truck stood waiting in the background. The beautiful shoes and wallets and handbags, the designer suits and coats and dresses, would be locked in the heavily reinforced evidence room. The jewelry, each piece, would be photographed, fingerprinted, and locked in the strong iron safe that was bolted to the floor there. Max didn't like having this kind of wealth stored in the department. As soon as daylight shone, the stolen goods, all inventoried, would be sent by armed guard to the nearest Saks warehouse.

Joe wondered, as he and Mindy and Zeb piled into Charlie's SUV and headed for the Pamillon estate, how Zeb would respond to Maurita. Would he have only disdain for the battered woman because she had been a thief, like DeWayne?

But why should he, when DeWayne had forced her to follow his orders? When DeWayne tried to kill her when she finally ran—when she was soon too beaten to fight back?

Maurita was still under protection. Even though DeWayne was dead, his scuzzy partners were not. This young woman knew enough about their past records to help convict them, and they could be as mean as DeWayne. Joe Grey hoped they would remain in prison, that they would not be free again—but until sentences were passed, or until some of them died of their wounds, he'd feel edgy for the young woman.

He thought Maurita and Zebulon had a lot in common, losing DeWayne even though they'd hated him. He wanted them to bond, to feel only tenderness for each other. And he was off on the kind of daydream that Dulcie or Kit might imagine, happy thoughts about Zeb and his newly discovered daughter-in-law. He was so involved in hoping they would become a real family that, traveling up the dark highway, they were at the mansion before he knew it. A soft light burned at the cat shelter, in the little office. They parked by the door. Charlie stepped out, Joe leaping past her. She knocked and called out.

The minute Scotty opened the door, bare legged and wearing a short robe, Joe Grey slipped past him into the office where the light burned, where Maurita's cot was neatly made up. As if she hadn't slept in it, as if maybe she had paced all night. Joe couldn't speak to Scotty, with Maurita present and with Zebulon standing in the doorway. She sat on the cot looking up at them, her expression both desolate and hopeful. She looked at Zeb and she knew who he was—and, from his look, she knew what had happened—and there was nothing she could say.

Kate appeared from the bedroom wearing an extra-long shirt of Scotty's, her short blond hair a tangle. Charlie, her red hair just as ruffled, moved inside past Scotty and into the little office. She sat down on the cot and put her arms around Maurita.

Maurita leaned against her. "It's come down," she said. "They took out Saks." She looked at Charlie. "When we passed their motel, the way the cars and limos were arranged, I knew. I couldn't sleep, for the scared feeling—scared that a cop would be hurt. I tried the radio but I couldn't get much but static." A tiny radio sat on the desk, turned low. It was more squawk than clarity and was, at the moment, occupied with a disgusting melody that no one wanted to hear. "When I called the dispatcher, she would tell me nothing. She said, 'I am not allowed to give out that information.'"

Charlie rolled her eyes. "EvaJean, the bitch." Then, in a kinder tone, "I asked Max to let me come out and tell you, though it's his job to do this."

Maurita's eyes looked deep into hers, waiting.

"Maurita, several of the burglars were killed tonight. DeWayne was shot when he charged two officers. He died at once."

The young woman leaned against her; she was shaking. Charlie didn't know what else to say. She had a right to cry; after all, he *had* been her husband.

But when Joe Grey jumped up and pawed at them, when Maurita turned to look at him, the tears in her eyes were a mix of not only shock, but laughter. Her expression was uncertain for a moment but then replaced by a deep and satisfying contentment. Joe wanted to shout, *You're free. He's dead and you're done with him, done with those brutes he ran with. They're either dead themselves, or will be locked away for good. You're free, Maurita, to do with your life as you please.*

Charlie was thinking the same: Maurita was free of her imprisonment, and there was one less scum in the world.

"But two fine young police officers were shot," Charlie said sickly, and she prayed that they had received only surface wounds, that they wouldn't go through the hell that some injured officers suffered.

That day at the mansion, and the night to come, turned into a tangle of emotions as cars began to arrive. Only Zeb, Mindy, and Maurita didn't know what the gathering was about as people began to pull in. Kate said, "I invited a few friends over, they're bringing takeout breakfast."

Wilma and Dulcie arrived with tears in their eyes, but they weren't crying for DeWayne. Lucinda and

Pedric and Kit and Pan drew up in the Greenlaws' Lincoln Town Car, their faces filled with sadness. They all knew that DeWayne Luther was dead and folks looked at Zeb shyly. They got back only a handshake and a nod. Ryan and Clyde slipped in, Ryan snatching up Joe Grey, crying into his fur.

But none of it was about DeWayne Luther.

John and Mary Firetti were right behind them, Buffin and Striker on John's shoulder. Dulcie mewed at them. Wilma, her gray hair tied back crookedly in its ponytail, put her arm around John. Wilma had helped Dulcie to raise the three kittens, but Dr. Firetti had helped to birth them—this gathering was about the girl kitten.

If Zeb and Maurita and Mindy guessed that the poignant celebration was because Maurita was free, they were right in part, but that was not the cause of the sadness that filled the little office—Maurita was free, but Courtney was not, and Ulrich might never stop looking for her. He and Fay might go to prison for involvement with the Luthers' crimes, or they might get probation and walk free, and Courtney could always be in danger.

Now, with the young calico's final and distant escape to come, her friends began the real grieving. For years hence, they would find that day resonating in waking memories and in nighttime dreams as real as this day itself.

As they all crowded around the table, Zebulon's mood softened and he laughed. Soon noise and laughter rocked the tiny apartment, driving away the sadness, but causing Maurita to draw back in shy silence. And still, during the friends' arrivals, no one had seen Courtney.

The six other cats ate their own takeout quickly, clambered down from laps and side tables and headed for the ruins. Still no Courtney. She would not show herself, thinking the Seavers might be out looking for her, not when Seaver might see all the cars up here and wonder. Who knew where they would choose to search? Courtney had no idea they might be in jail.

Down in the depths of the ruins, the cats spent a long time with Courtney alone. There wasn't much time left together. Now, when folks began to leave, Wilma took all seven cats to her place to wait for dark, for a last visit, where the three kittens had been born. In their own first home, they curled up on the couch with Wilma, a gentle fire burning on the hearth, Joe Grey and Dulcie snuggled close to their calico kitten, Buffin and Striker lying nearly on top of her. Kit and Pan lay sprawled on her other side, their noses against her calico coat.

Only after supper, when darkness fell, would they all go together, the cats and their families, back to the

Pamillon ruins. There they would say good-bye to Joe and Dulcie's calico daughter.

Zebulon, before leaving the Pamillon estate after breakfast, took Maurita's hand solemnly. "Will you come home with us? Will you be part of our family— will you want us, the same as we want you?" He put his arm around her. "We need you, Maurita."

"And I need you," Maurita said softly. "I've never had a family."

We're lucky, Mindy thought. *And we'll be happy—if Mama and Varney get hauled off to jail and can't come bothering us.*

"It might be well," Charlie said, "if you three stay at our house for a few days, where Maurita will be safer until we're sure those men are all in custody."

Maurita hugged Charlie; she had begun to feel more at ease, more in charge of herself. As if she had found something of herself that was lost—lost or maybe never discovered.

"Meanwhile," Charlie said, "we can dust up your house a bit, change the sheets, get in some groceries." And the four of them headed for Zebulon's place, to brighten Maurita's new home, to make it ready and welcoming. Mindy and Maurita, Charlie and Zebulon worked for the rest of the day, washing windows, cleaning the kitchen. Rearranging Maurita's new room, which had been Nevin's. The room of no-good Thelma's husband, but that didn't bother Maurita.

With freshly washed curtains and clean windows, she would see, in early morning, the sun rise over the eastern hills, would see at night the sun set above the sea. Looking around her, she felt clean, she felt new. The way she used to wish life would be. All she'd needed was a little help. The terror of DeWayne's brutality was beginning to fade, wiped away by human friends, human love. By the surprise of being part of her own family. And, earlier, by the warmth of those long, quiet days of cat love.

When Charlie and the Luthers arrived back at the Harper ranch for an early supper, Max's truck was parked by the house. "I took off early," he said, coming in, yawning. "Handed it over to Cameron for the night—all those bastards are snug in their cells. Dallas and I are on call."

Across from the house, above the hay barn, the Luthers' beds were already made up in two rooms next to Billy's. Both Zeb and Maurita found they were able to handle the stairs, with Mindy's help; and Billy Young had been busy. The outside alarm was set, two loaded firearms stood inside Billy's and Zeb's bedroom doors, and the two big dogs ran loose and watchful in the fenced entry yard. Mindy had strict instructions not to touch the shotgun and rifle. "When you are old enough," Max said, "and that will be soon, you will have the same safety training as Billy is getting. Maybe even take the same classes as a police cadet, if you like."

Mindy grinned at him with delight, and so did Zebulon. Zeb would much rather have her thoroughly trained by a professional, than to do a bad job himself.

It was that night, during supper, that the earring appeared.

Supper was a tamale pie that Charlie had taken from the freezer, and a salad that Mindy made. They had just sat down when they heard Jimmie McFarland's car pull up in front, parking next to Max's truck. Charlie let him in and asked him to join them. He was carrying a small white box. He said he had eaten, but accepted a slice of lemon pie and coffee. Jimmie, glancing kindly at Maurita, held out the box to Max.

"Dallas found this, just a little while ago. Or, Joe Grey found it."

"Joe Grey found it," Max said in a flat, uneasy voice. Charlie's stomach lurched. Max said, "Let's hear it," in that same suspicious tone.

They all knew the Saks crime scene extended from the store itself to the pile-up of cars being hauled away on the highway; but that it also included the motel rooms where the burglars had stayed as they posed as limo drivers. The sun was setting when Detective Garza and Jimmie McFarland went to work on that part of the scene. At the same moment, Joe Grey was running the rooftops, working off some of his grieving before they all returned to the Pamillon estate to bid Courtney a last good-bye. Racing the shingles among the smell of restaurant suppers, he saw a squad car and Jimmie's car below him and yellow crime tape strung around the motel and parking lot. He backed down a young acacia tree and was about to slip into the motel to see what Jimmie was doing, when, deep in the flowery ground cover, he stepped on something that hurt.

Something hard but delicate, buried deep among the blooms. He pawed it gently out.

There was the earring.

The ornately fashioned gold loop looked, indeed, as if it had been made by Peruvian hands, like pictures of that ancient jewelry he had seen, an intricately carved crescent moon hanging from its center. He was sniffing at it when he heard footsteps.

Dallas Garza stood over him.

He looked up at Dallas and pawed at the earring as

if playing, as would a kitten with a toy. Dallas looked back at him with all the suspicion he'd ever felt about Joe Grey. Not cold, cop suspicion, but startled disbelief.

The detective turned away, fetched a small box from his glove compartment, emptied it and lay the earring inside, then slipped the box into a small evidence bag. Returning to Joe, he called Jimmie over. "Take this up to Max. He went home early."

Now, at the Harpers', before Jimmie tied into his pie and coffee, he handed the box to Max. "Dallas found this near the motel. They're finished with it, fingerprints, DNA, photos—didn't take long. He thought Maurita might want it."

As long as DeWayne was dead, and Maurita hadn't wanted to press charges, there wasn't much point in keeping this one piece of evidence. They had the bloody pictures, the doctors' reports, the other, smashed earring. And DeWayne's accomplices had plenty of other charges against them, in case they were involved.

Max took the box from Jimmie and opened it. He studied the contents, then held it out to Maurita. She accepted it, looking sick. The earring lay on a clean cotton pad, it was battered only a little, an ornate gold loop with an intricate crescent moon suspended inside. She touched the scar down her torn ear, felt the surgeon's stitching. She sat looking at the earring for a long time, thinking, then looked up at Max. "Do you have a spade, or a short shovel?"

Max rose from the table. But Jimmie said, "I know where they are," and he was out through the tiled mud room that served as the house's one entry. Heading for the stable, the two big half-Danes leaped all over him barking and licking his face. Jimmie ruffled their ears and told them to get down. They obeyed him, watching as he put a shovel and a spade in his car, then stood waiting for Maurita.

"We won't be long," Maurita said in the doorway as she stopped to hug Charlie. "I'll do dish duty tomorrow, and I'll cook." Zeb and Max watched her with interest. Already she looked stronger, as if doing a day's work, as if beginning to make a new home, was already driving back the weakness that had overwhelmed her.

In Jimmie's car, they turned north up the highway, then left down Ocean Avenue to the beach. Here it was darker as thick fog rolled in, hiding the last of the sunset. Jimmie opened the trunk while Maurita prowled the sandy park, stepping carefully, looking down at the sand and the way the fallen trees lay. When she had her bearings she took the shovel, and slipped the spade in her belt. When he moved to help, she looked at him with an expression he couldn't read.

"I want to do this, Jimmie."

She dug for a long time, but the sandy dirt was soft. She dug nearly as deep as she could reach, then she used the spade to make a tiny hole. She dropped in the box. She wrote nothing on it, she said no word. She filled in the little hole, pounding the dirt with the handle of the spade, then shoveled back the dirt she had removed. She smoothed it over roughly with the shovel, then walked across it a few times, kicked some grass across it and tossed on a few small stones so it resembled its surround, matching the rest of the park.

She cleaned off the tools with a tissue and put them back in the trunk. He closed the trunk and took her hand. They walked across the little road that ended where the beach began; the waves were high, crashing in. They climbed the cliff high above the sand, sat hand in hand, in silence, Maurita's long black hair blowing in her face. Her expression was a church kind of look, deep and thankful. As if she had buried the last of her hatred. As if her anger and resentment would lie there deep beneath the earth until time ended, completely removed from her. She looked past the breakers to the soft blanket of fog, and she leaned silently against Jimmie.

29

It was dark when the cats gathered in the mansion's north grotto, deep down but where, in one adjoining alcove, their human friends could crowd in. Those who could speak to them, who could say good-bye to Courtney and the ferals. The ferals had, most of them, promised to return. Courtney made no such promises. She said only, "I'll try. I think I will come back."

Lucinda and Pedric Greenlaw had picked up Dulcie and Courtney and Wilma at her cottage. Ryan and Clyde and Joe Grey had squeezed John and Mary Firetti and the two boy kittens in the back of Clyde's Jaguar. Kate and Scotty had walked down through the ruins and were already in the cavern. Charlie was absent but she had sent a loving message by way of Ryan; there was no way she could leave her new guests tonight when they needed the warmth of friends around them. And no way she cared to leave Max when he was still scowling with suspicion about Joe Grey.

Dulcie was crying as they gathered in the grotto. Kit was crying so hard she had to keep wiping her nose on Pan's golden fur, which didn't please him. His own eyes were both sad and yearning. He'd very much like to go back with Courtney, as would Kit. They had traveled to the Netherworld, they had thrilled and shivered at its wonders and they were sharply drawn, now, to return with the calico and the ferals.

But Kit couldn't leave Lucinda and Pedric a second time, nor could Pan. How many years did their old couple have left? When she watched Courtney's two brothers licking and snuggling their sister and listened to their sad mewls, it was too much. Kit yowled until Pan cuffed her and she went silent, pressing against him; and Courtney watched them all with painfully mixed feelings.

She knew she had to go down, she wasn't safe here. She knew there was a place for her, a special place for the calico with the three bracelets, she believed what the ferals had told her. She was filled with excitement at what she would discover in that new world, and was terrified at what she might confront. She looked helplessly at her family and friends, confusion boiling in her heart—but something called to her, from that world. And she was glad the ferals would be with her, she would be terrified to go down alone.

She rose. She faced her parents and her dear friends. She whispered, but then she said boldly, "Good-bye. I love you. I love you all as I love the spirit who made us. I will come back to you." Turning, not looking back again, she headed for the little hidden cave that would drop down to the rocky tunnel that would lead, by morning, into the Netherworld: the ferals were all around her, some disappeared ahead of her, racing down into the black tunnel, dropping down and down, abandoning the upper world.

They were gone. Courtney was gone.

Courtney's friends and family went away silently, in twos and threes, back into the village where the calico would no longer be present; leaving the Pamillon estate where there would no longer be any speaking ferals. Everyone was crying, Scotty and Clyde hiding their tears.

What would occur in the world of speaking cats, in the future, no one knew.

That night, Joe and Dulcie sat together atop Wilma's roof looking east toward the hills where hidden chasms fell down into that other world. There was fog low over the hills, veiling a thin smear of moonlight. They didn't speak. Until Dulcie said, "We raised a strong girl. What amazing things will she do there?"

"We raised three strong kittens," Joe Grey said. "Each has chosen a useful life, each will make their mark. This is not the end. This is the beginning."

But there would be many nights when they would sit together brooding, looking up at the hills or out across the sea. Or they would sit with Wilma watching the moon rise, contemplating the lives that had come before and those that will come after. Knowing there was cruelty and pain in this world, but knowing this wasn't the last life. Knowing that the true living spirit was courage, mixed with love, and Courtney had that. And, as Ryan and Clyde reminded them, the calico carried within her the genes of their own spirits. A part of Joe and Dulcie would always be with her.

About the Author

Shirley Rousseau Murphy is the author of twenty-one mysteries in the Joe Grey series, for which she has won the Cat Writers' Association Muse Medallion eleven years running, and has received ten national Cat Writers' Association Awards for best novel of the year. She is also a noted children's book author, and has received five Council of Authors and Journalists Awards. She lives in Carmel, California, where she serves as full-time household help to two demanding feline ladies.

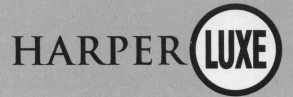

HARPER (LUXE)

THE NEW LUXURY IN READING

We hope you enjoyed reading
our new, comfortable print size and found it
an experience you would like to repeat.

Well – you're in luck!

HarperLuxe offers the finest in fiction and
nonfiction books in this same larger print size and
paperback format. Light and easy to read, HarperLuxe
paperbacks are for book lovers who want to see
what they are reading without the strain.

For a full listing of titles and
new releases to come, please visit our website:

www.HarperLuxe.com

HARPER (LUXE)

SEEING IS BELIEVING!